Total-E-Bound Publishing books by Gwen Masters:

The Green Room

A WEEK IN THE SNOW

GWEN MASTERS

A WEEK IN THE SNOW

Dedication

For my Patrick Jane,
who turned a spark into a raging fire.

Chapter One

"You sound happy. Are you?"

Rebecca smiled and shifted the phone on her shoulder. She stared at the single candle on the mantel. The clock had just chimed midnight. "Yes."

"Tell me."

"This isn't just a want. It's a need. It's like breathing, or my heart beating. I can feel it right now, between my legs." She slid a hand down her naked belly. "I want to lie underneath you and open my legs for your hand, at the same time as you slide your cock into my mouth."

Her own words turned her on just as much as his did, and she let her fingers walk farther down, until she was brushing the neatly trimmed hair at the apex of her thighs. Her nipples were sensitive and tingling, and the cool breeze from the air conditioner kept them hard. She curled her toes against the end of the couch as she listened to his voice, coming low over the phone line.

"You like that, don't you? My cock in your mouth? You like it when I pull your hair and hold you there and make you take it, don't you?"

She touched her clit with her fingertip, then dropped her head back and moaned.

"And at the same time, I'm pushing two fingers into you—no, how about three?—just slamming them in, because you're so wet already, and I'm driving them in and out, and every now and then I press on your clit, right there. You like that? I can hear you panting for it. You wouldn't be panting if my cock was in your mouth, would you? You would be fighting to breathe while you came and came and came."

Rebecca ran one finger on either side of her clit, scissoring it gently, rubbing up and down. The tingles got bigger and her mind started to venture off into the fantasy, the thought of his hands doing those things to her. She imagined her own hands would be on her nipples, playing with them while she bent her head back just so, taking his cock in deep enough to please him, but not deep enough to gag. His fingers would be working magic between her thighs, sliding into her when she needed to be filled, pulling back and teasing her before she could come, making her beg with moans before he slid his fingers in again. That delicious stretching would overcome her and she might forget the motion of her mouth, forget the way she was supposed to move, and he would have to pull on her hair to get her attention again.

That was what did it for her this time—the thought of him pulling on her hair, maybe a little bit frustrated with her, demanding she pay attention to his cock. She imagined the velvet skin sliding between her lips, the tense muscles in his thighs, the way he would look at her as he came. She imagined all of it, except the one part she didn't have to imagine.

"Oh, fuck, Becca — I'm going to come!"

He hollered when he came, his voice loud enough to make her pull the phone away from her ear. He held his breath for a moment, then let it out on a moaning exhale. Rebecca smiled as her own orgasm hit, right in time with his. She arched under her hand, everything but the voice in her ear forgotten, as the orgasm swept from her middle and out to her fingers and toes. Her whole body tingled, her nipples hard enough to hurt, her clit humming under her fingers.

When she relaxed and opened her eyes, she saw the candle. It had burned halfway down, the flame dancing on a small breeze.

"Was it good for you?" he asked, his voice low and dramatic. As if on cue, Rebecca giggled. She always giggled after a really good one, and that was right up there in the top ten. He laughed with her, and that made her feel warm inside. So what if he was thousands of miles away? At moments like this, he felt close enough to touch.

After long minutes of talking about what had just happened, he yawned. She knew he would be going to bed soon, and, even though her time zone put her an hour ahead of him, she would be awake for hours yet, thinking about the coming week and what it might have in store.

He was thinking of it, too. "Have you decided what to pack?" he asked.

"I've already packed one bag with the essentials." She stretched, delighting in the feel of her legs, a little too tense, reminders of what she had just done. The orgasm still thrummed through her now and again. "It's going to take two bags, though — I'm doubling up on everything to survive those chilly temperatures."

"Iowa is chilly in the fall," he agreed.

"You can keep me warm."

"Don't forget the vibrator," he teased.

"Gene," she teased right back. "I thought we were just going to have coffee."

"Of course we are. The morning after."

She giggled again and nestled deeper into the couch. The thought of going to see him was like an adventure. She was always the good girl, the one who was reliable and safe and careful, and this felt like doing something she had always wanted to do, but had never had the nerve. She was going to meet her online boyfriend and she was going to fuck him silly, and then she was going to fuck him some more, and to hell with the good girl act.

"The morning after sounds good," she said. "Are you going to make it for me?"

"You're the woman," he replied. "It's your job."

That was the only thing about Gene that drove her crazy. She always hoped he was joking about the macho way he viewed things; that he really did believe in equality, that he wasn't as chauvinistic as he seemed. But the more time went on, the more she thought maybe he really believed a woman's place was in the kitchen, barefoot and pregnant. Each time the thought came up, it made her wonder: what in the world was he doing with a woman like her, who ran her own business and was determined to make a name for herself?

"Speaking of jobs, mine is waiting on me, and I need to get a few things done before I go to sleep," she said, dangling more bait. "I have to wrap up this latest project before I come to see you."

Gene yawned, as though the project she had going wasn't interesting in the least.

"Okay, babe. I'm going to go to sleep. You might want to get some sleep, too, so you can make that drive."

"I'll be all right."

"Are you sure you won't fly?"

She didn't want to fly, and she had told him that over and over. She wanted to drive her way up from Florida to Iowa, her camera on the seat beside her, ready for good light. She could already imagine all the farms along the way, the old barns begging for a picture, the town squares that deserved to be caught by her lens. The point of the trip was to see Gene, but what was wrong with taking some time of it for herself?

"I really want to take some photographs on the way up." She had said it a hundred times if she had said it once, and she was getting tired of the same old saw. She carefully filtered the note of wariness out of her voice.

"Okay."

His tone was curt, almost hurt, but she stood her ground. "I'll leave tomorrow, and I'll see you on Friday. Want me to call you before I leave?"

"Before you leave, and while you're driving, and while you're at the hotel, and everywhere in between," he said. "I can't wait for you to get here."

No matter their differences, she knew that much was true, and it warmed her from the inside out. "I can't wait, either."

"Goodnight, Becca-girl."

Before she could say anything in response, he hung up. She clicked the phone closed and dropped it on the table, where it slid to a stop against a stack of photo proofs. She stared at the candle until it started to blur, trying to hold on to the good sex and the even better orgasm, but it was already a distant memory. Now she was thinking about the hours of work still ahead of her, the proofs to organise and the mailings to be done. Just thinking about it made her tired.

She sat up on the couch. The sudden wetness between her thighs reminded her of what she had just done with Gene, and what she could expect to do much more of as soon as she got to his house in Iowa. She padded to the bathroom and cleaned up, smiling as she thought about climbing into the shower with Gene after making love, washing away the remnants of him, leaving only the tiny little bruises and love bites that would remind her for days of what they had done.

But first, she had work to do.

Rebecca grabbed the proofs from the living room table and took them to her office, where she sat naked at her desk and pulled out the envelopes. Taking pictures of school kids and dogs and families was the way she paid the overheads, but her real passion was creative photography. In between the shots that took her breath away, she had to do the monotonous jobs—like stuffing four hundred proofs into mailers and getting them ready to drop off at the county school.

She studied the envelopes, glanced at the clock and got to work.

By the next nightfall, she had made it to the Georgia border. It would take another two days of steady driving to get into Iowa, but she felt more than up to the task. As she watched the sun set over the foothills of the Appalachian Mountains, she thought again how good it was to drive the stretch. She pulled over to the side of the road and took pictures until the sun went down, then headed into town for a motel.

She called Gene as soon as she got to her room. He was already asleep, so she quickly told him she was safe in Georgia, and let him go back to dreamland. When she hung up the phone, she crawled under the cool, impersonal covers. She tried to sleep but soon found it impossible—the excitement of the day, the travel, all the new things she had seen, flashed through her head and refused to give her rest. The anticipation of seeing Gene for the first time was the thought that came to her most often, and she finally kicked down the covers, resigned to not going to sleep for a while.

She flipped through the television channels and watched the local news, which was not so different than the news in Miami, though the accents of the newscasters were decidedly different—not as slick and careful, somehow. She watched a bit of a movie, something she vaguely remembered from years ago, but quickly tired of the drama.

She turned the channel again and this time she hit the pay-per-view section. She looked at the listings, and one of them caught her fancy: *Sebastian's Hot Ride.*

She laughed out loud at the name, but that didn't stop her from clicking on the title. When it asked if she was sure, she clicked on the button that said she was, though she had no idea what she might find. When the images filled the screen, she dropped the remote on the bedside table and stared.

"Jackpot," she whispered.

The man on the screen was tall, broad-shouldered, unbelievably buff, the kind of man who graced the cover of romance novels. The woman with him was impossibly tiny, her breasts much bigger than God had intended, and she wore nothing but blood red lipstick.

Rebecca watched as the woman lay on the bed and pressed her ample breasts together with her hands, her come-hither eyes making it very clear what the tall stud was supposed to do. He crouched over her and slid his long, thick cock between the white globes. The woman lifted her head a bit, and the camera watched from behind as she sucked his balls into her mouth and worried them with her tongue. The sounds of moans filled the air.

Rebecca's own moan joined in as she slid a hand between her thighs. The movie was unreal, completely over the top, but that didn't stop her from looking at the dick and wishing she had one right now. When the man changed positions and got on top of the woman, lifting her legs high in the air and slowly impaling her with his impossibly perfect cock, Rebecca slid a finger inside herself. She imagined the couple on the bed were really her and Gene, and she watched with fascination as they went through every position imaginable. She played with her clit the whole time, backing off when she got too close to the finish, wanting to make it last.

When the man on the screen held the woman by the hips and slowly pushed his dick into her tight ass, stretching her with it, Rebecca came so hard she felt lightheaded.

She watched the movie to the end, hoping to garner some new and interesting positions to use during her time with Gene. When it was over she flipped off the television and lay awake in the darkness, thinking about Gene, and almost wishing she had taken the plane after all.

During the journey, Rebecca stopped often to shoot images that struck her. A field of late-blooming flowers caught her attention, and so did a huge group of wild turkeys. In Tennessee she took pictures of the soaring bridge over the Natchez Trace Parkway. She stopped at a cafe in Kentucky and took pictures of the tractors outside, the farmers at the counter and the waitress who gave her a free scoop of ice cream on top of her apple pie. In Illinois she caught an impressive mass of dark clouds over the flat corn fields while she listened to dire accounts of severe weather on the FM radio stations.

She found old barns everywhere and took enough pictures to create a whole book of them, if she was so inclined. Some of her favourite photographs were those she snapped of the giant windmills. The steel rose imposingly from the ground, at definite odds with the century-old silos and small, squat farmhouses.

She spent the night in a little motel that offered only three channels on the television, no room service and a heater that worked only half the time. There would be no pay-per-view this evening, but she was too tired to care. She cuddled up under the blankets and fell asleep to the buzzing of a neon Vacancy sign outside her window. The new morning dawned crisp and clear, and the neon buzz was replaced with the sound of chirping birds.

In northern Illinois she saw her first snowfall.

Rebecca pulled over to the side of the road when she saw the little white flakes. She stared at the windshield as the snowflakes fell, stuck to the glass for a moment and melted into a drop of water. She was stunned by how pretty they were. She had lived all of her twenty-something years in sunny Miami, where the thermometers never dropped below the fifties. Now that she was seeing snow for the first time, she was utterly fascinated.

Rebecca got out of the car and stood in the cold air, surprised that the temperatures had dropped so quickly.

She grabbed her camera, focused on the trunk of her car and tried to get shots of individual snowflakes before they melted. She found it much harder than she had imagined it would be. Finally she put the camera away and simply stood in the softly falling snow, listening to the world around her and breathing deep of the crisp air.

By the time the sun went down, she was crossing the Iowa border. Small farmhouses dotted the landscape, their porch lights shining in the twilight darkness. The snow was falling harder now, and Rebecca drove with her windshield wipers on. The heater in her car had never been used before — why would she ever need it in the Sunshine State? When she turned it on, a burning smell blasted out of the vents. Once the dust was burned away, there was nothing but the blessed heat blowing over Rebecca's face and feet.

The farmhouses became few and far between, and the road was darker than ever without streetlights to help guide her way. The snow came down furiously, drifting across the road, piling up in the ditches. Mixed in with the snow was a hard ticking sleet, the tiny pieces of ice pinging from her windshield. Her headlights shone on a fury of white as she looked for another porch light, and became increasingly worried when none appeared.

When she glanced down at the gas gauge, that worry turned to near-panic.

She pulled carefully to the side of the road and reached for her cell phone. She dialled Gene's number and immediately got a beep, followed by another, louder one. She looked at the little glowing screen.

Call failed.

She tried it again, with the same result. There was no signal.

Think, Rebecca. Think. What's the best thing to do now?

She knew she was on the right road — she had turned on to it several miles back, but she was still a good thirty miles short of where she needed to be. Glancing at the gas gauge one more time, she decided to drive on until she came to another service area. Then she would call Gene, tell him her situation, and ask him to come out and meet her. He knew the roads better than she did, and he knew how to drive on snow. She hadn't the faintest clue.

Comfortable in her decision, she carefully pulled back on to the road. At first she kept her speed at a crawl, but as she grew more confident in her abilities to drive on the snow-covered road, she pressed harder on the gas pedal.

The tyres lost their grip and the car began to skid.

Rebecca tried to remember what she had learned about snow, and whether she should turn into the skid, or away. Before she could decide, there was a dull thud, and the rear of her car bounced. Another thud, and the car slid into the ditch with an air of finality. The engine stalled, sputtered and died.

Rebecca sat behind the wheel, her knuckles white, staring out of the windshield. She took a deep breath. She closed her eyes as the shakes set in.

It had all happened so fast.

Her hands still shaking, Rebecca reached again for her cell phone. She pressed the button and the blue light of the tiny phone filled the car.

No service.

"Damn it, not now!" Rebecca punched buttons on the phone, as if that would make a difference. She threw it on the dash, grabbed the keys, turned the ignition and heard the satisfying roar of the engine. She cranked up the heat, held her hands in front of the vent for a moment, then put the car into gear. Gingerly she pressed on the gas pedal and felt the tyres catch. They gained traction for a moment but almost immediately slipped again, dumping the car back into the ditch. Rebecca put it in reverse and tried the same thing. No luck.

"Damnation!" she hollered.

She shoved open the car door and climbed out. The ditch was deeper than she had thought and the car was on an angle, so getting to the road was a bit of a struggle. When she turned to look back at the car, she realised it would never come out of there without the help of a tow truck.

The snow was coming down, obscuring everything. It was frigidly cold, like standing in a refrigerator. She got back into the car and slammed the door shut behind her. At least the engine was still running — she held her hands in front of the heater vents, trying to stay warm while she took stock of the situation.

Her phone didn't work. Her car was definitely stuck. It was still snowing, and now the world was so white she couldn't see the yellow lines of the road, though she knew they were only a few feet away. There hadn't been a porch light for miles. She knew which road she was on, but that was all she had in the way of direction.

She was already getting warmer, though. The car's heater was a dragon of a thing, and would probably keep her toasty warm until the gas ran out.

The gas.

She stared at the gauge. It was sitting at just below a quarter of a tank, which was enough to last for a while, but not nearly enough to last through the night. If she were really as stuck as she seemed to be, that gas wouldn't hold out long enough.

"Think," she whispered, fighting against panic. "Think."

She could walk as soon as the snow let up, and try to find the nearest house. She was wearing tennis shoes, two shirts and jeans — not heavy enough to fight the cold of the snow. She had other clothes in her trunk, including a coat. She could layer all of them if she had to.

But first she would wait for the snow storm to let up, so she could see where she was walking when she did venture out of the car.

Rebecca laid her head back against the seat. The engine was still humming along and the heater was blowing full blast. She was warm in her little cocoon of a car, and for a while she simply watched the snow fall outside the window. She even admired how pretty it was, even though she was scared to death of what might happen if it didn't let up soon.

When she looked back at the windshield, it was covered. Panic sliced through her, clean and sharp as a razor blade. She sat up to stare at the white. How much snow was out there? She opened the door a bit and watched as it cut a path through the white drifts, proof that the snow was at least a foot deep, maybe more.

Deep enough to cover the tailpipe?

The sobering thought sent her out into the snow in a hurry. Rebecca pushed the door open all the way, climbed out into snow that now came up well past her ankles, and struggled to the back of the car. The tailpipe wasn't blocked, but it was close. She knelt in the snow, cursed as it soaked through her jeans, and pushed handfuls of it away with her hands. It was still coming down, hard enough to make her efforts seem lost in the blizzard.

"That's what this is," she murmured to herself, her teeth already chattering. "This is a blizzard."

She cleaned around the tailpipe as well as she could, then trudged back to the car, where she leaned towards the heater vents. Her hands were already numb. The cold had seeped through her jeans and now seemed to cool her whole body, making her tremble from head to toe. The heater warmed her quickly, but she knew any chance of finding a house with a glowing porch light was quickly disappearing under the threat of that heavy, wet snow.

She gripped the wheel, leant back against the seat and hollered her frustration at the top of her lungs. The sound filled the little car, but did absolutely nothing to make her feel better. She slammed her fist down on the dashboard, and that immediately made her feel guilty. The car was doing a good job of keeping her warm, after all. She laid her head on the steering wheel and squeezed her eyes shut.

"I will not cry," she chanted. "Will not, will not, will not."

Outside the snow kept falling, turning the landscape into an endless world of white.

Chapter Two

Richard Paris strapped on his helmet and eyed the snow. The forecast hadn't anticipated this much, but he wasn't surprised—when Iowa decided on snow, nobody knew when it would end, not even the meteorologists. Tomorrow morning there would be abashed apologies about the forecast on the morning news, but nobody really minded. There was nothing more unpredictable than Mother Nature, especially in October.

The snowmobile had been sitting idle all year, just waiting for a night like this. The highway patrol had closed down the roads, which was a moot point, because the roads were impassable by now anyway. Only snowmobiles could make their way through until morning, when the road-clearing equipment would come out with a vengeance, ready to do battle against all the white stuff. From the looks of things already, the roads would be impassable tomorrow, too.

Richard climbed on to the big machine with a grin of anticipation. He remembered this feeling from being a kid, when the snow would come down and school would be cancelled. His mother would make him bundle up in layers and layers of clothing, so much fabric he could hardly walk, and he would waddle down to the garage and find the sled. Long, sleek, long ago painted yellow but now a mellow gold colour, it would beckon him from the corner. After moving away a year's worth of stuff — in his father's garage, there was always a mountain of odds and ends — he would set the sled on the snow. He remembered how it would slide out of his hands almost immediately, ready to run on the ice.

Though it had been years and years, he'd never forgotten what it was like.

Richard turned the key in the ignition and the snowmobile gave a mighty roar. It choked out a bit of smoke before it ran clean and easy, a finely-tuned machine ready to have some fun. Thirty years fell away as Richard leaned over the handlebars, released the brake and cranked up the gas.

"Yeah, baby, run!"

The snowmobile shot out of the driveway like a machine possessed. The blades slipped across the snow and the engine hummed as Richard turned into the road, fishtailed a little, then straightened up and gave it more power. The snowmobile gained in speed and Richard put his head closer to the machine, peering through the windshield as he left tracks on the pristine snow.

He was flying, his speedometer hovering at just under ninety miles an hour, when he saw a flash of red in his headlights. It was so quick that if he hadn't been looking at the right side of the road he would have missed it. He kept on going but the flash of colour stuck with him, and a few miles later he slowed down. The machine whined in protest as he turned around and found his tracks, following them the way he had come, much slower now that he had something to look for. It might have been nothing, maybe just a kid's bike left on the side of the road, or maybe a mailbox he hadn't noticed before. But in weather like this, it might have been something else, and he had to go back and make sure.

He slowed to a crawl when he got closer to where he had seen the flash of red. The snowmobile idled, just sliding along on the ice, when he saw it again. It was definitely red, and it was definitely not a bike. It was far too big to be a bike. A few feet closer and Richard saw more red, this time peeking from the top of a snowdrift.

"A car," he said to himself, and pulled up alongside it.

The drifts already covered the body and almost obscured the top. Richard geared down the snowmobile and climbed off, trying to peer into windows that had too much snow over them. He walked closer to the car, searching for a door. The car was completely encased in snow and probably no one was in it, but he had to check. With one gloved hand he brushed snow away from the window and tried his best to peer inside.

The interior light snapped on.

The sudden burst of light damn near scared Richard to death. He actually stumbled backwards, cursed himself for being a sissy, then started to dig around the door. Someone was obviously in the car, and they might be toasty warm in there, but they were probably close to running out of oxygen.

"Help me!" The voice belonged to a woman. Richard dug harder, finally clearing the window. There was no way he could reach the door to open it — that would take an hour of digging.

"Can you roll down the window?" he yelled.

"It's electric!"

"Okay. Will the engine turn over?"

"No."

That answer was not what he wanted to hear. He stared at the snow and tried to calculate the hours it would take to dig that car out. Whoever was in there would need their freedom long before then.

"Are you all right?"

"Yes," she said, though he could hear the sobs in her voice, the crying barely held in check. "But I'm scared and cold and hungry, and I really want out of here!"

He brushed more snow away from the window, and now he could see her. She was small, with brunette hair and large, frightened eyes. She was wrapped up in clothes and a coat and she looked warm enough, but Richard knew very well how fear could make all that warmth disappear.

"I'm going to get you out," he said. "You hang on for just a minute more."

He went back to the snowmobile. The snow was still falling, but now it was a gentle rain of it, a break in the blizzard that had turned his corner of Iowa into a barren world. He opened up the pack on the back of the snowmobile and pulled out the wrench. It was good to have when the snowmobile needed adjustments, and it was especially good now, when it needed to break a sheet of glass.

"Get over on the other side of the car," he said to the woman behind the window. "I'm going to have to break this glass to get you out."

She nodded and climbed over the gearshift. He waited until she was huddled against the door, her face turned away in anticipation. With a deep breath and a mighty heave, he slammed the wrench down hard against the window. He was gratified by the sound of crashing glass.

"Good thing that wasn't safety glass," he said with a smile, peering into the car. "If it had been, it would have been a real bit of work to get you out."

The woman inside suddenly burst into tears. "I was so scared..."

Richard grabbed the small shards of glass that were left around the doorframe. His gloves were thick, and the pieces didn't penetrate. He threw the sharp bits away from the car and reached in a hand, offering her help in climbing out.

"Let's get you warm."

Rebecca took his hand and climbed out of the car. When she finally stood on top of the snow, she was surprised to see that her tennis shoes barely made a dent in the surface. She lifted her face to the sky and felt the cold flakes, still coming down. The deep breaths of cold air burned all the way down, but she found herself grateful for the sliver of pain in her lungs, quite happy to be out of the car and with someone who could help her.

She took one step and sank to her knees. She yelped in surprise, and the man grabbed her, hauled her up, and helped her walk to the hulking machine that sat idling in the middle of what used to be a two-lane road. She climbed on the back of the snowmobile, glad to be on something solid. She pulled her coat tight around her.

"I'm Richard," the man said, and she looked up at him. His face was mostly obscured by a toboggan and scarf, and his body was covered in layers and layers of clothing.

But she could see his smile, broad and happy, and she couldn't help but smile back.

"I'm Rebecca," she said. "I'm from Miami."

Richard's smile faltered a bit. "Miami? What are you doing here?"

"I was coming to visit someone. I had no idea the snow would be like this."

"Apparently, neither did the forecasters on the local news." Richard was peering back into the car. "You're the only one?"

"Just me."

"Anything you need from in here?"

Rebecca nodded. "My purse is in the front seat. And there is a small blue bag. It's in the backseat. You can reach it through the window, I think."

Richard found it and pulled it through. He then grabbed the purse and stepped back to watch as the snow settled on the console of the car. The interior would be ruined by morning if he didn't do something. He reached in again and turned off the interior light, hoping to save the battery, at least.

Richard carefully tossed the bags to Rebecca and dug into his pack, searching for the emergency blanket he kept there. He unrolled the thin blanket and stuck it over the window as best he could, weighing the edges down with wet snow. Finally satisfied that he had done what he could for the car, he turned back to the woman on the snowmobile. She was shivering with the cold, her arms wrapped around herself.

"Scoot back a bit more and let me on. We'll be at my place in a minute."

Rebecca held on to his waist as the snowmobile roared to life. She watched as her little red car disappeared in the distance, then buried her face against the back of the man who had just saved her. The wind whipped over them, cutting like a thousand tiny knives. Rebecca could hardly breathe for the cold.

As they finally approached the cheery light of a farmhouse, Rebecca fought back tears of relief. The man stopped in front of the house and motioned towards the door.

"Get in and get warm," he said, and she climbed off of the snowmobile. The snow here wasn't as deep, but she still sank to her ankles. The golden glow of light from the windows fell over the yard and the snow was a dusting on the covered porch. It looked like the front of a picture-perfect postcard.

"Thank you," she said, her teeth chattering.

"You're welcome. Now get inside. Door's unlocked."

He watched until she was safely inside the door. Sighing, he looked back at the snow. The moon had come out, glossing the world with a brilliant shine.

"This is just what I need," he muttered.

Rebecca stepped in the front door and looked around. "Hello?" she called, and got no answer. She closed the door behind her and took a deep breath, the warm air already soothing her cheeks and making her hands tingle. The roaring light of a fireplace beckoned her, and she rushed towards it like a moth to flame. She put her hands close, almost too close, and watched as the flames licked at the wood.

She really did start to cry then, long and racking sobs that frightened her. She had been out there in the car all evening, afraid to look at her watch, unable to dig out from the snow that had got too deep, too fast. The gas had run out with a final sputter of the engine, and that was when the panic had set in. She remembered fighting to open the door, pushing helplessly against the impossible weight of the snow, crying and sometimes screaming. Now she was crying again, and she was starting to wonder just how many tears the human body could have inside it. She was surely reaching her limit.

That was how Richard found her — standing in front of his fireplace, warming her hands over the flames, tears dripping from her cheeks. He watched her for a moment, giving her time to get herself under control. He didn't blame her for crying, and he didn't want to embarrass her. He gently laid her blue bag and purse on the couch, then stepped to the kitchen and started a pot of decaf, listening for any sound from the living room. He made quite a lot of noise himself, so as not to startle her with his presence.

When he finally did come back into the front room, she turned to face him, her back to the fire. She had slipped off her coat and now stood a few feet away from the fire, her shivering gone in the heat of the flames. She gave him one of the most brilliant smiles he had ever seen, even though there were still tears on her cheeks. She made no attempt to hide them.

"Thank you," she said, and somehow that opened the floodgates again. She buried her face in her hands and this time Richard didn't have the heart to leave her alone. He crossed the floor in three long strides and wrapped his arms around her.

Rebecca buried her face in his shoulder until her tears tapered off again. When she looked back up at him, her nose was red and her lips were swollen. She moved away slowly, carefully, as though he were her centre of equilibrium.

He found a box of tissues on an end table. She gave him a grateful smile when he handed them to her and tactfully turned away, giving her a bit of privacy.

"I don't think we've been properly introduced," he said, holding his hands out to the fire. "My name is Richard Paris. Welcome to Crispin, Iowa."

She laughed — the sound was light and airy, the kind of laugh he hadn't heard in a long time. "My name is Rebecca Connors," she said, "and I'm not sure Crispin and I get along."

He nodded. "You're a long way from home."

"I came up here to meet someone, but then the snow started, and somehow I managed to slide my car right off the side of the road," she explained. She thought for a moment and shrugged. "The snow helped me a little bit with that one."

"I can imagine it did."

They looked at each other for a while, neither of them sure of what to say. Richard saw a pretty young woman, one who was trapped by circumstance far away from home, who held herself with dignity even though he could tell a part of her wanted to break down and sob some more. Rebecca saw a tall, handsome man with a weathered face, one who wasn't quite sure what to do with this woman in his house, but whose smile was kind.

"Coffee's hot," he said, and at the mention of something to fill her stomach a deep rumble came from her belly. She slapped her hand over it and blushed as Richard laughed.

"I'm starving," she admitted.

There wasn't much beyond breakfast foods in the refrigerator — Richard usually took lunch at his office and dinner somewhere in town — but there was a loaf of garlic bread in the freezer and some spaghetti sauce in the cabinet. He put a pot of water on the stove to boil and turned on the oven.

Rebecca sat down at the kitchen table, a cup of steaming coffee in her hand, and watched him as she took the first sip. The heat of it warmed her from the inside out, and finally she could think of something other than the terror of being in her car and watching the drifts pile up around her. "I didn't expect the storm," she said. "The forecast for Iowa was clear when I left Florida."

"It was clear," he agreed. "On the morning news they thought we might get about six inches. Around here, that's not much more than a sputter." He glanced at the wide kitchen window and raised an eyebrow. "The weather guy has a lot of explaining to do."

She watched as he stirred the spaghetti into the pot and put the garlic bread in the oven. The spaghetti sauce went into the microwave, and soon the smell of dinner was making her stomach rumble even louder than before.

"Not long now," he said.

When the food was on the table, Richard offered her a glass of iced water. She ate quickly, devouring the first plate and reaching for seconds. She thanked him over and over as she ate, declaring it the best food she had ever tasted. Richard was full of questions but she seemed to be so overwhelmed, so tired, that he bit his tongue and let them go. He could offer her a place to sleep and tomorrow he could help her pull her car out of the ditch, but beyond that, he doubted he would ever see her again. Who was he to pry?

Rebecca finished her dinner and pushed her plate back with a satisfied sigh. Richard sat the dishes on the counter, poured them both a final cup of coffee, and declined her offer to do the dishes. They both wandered out to the fireplace, where they stood side by side and watched the crackling of the fire, sipping their coffee and not saying much.

Finally Richard chuckled uneasily and looked at her. "I don't know what to say to you."

She nodded. "I just want to keep saying thank you, over and over."

"Please...you're welcome."

"Thank you."

He grinned. "I know this is awkward, Rebecca, but I'm glad you're safe."

She smiled and relaxed, her shoulders sagging. "I'm glad you came along."

"Listen...it's late. You've had a very long night. What do you say we both just go to sleep, and worry about everything else tomorrow?"

That sounded like the best idea Rebecca had heard in ages. "Sleep, yes. That sounds heavenly."

"The guest room is down here," he said, and led her to a little room off of the living area. In it was a bed covered with quilts, a dresser, an old armchair that had seen better days and a small television on a low table. The bathroom was the next door down the hallway, furnished with a deep claw-foot tub and a corner shower with tall glass doors. "If you want to get a hot bath, go ahead," he said. "And if some of your clothes need washing, put them in the hamper and I'll get them in the morning. The bag you wanted from the backseat of your car is on the couch in there, and your purse is too. My bedroom is upstairs, and, if you need anything, you holler."

Rebecca nodded, too overcome with gratitude to say all the things that were racing through her head. She settled for another whispered thanks. Richard gently closed the door behind him.

As soon as he was out of the room she sank down on the welcoming bed, the long hours finally catching up with her. She closed her eyes and took a deep breath, then another, trying to clear her mind. She ran her hand through her hair, winced at how tangled it was, and decided a shower would be a good idea.

Once under the warm water, with her body clean and her mind finally catching up to all the events of the evening, she marvelled again at the fact that she was alive and well. It could have turned out so differently. She tried to think of what the alternative scenarios might have been, but quickly abandoned that line of thought. She decided simply to be grateful she was still around.

The shower had two showerheads, water coming from both directions. She revelled in the feeling of it, like a massage, very different from the single showerhead in her tiny Miami apartment. She pressed her fingers against the back wall and arched into the water, concentrating on the way it slid over her body, the way it trailed from her neck to her back and down to her legs, then swished around her toes before gurgling down the drain.

It was hard to believe this shower could be so warm, while, just outside the window, the air was so impossibly cold.

She suddenly thought about where she was supposed to be, and what she was supposed to be doing there. She should have been in Gene's arms, in his bed, doing all sorts of wild and passionate things with him, just like they had both dreamed about for long months. Instead, she was stranded in the middle of a little nowhere town. Gene had no idea where she was.

She pictured him as well as she could, drawing on her memory of those photographs he had sent her over the Internet connection. She envisioned his broad chest, the smattering of black hairs, the almost-flat stomach and the strong, shadowed jaw.

She also envisioned those pictures of his long, hard cock, the photographs that filled the computer screen when she opened the file, the ones that made her mouth water and her heart pound. The thought of having that in her mouth or between her thighs had kept her dreams in high gear. Now he was within less than an hour's drive, but there was no way she could get to him.

But she did have him in her head, didn't she?

Rebecca grinned and rested her forehead against the cool wall of the shower. The emotion of the evening caught up with her again, but instead of the urge for tears she felt the urge to do something that proved she was alive — something vital, something powerful. The water slid down her back, arrowed down over her ass and dripped from her pussy. She let her breasts brush that shower wall, too — and though the water was incredibly hot, the wall was still cool. The rush of sensation was heady, made more powerful by the emotion of the evening. She pressed harder, until her nipples were flat against the wall, hardening at the contact, her breasts tingling with the pressure.

She took a deep breath and arched her back, pushing her head under one of the streams of water. It cascaded over her face. She held her breath as long as she could. When she pressed her forehead against the wall again, she was breathing hard. She spread her legs a bit wider, and suddenly she could see the picture in her head of what she must look like: a young, sexy woman dripping wet, her legs open, her whole body braced, waiting for whatever a lover might do to her.

Rebecca stood under the water and let the feeling build. The fantasy took flight, the images of Gene's cock in her head adding fuel to the fire. She thought about the way he sounded when he came, so strong and vulnerable all at once, and that alone was enough to send a surge of wetness between her thighs. She slid her hand down her flat stomach and rested it there, right below her belly button.

The water cascaded over her fingers as her thoughts took a different turn. She imagined someone was watching her, someone she didn't know, and her thoughts of Gene slipped away to be replaced by this new, intriguing fantasy. She pictured a man behind her, watching her while she went about what she was doing right then, which was sliding that hand even farther down.

She brushed the inside of her thighs and pressed her breasts harder against the wall, pushing her ass out, bending her knees just a little to make more room for whatever fantasy man might be watching her. She imagined he could see everything, her pussy open and dripping, a blatant invitation to the cock that might want to slip into her tight, wet hole.

Rebecca pressed her hand against her pussy and rocked. She bit her lip to hold in the long, low moan. The adrenaline of the night was now heading in a decidedly more sensual direction, and she let all the emotion flood her, let it turn into passion as she rode her own hand under the dual showerheads. She slipped two fingers into her cunt and imagined the fantasy man behind her, watching as her fingers disappeared inside her, maybe moaning his own pleasure as he stroked his hard cock. She slid her fingers out, stretching her pussy for his gaze, inviting him to put something of his own in there.

Her fingertips danced across her clit as she imagined that fantasy man moving up behind her, slowly, giving her time to move away if she was so inclined. She imagined his tongue on the back of her neck, tasting the water that ran from her skin. She could almost feel him placing his hands on her hips, holding the swell of them, and pressing the head of his hard dick against her opening.

He would slide in slowly at first, testing her acquiescence, but soon he would be overcome by how slick and hot she was. He would start slow and gradually move harder, faster, until he was almost ramming her, lifting her feet from the floor with his thrusts, making her struggle for balance as he began to ride her.

With a quiet groan, she pushed two fingers into her pussy. As she pulled them out, she stroked her clit, then pushed them back in. She kept it up until she was panting and trembling. The water slid down her body and she imagined it was the gaze of her mystery lover, watching everything she did, every move she made. She envisioned him waiting, holding back, and finally feeling those first contractions of her pussy around him, announcing that she had reached the pinnacle of pleasure she deserved.

She imagined the spurt of his cream, so much hotter than her own wetness, and that was the final edge of fantasy it took to make her come. She bit her lip at the last moment to keep from screaming out her pleasure as the orgasm swept over her, reducing her to whimpers and moans.

Her knees gave way and she slid to the floor of the shower. Her body thrummed with pleasure. It was enhanced by the adrenaline of the evening, strong enough to make her gasp for breath. She burst into laughter, her mouth muffled by her hand, trying to keep quiet, mindful of the man who was somewhere in the house with her.

She had never felt so alive.

When the pleasure and laughter were finally over, she was utterly exhausted. But there was still one other thing she had to do before she crawled into bed.

Chapter Three

Upstairs in the room above Rebecca, Richard stared at the shadows on the ceiling. It was strange to have someone in his house again, especially a woman. He hadn't had a woman around in at least three years, since the day Amanda had claimed she needed to find herself and had taken off for parts unknown. He had stopped wondering about a year ago, when another Christmas had gone by and he was alone, without even a card from his wife arriving in his mailbox.

Lately he wondered if she was really still his wife, or if there was some precedent that ended a marriage when someone just upped and disappeared.

He had read about divorce on the basis of abandonment, and more and more the thought had crept into his mind. He hadn't pursued it yet for a variety of reasons. He still loved her, for one, and it was very hard to contemplate divorcing a wife he still loved.

Secondly, he didn't know how to go about it—what would he say to an attorney?

Most of all, his very traditional family didn't believe in divorce, and slyly questioned why she had run away. They gave him sideways glances when he mentioned her, as if asking what he had done wrong to make her go, and so he had stopped bringing up her name at all. That made them even more suspicious. His mother had taken lately to quoting biblical verses, telling him how a man should cleave to his wife, and how once a marriage was sworn before God and man, it was the real deal, complete and never to be broken.

She was telling him, in no uncertain terms, to put his life on hold and wait for his wife to return.

As time went by, Richard wasn't happy with the idea of being alone for years, but the idea of divorcing Amanda and alienating his family was even worse. So he found himself sitting still while life passed him by with frightening speed. He thought about Amanda quite a bit, but he no longer jumped when he heard a car in the driveway, and he no longer went to the mailbox in anticipation of a postcard or a letter. She was never on the other end of the phone line, and nobody down at the cafe ever saw her. After a time the work of the newspaper had taken over his life, and the townspeople had simply assumed she would never come back, so they had stopped talking about her. Richard was just fine with that.

Now he listened to the water running downstairs and thought about the young woman in the shower. She had been through hell out there in that car—that frightened look in her eyes spoke volumes, even when she was warm and safe in his house—and he was glad he had taken the time to drive back. What would it have been like to read of her untimely death in the paper, when he had zipped right past her on his snowmobile? The guilt would have eaten him alive.

He looked at the clock and considered going out on the snowmobile again, but, just as quickly as the thought came, he decided against it. It would probably be incredibly bad form to tell the woman downstairs that he was going to go out for a joyride in the very conditions that had caused her so much fear and worry.

But the desire to go back out there was strong, the memory of all those childhood winters coming back, the thrill of making those first tracks in the pristine snow. There were lots of other snowmobiles out there, and plenty of people would be out by the light of the moon tonight. He loved to see the snow clean and unmarked in front of him, just like it had always been when he was a kid.

He rolled over in bed and looked at the bookcase, all the books he had read a dozen times, and contemplated which one he wanted to open up tonight. He would forget all about the snow. He would fall asleep while reading, and get up early in the morning to make breakfast. Then he would help the young woman make her plans for getting back on the roads as soon as they were passable again.

He studied the books for a while, but reading wasn't what he wanted. He rolled back over and looked at the ceiling, thinking. The excitement was still begging for an outlet. His hand moved down his body, the motion entirely natural and familiar. Since Amanda had left, it had been only his hand for company, and he needed that company quite often.

Usually the fantasies that filled his mind were of a nameless, faceless woman, maybe dressed in leather and wearing high-heeled boots, daring him to come and take her — if he could. Sometimes it was a trip to the sex toy store, where the clerk behind the counter was more than willing to try out all the merchandise with a good customer. When nothing else worked, he thought about two women, and that always seemed to trip his trigger.

This time it was the sex toy store. He slid his hand up and down, not quite ready to start stroking yet. He thought about sex toys hanging in neat rows on the corkboard walls. He imagined browsing through all the dildos and vibrators, not all that interested in buying one but intrigued by the different shapes and sizes. Then he would find the row of plastic pussies, the holes inviting him to stick it in, and the clerk would ask him what kind he liked most. Soft and slightly loose? Tight and a bit hard? Maybe really, really tight, the kind of pussy that would suck your dick even as you fucked it?

He started to stroke his cock when the clerk leaned over the counter. Her low-cut blouse rode even lower, and he got a good view of two large, round nipples. "I can help you find one you like," she said. She licked her cherry-red lips as she looked at his crotch.

Richard made a fist and pushed harder into it, imagining how tight the clerk's pussy would be, and how she would use it to great advantage. He pictured her bending over the racks of cock rings, helping him test one out as he pounded her from behind. He secretly hoped someone else would come into the store, a man perhaps — one who would gauge the action with one look and decide that maybe that clerk needed a bit more than she was getting.

Sure enough, in fantasies, dreams come true. The man who walked into the store wasted no time in dropping his pants and offering his cock for the clerk's mouth. She took it, moaned with approval, and rocked back and forth on two dicks. It was Richard who had made her want that, Richard who had the best of things, who would fuck her pussy until he made her come.

He tightened his fist and in his head the clerk moaned, her pussy getting tighter, almost ready to come by the sheer pleasure of his thrusting. He didn't even have to touch her — she was just that close, that fast.

In his bed, Richard arched his back and gritted his teeth, the orgasm right over the horizon, almost within his reach. He envisioned the clerk reaching back, between her legs and underneath herself, to cradle his balls in her hand. She would pull them gently, knowing just what a man liked, and when she did it would make him come...

Tap, tap, tap.

Richard froze in mid-stroke. His mind was pulled from the sex toy store back to the here and now, where he lay on a lonely bed with his dick in his hand. That dick was throbbing, right on the verge of exploding. The clerk vanished with the sound of another knock on his door.

"Fuck," he whispered. "Fuck, no. This isn't happening."

There was another tap on the door, this one a bit more hesitant.

He sat up on the edge of the bed, his dick protesting every movement. The erection that had been so enjoyable a moment before was now a source of pain as he grabbed his robe from the foot of the bed. He slipped his arms into it, hoping she wouldn't open the door. "Yes?" he asked, and blushed in the darkness at the sound of his voice, so rough and raw.

"I hate to bother you," the woman said from the hallway, "but I need to use your phone. I need to call my boyfriend. Is that all right?"

Richard almost laughed out loud. She'd interrupted him for that?

"Sure. The phone is in the kitchen."

He listened as she hovered at the door. Richard was breathing too fast, too hard, and he tried to control it so she wouldn't hear. He wondered how much she had heard when she came up the stairs. Had she been smiling as she listened to him panting with approaching orgasm? Or had she been oblivious to what was happening on the other side of the door?

"Thank you," she finally said, and he listened as she walked down the hallway. She stopped at the top of the stairs, as if she were looking back and thinking of something else to say. For a long moment Richard held his breath, wondering what she would do.

When he heard her feet on the staircase, he breathed a sigh of relief and fell back on to his bed.

He had never been interrupted while masturbating before. He slid his hand back down and found that his dick was still rock hard, a surprise, since he had been sure the shock would have made him soft. He started to stroke again, but this time when he conjured up the image of the clerk at the sex toy store he got an image of Rebecca instead.

Richard moved his hand away. His dick strained in the night air, throbbing. He felt guilty for thinking of Rebecca that way, especially after her ordeal of being trapped in the snow. She deserved a certain level of respect for that, and picturing her bent over in a sex toy store, taking his dick from behind, just didn't seem to qualify.

Even so, he couldn't shake the image. His hand crept back to his cock, matters of the body taking precedence over matters of right and wrong. He started to stroke and this time he let the clerk become Rebecca. He fucked into her from behind, hard and fast, and watched as the other man in his fantasy moved forward again, offering his dick for her hungry mouth.

Richard was closer than he thought—his balls tightened and his heart started to race as he imagined bracing himself behind her, thrusting upward to get the best friction, making her cry out his name even as she tried to suck that stranger's cock. He imagined fucking her so hard that she had to push the other guy away, had to give herself more room to move. He would come inside her, and she would moan with the pleasure of it, and then she would come, too.

Richard gritted his teeth as the cum shot out of him, covering his hand. He stroked until there was nothing left in him, until the sensation faded and the fantasy clicked away, like a light turned off with a flip of the switch.

He was suddenly very, very tired.

He reached over to the bedside table and pulled a few tissues from the box. Cleaning up, he thought about Rebecca, the woman now downstairs on his phone, talking to her boyfriend. He wondered how long she had been with that boyfriend, and what he was like, and if he made her happy.

Banishing such thoughts from his head, Richard crawled under the covers and let sleep overtake him.

On the phone downstairs, Rebecca was definitely not happy, and that boyfriend was the reason why.

"I told you to fly!" he shouted at her through the phone line. "You should have listened to me!"

Rebecca sat on the strange couch and wrapped her flannel shirt around her. It was a good thing she had layered up in the car, because now the only clothes she had were the clothes on her back. She wondered if perhaps Richard would be willing to take out the snowmobile again tomorrow, to pick up some of her things. She hadn't thought about clothing—she had just thought about saving her camera from the elements. It was sitting on the dresser in the guest room, just as safe as she was.

She had turned on the television, and even with the sound on mute, so as not to disturb the man upstairs, she understood the situation was dire. Schools were already cancelled for the rest of the week. She watched as the statistics flashed on the screen. This was easily the most snowfall in a twenty-four-hour period that Iowa had seen in over eighty years, and in October, no less. How did no one see it coming? The meteorologists all looked a little sheepish.

It was still snowing out there, and Gene was still yelling at her.

"I told you," he said again.

"You're right," she said to Gene, and she meant it. If she had flown, she would be safely snowed in with Gene, not snowed in with a complete stranger who just happened to come by in time to save her life. Gene's tone rankled, but she had to admit that, this time, he really was absolutely right.

"Of course I'm right," Gene said with enough arrogance to make her roll her eyes. "You've been too headstrong, Becca. You never listen to me. Maybe now you will settle down a bit and listen to me when I'm talking to you."

She didn't like his tone, but she bit her lip and refused to answer to it. She wasn't happy about the situation either, but that didn't make him the absolute authority. Gene liked to be listened to, and anyone who doubted his opinion was just flat-out wrong. As she listened, she flipped through the channels, watching each for a few seconds before moving on.

She stopped at FOX News. The man on the screen was berating someone for their opinion, and that's when it hit her: Gene reminded her of Bill O'Reilly.

The thought made her giggle. Gene heard it, and the response from him was the last thing she expected to hear.

"You're a fucking idiot, Rebecca."

Her whole world slowed to a standstill. She caught her breath, hearing the words over and over in her head, and thought surely she had heard him wrong.

Surely.

"What did you just say?"

"You heard me," he growled. "I said you're a fucking idiot."

The world started spinning again — this time, so fast she could hardly think straight. The fury was immense. Had he really just talked to her that way? Had he really found the nerve?

"You son of a bitch."

There was a long silence on the other end of the line, but Rebecca could imagine the anger building. She could almost feel it.

"What did you say?" Gene thundered.

She could not believe the man she might be in love with, the man she had been so eager to see, was saying such things to her. She would never tolerate anyone talking to her that way, and especially not someone who professed to adore her. She was not the kind to take it lying down, so she gave it right back to him: "You high-and-mighty, self-centred, chauvinistic son of a bitch."

The silence came again, but this time she was sure it was sparked by shock. She imagined his face turning red, his hands clenching into fists. She imagined him trying to think of what to say to bring this young lady once again to heel, like a dog that had done something wrong, and she was having none of that.

"I got stranded on the side of the road in a snowstorm," she said, biting out each word. "And you sit there and tell me I should have listened to you? What you should have said was how glad you were that I'm all right, and how much you want me there with you, and how your world would have ended if anything bad had happened to me. That's what you should have said, but instead you have to act the asshole and treat me like I need a good slap upside the head before you drag me back to the fucking cave where I belong."

"Now, Rebecca, just calm down."

His tone was superior, authoritative, leaving no room for argument.

That was just fine. She wasn't about to argue about anything with him anymore.

"I'm calming right down, Gene," she agreed. She was surprised to hear her own voice, so light and airy, almost happy. "I'm calming down. I'm also coming back down to earth. You are a sick, sad little man with no hope of ever having a fulfilling relationship with a woman, and, now that I know that, I'm not going to be coming any closer to you. In fact, as soon as this snow clears, my little car is headed as far away from you as possible. Don't ever think for one second that I'm the kind of woman who will move along blindly behind you, like one of those cows on your farm. You aren't worth the breath I'm wasting right now to explain all this to you."

The picture must have been abundantly clear to Gene, because he immediately started to plead. It was almost sad, hearing such a man beg for forgiveness, mostly because she knew it was entirely false. Gene wasn't sorry. Gene wanted to get her closer to him, so that maybe she couldn't see the flaws so readily, and bend her to his will.

Gene wanted to talk some sense into her.

"Don't ever call me again," she said.

"No, Rebecca, what the hell are you doing? You're acting like a child!"

"Goodbye, Gene."

"Damn you, woman, listen to me!"

She hung up on him. The only sound in the living room was that of the fire, crackling merrily away at the logs of wood. She waited, staring at the phone. He had caller ID, and he would probably ring back. She prayed the man upstairs didn't have a phone in his room, so Gene wouldn't wake him when he called back and tried to talk some sense into her again. When several minutes passed and the phone didn't ring, she was both confused and relieved.

She flipped off the television and stared at the blank screen, stunned at what had just transpired. It took only a moment to see the true colours in someone. No matter how well they tried to hide it, at some point their true nature would always come out. She had always known that, deep down, but she had never experienced it until now.

Outside the window, the snow had finally stopped.

Rebecca dragged herself from the couch, grabbed her bag and her purse and wandered into the guest room, where she took off her clothes and slipped between the covers. The light of the moon cascaded through the windows, bathing the room in otherworldly light.

Rebecca stared at the camera on the dresser. There were some beautiful shots on that film, images of farmland and sunsets and old barns and even people, pictures that might one day wind up in a magazine or on a gallery wall. But, as she gazed at the closed eye of the lens, all she could think about was how she would view those photographs later. Would they be forever tainted by the anger and sadness she was feeling right now?

Rebecca turned over, laid her head on the comfortable pillow, and pulled the old, worn quilt over her shoulders. She was warm, safe and secure, and grateful for it. She didn't shed a single tear over Gene, and that might have bothered her, had she been awake to think about it. Instead, she was asleep in seconds, and didn't move until the morning sun streamed through her window.

Chapter Four

Richard was up before the sunrise, reading the two-day-old paper from Des Moines and planning his day. He was also frying bacon and sausage, certain his visitor would want something to eat when she got up. She had eaten her fill last night, but Richard hoped she would be more than ready to partake of a full spread for breakfast.

What had she said her last name was? He had tried all morning to remember but that little detail had slipped his mind. He knew her first name was Rebecca and she was from Miami. He also knew she had pretty blue eyes. Between them, she had the cutest smattering of freckles on her nose. They gave her a youthful appearance, and, though she certainly wasn't a kid, looking at those freckles made him feel old. On cold mornings like this one, his forty-four years made themselves known with a bit too much creaking and aching when he climbed out of his warm bed.

He flipped through the pages of the paper, distracted when he should have been paying attention to what the competition was doing. He doubted there would be a chance to get to the office today, as the roads were still closed by the State Patrol, but maybe the sheriff would make an exception and let him take his snowmobile to the town square. The offices of the *Crispin Tribune* were right across from the courthouse, which would have served well for a John Grisham novel, had they ever had an interesting trial. In Crispin, the most trouble anybody ever got into was a bar fight on a slow Saturday night, which usually made the very small police blotter section of the newspaper.

Richard covered the basic things that any small town loves to hear about—the local fair, the dairy prices, the beauty pageants and the honour roll, all just as important as the minutes of the community meetings. For the rest of his content he got creative, and usually a human interest story topped the front page. He loved to get to know people and to write about their troubles or their victories, whether it was the champion of the third-grade spelling bee or the farmer struggling to hold on to land that had been in his family for half a dozen generations. Stories like that brought the community together.

As he flipped through the paper and looked at the ads for used cars, telemarketers and construction workers, he wondered what kind of story Rebecca would have to tell, and if she would let him tell it.

At that moment the object of his thoughts came down the hallway and peeked into the kitchen. The sharp smell of coffee and the sweet smell of bacon had made her stomach rumble even before her eyes had opened. She stepped into the kitchen and Richard turned to look at her, his smile far too broad for this early hour.

"Good morning," he said, his voice booming.

"Good morning."

"Breakfast is almost ready."

Her stomach rumbled again. "I'm starving."

"Good. I've got everything you can imagine for breakfast. I hope you're not a vegetarian?"

She laughed. "No."

"Get some coffee and have a seat. Juice is in the fridge, if you would rather."

"Can I help?

"Thank you, but no need. It's almost done."

Rebecca pulled a chipped mug from a hook underneath the cabinet and poured a cup of scalding hot coffee. She gingerly took the first sip. The coffee last night was simple and serviceable, but this was a surprise—it had a deep, rich flavour, complemented by just the right touch of hazelnut.

"This is delicious," she said, braving another sip. The coffee lit warm embers in her belly.

She sat down at the table and looked around the country kitchen. Everything from the night before seemed like a bit of a blur, and she hadn't taken the time to appreciate the room until now.

The stove was working hard, all four burners going with something good in the pans. Copper pots hung from a decorative rack above the stove. In the pitcher on the counter there were a dozen wooden spoons, stained and well-used. The counters were spotlessly clean, and the table was big enough for a family, though it appeared Richard lived here in the big house alone. She hadn't seen a single picture of kids or a wife, and he wasn't wearing a wedding band.

"It's just you in this big house?" she asked.

"Yep. Just me."

"Thank you for letting me stay here last night."

Richard smiled as he flipped a slice of bacon. "You really need to stop thanking me."

"I will eventually."

He laughed, the sound hearty and strong.

"Is it really as bad as it looks?"

She was gazing out of the window at a world of white. Trees dotted the landscape. They looked like big, abstract snowmen.

"It's worse," he said. "The roads are still closed down, and probably won't open today. Emergency vehicles only."

Rebecca sighed, staring into her coffee cup. "I'm sorry to be a burden."

Richard turned to look at her. She was sitting in that chair as if she wished it would swallow her up. There were dark circles under her eyes. She met his gaze as she took another sip of coffee.

"Why would you think you're a burden?" he asked her.

"It must be hard to have someone invade your house like this," she said. "I'm sure you weren't expecting company, especially company that might stay a while."

Richard put the last of the bacon on a platter, next to the sausage, and gave the gravy a stir. He opened the carton of eggs. "How many?"

Her stomach was still rumbling despite the coffee. "Three. Over easy, please."

Richard cracked eggs into the pan. They sizzled for a moment before he moved them around a bit with the spatula. "I hadn't expected company, no. But you're safe and warm here in my house, instead of freezing to death in that car out there. I'm happy to have you here, Rebecca."

She smiled, feeling the first flood of emotional warmth since her fight with Gene last night.

Richard pushed bread into a toaster and gave her a sheepish grin. "I'm pretty good in the kitchen, but homemade biscuits are where my expertise ends."

"It's fine," she assured him. "It's all fine."

Minutes later they were sitting together at the kitchen table, eating breakfast and not talking much. Rebecca was too busy appeasing her hunger, and Richard was too busy watching her do it. She seemed rather quiet and shy, something he wasn't accustomed to seeing. Everybody in Crispin knew who he was and nobody was ever shy about talking to him, especially when they had something to say about the paper.

"What do you do for a living?" he asked her.

"I'm a photographer."

That piqued his interest even more. "How long have you been doing it?"

"Ten years now. Since high school."

So she was in her late twenties. Richard nodded. "I know what it's like to start young. I've been the editor of the newspaper here since the day I graduated college."

Her smile lit up her whole face. "Somehow I knew you were the creative type. There's a certain vibe to us artsy ones, isn't there?"

"Absolutely."

Happy to find a kindred spirit, Rebecca started to talk, telling him all about the pictures she had taken on her way up to Iowa. When she told him about the gorgeous mellow light of southern Illinois, and the juxtaposition of an old, weathered silo beside a tall and modern windmill, she came alive with passion for what she did. She told him about taking pictures of kids who didn't want to have their pictures taken, or about taking pictures of CEOs for their company brochures, and explained how those were the things that paid the bills—the real thrill was in the creative work, and she was becoming better at it every day, and making a name for herself.

He told her about the paper, about finding a niche that allowed him to compete with the huge papers in Des Moines, and how he loved to write about the most unexpected things. Sometimes he came across a difficult or even heartbreaking story, but he tried to write it in such a way that the townspeople were inspired to help, as they so often did. He talked about going to college and planning on being in the big leagues, but after a few years spent at the *Chicago Tribune*, he'd decided the smaller towns and simpler life were what suited him best.

Over eggs and bacon and toast they got to know each other, and by the time the plates were clean they were talking about everything under the sun. Their common ground had broken the ice.

Then Richard asked her if she had made that call last night, and if her boyfriend was worried. A dark shadow descended in her eyes.

"He's not my boyfriend anymore."

Richard raised an eyebrow in surprise. "That was fast."

"It was long overdue."

"I'm sorry, regardless."

Rebecca's smile was sad. "It was my choice."

An awkward silence took over. Richard started to clear the table of their plates. He had no idea what it was like to make the choice to end a relationship, because he hadn't been the one to end his. Amanda had taken off for parts unknown and left him with very little choice in the matter.

"Does that make it easier?" he asked. "That it was your choice?"

Rebecca sighed. "No."

Richard set the plates in the sink and ran hot water over them. He opened the dishwasher. Rebecca watched him as he moved. His motions were deliberate, but not slow. He seemed the kind of man who wanted to make sure a job was done right the first time. His body was long and just slightly overweight, but not enough to detract from how handsome he was. His brown hair was cut close to his head, his face neatly shaven. He looked like an accountant, or a banker, or exactly what he was — the editor of a newspaper.

When he looked at her the way he had over those plates, studying her and completely absorbed by what she was telling him, his eyes lit up and made him look much sexier than he first appeared.

She contemplated this as he refilled her coffee mug and started the dishwasher. When there was nothing left in the kitchen to do, he rested against the counter and looked at her. They studied each other openly, without any words, while the sunlight streamed in from the wide windows.

"I might try to go into town today," he said, almost to himself. "I'm sure there are things you need, either from your car or from the store."

"Yes, but there's no hurry."

"Want to see the rest of the house?" he asked, suddenly remembering he hadn't shown her where things were.

Rebecca rose from the kitchen table. When she walked past him into the hallway, he caught a whiff of her hair, clean and smelling of his own shampoo. For no reason whatsoever his heart began to pound and certain other parts of him began to respond in kind. He tried to think of anything else, but the images of his fantasy from the night before came back with a vengeance.

As she looked over the dining room he wondered, for the briefest of moments, what it would be like to bend her over the table.

Rebecca didn't think anything out of the ordinary until they went up the stairs, where they looked at his office — quite messy compared with the rest of the house — another large bathroom, and the bedroom where Richard slept.

He hadn't intended to show her the room, but she opened the door as he motioned towards it, and what was he supposed to do? Shout out for her to stop? She stood in the doorway and looked at his most private space. The bed was unmade and the pillow still held the indentation of his head. On the bedside table were a small lamp and a few books, and beside the bed was a bookcase, every available inch crammed with the printed word. The door to the closet was open and, though clothes were hung neatly on the bar inside, the floor of the closet was covered with clothing, obviously waiting for a washing machine.

Rebecca grinned when she saw that, and she turned to make a funny comment to Richard about it. But before she could say anything, she suddenly realised they were standing in his bedroom door, and he was looking down at the floor, shy and uncertain, almost like a schoolboy who had been caught doing something wrong.

God, she wanted him.

The thought came out of nowhere and made her forget what she was going to say. She immediately began to discount that moment of attraction. He had saved her life, so of course she should be attracted to him, right? Besides that, she had intended to spend the evening with Gene last night, getting laid in every position imaginable and some that were not, and her body had been amped up with anticipation for weeks. Richard was the man who happened to be there, and her body was still craving a touch...so it made sense, right?

She had almost talked herself out of it. She had almost regained her composure. Then she chanced a look at Richard again.

He was staring at her with raw, untempered lust.

Rebecca actually took a step back from that gaze, startled by it, but more shocked by her own reaction—her body tingled in the most inappropriate places.

Richard immediately looked away. They stood together at the threshold of his bedroom, neither of them sure what to say. The longer the silence stretched, the guiltier Richard felt. He took a step back from her, then another, using distance as a barrier.

"I'm sorry," he finally said. "I haven't had a woman in this room in years."

Rebecca stared at him for a moment longer, her thoughts running rampant. He wasn't denying what she had seen, and strangely enough that thrilled her. Most men would have hemmed and hawed and tried to cover up what they had just done, but Richard didn't make an attempt. Instead of being offended by the way he had looked at her, she found herself impressed by what his response told her.

Richard was an honest man.

And, after all, hadn't she been thinking the same things?

"Thank you," she said.

The words from her made Richard look up. He gave her a grin. "I told you to stop doing that."

"Thank you for being honest with me."

Richard shook his head, amazed that he wasn't on the receiving end of a lecture. He deserved a good slap for the lecherous way he had eyed her. "You did catch me in the act, Rebecca. I wouldn't insult you by telling you otherwise."

"Thank you," she said softly, "for looking at me that way."

Now the silence came from Richard's side of the conversation, and the blush came from Rebecca. He studied her for a while, not sure what to say, so he did the only thing that felt right. He said the things that sprang to mind, all of them the truth. "It really has been a long time. Years. To see a beautiful woman in my bedroom after all that time, well...that makes me remember what I've been missing."

Rebecca blushed harder when he said she was beautiful. "I've been missing it, too."

"But you said you had a boyfriend?"

Ah, here was the tricky part, the thing she didn't know how to explain.

"I had a boyfriend for a while," she said. "But we never actually slept together."

Richard blinked at her for a moment, taking that in. "How is that possible?"

Rebecca shrugged. "We met over the Internet."

It all became clear to Richard then. He had never had a true relationship blossom over an Internet line, but there were people he talked to on the phone quite often for business, people he had never seen before, and he knew little details of their lives—the names of their kids, for instance. Over time, he came to care about them, and never failed to ask how their lives were going outside of work. He knew how easily a cordial discussion could turn personal, and how natural it was to come to care for someone, even if he had never met them in the flesh.

"I understand."

Rebecca didn't say anything else. She stood there, staring at Richard, thinking things she knew she probably shouldn't be thinking. She waited until he met her eyes, then she gave him a small smile.

"I know it might be too forward..." she started, but found she couldn't go on. My God, what was wrong with her?

She let the words hang there between them and watched as his mind caught up to what the rest of the sentence would have been. She watched as he considered how to answer.

The meaning behind her words plunged Richard into a sea of confusion. He was still married, wasn't he? Just because his wife had been gone for three years didn't mean he wasn't still bound to her, by the laws of both God and man. But it had been such a long time, and often he wondered if his wife had slept with someone else in the time she had been gone. In fact, more and more he wondered if her version of "finding herself" had more to do with spending time with someone else. That would never excuse him from doing the same thing...or would it?

Especially if nobody would ever know.

Rebecca was offering him a few stolen moments of passion—if he was reading her right, that was—and what was wrong with accepting something that would make him feel more alive than he had in a very long time?

"It might not be too forward," Richard finally said.

Rebecca wasn't sure whether to laugh or cry. What in the world was she thinking? She suddenly buried her face in her hands and let out a nervous, high laugh. "I have no idea where that came from," she said.

"Please don't apologise."

"It just popped out."

"Rebecca."

She dropped her hands and looked at him. He reached out and touched her for the first time since he had pulled her from her car. His hand caressed the side of her face.

Overcome by the simplest touch, she turned her face into his palm and breathed of his skin.

This was all kinds of wrong. Wasn't it?

"Yes," she said.

Richard couldn't believe his ears.

"Do you want this?"

She took a deep breath.

"Yes."

The answer was so simple, so easy and so completely crazy. She wasn't this kind of woman, and she was pretty sure he wasn't this kind of man, but with the bed only a few steps away and his warm hand touching her so gently, it suddenly seemed like the sanest thing in the world.

Richard paused, not sure how to say what was on his mind, but certain it had to be said before he lost himself in her the way he really wanted to. "I told you it's been a long time," he reminded her. "I'm not...prepared."

She looked up at him, her eyes wide. "I am."

Richard moved closer to her, unsure how to go about what he wanted, but Rebecca had no such qualms. She put a warm hand on the back of his neck, tilted her head up and pressed her lips to his.

The touch of a woman had been missing from his life for longer than he liked to think about, and now the return of it made his heart pound. He actually went weak in the knees, a fact that would have amused him greatly if it were any other time. He wrapped his arms around her to keep some sense of equilibrium. Her body nestled against him like it was meant to be there, and when she slipped her tongue into his mouth they both moaned with the pleasure of it.

The memory of the night before came to Richard, when he had thought about her as the orgasm overtook him. He had never imagined then what would be happening now: the woman he had fantasised about taking his hand and leading him to his bed.

She sank down on the mattress and pulled him to stand in front of her. She bent her head and rested her forehead against his belly, her hands on his thighs. She sat there for a long moment, breathing deeply, while he ran his fingers through her hair. He made no move to rush her. When she ran her hands up his thighs and found the buckle of his belt, he pulled his T-shirt over his head. Rebecca pushed his jeans down his legs and smiled at how ready and willing he was. She licked her lips and looked up at him with wild eyes.

"How long did you say it had been?" she asked directly, and he blushed as he thought of the answer.

"Over three years."

Rebecca was surprised, but a part of her was delighted. After so long without the touch of a woman, he would respond to every breath and kiss as though it was food to a desperately hungry man. All her hesitation fled as she thought about how much they would both enjoy this.

She moved to the edge of the bed, grabbed his ass with her hands and pulled him forward into her wet, open mouth. At the first taste of him she thought of Gene, expecting a tiny sliver of guilt at the very least. There was none — and so she took Richard deeper into her mouth, tasting more.

Richard shuddered at the first touch, then groaned as her mouth enveloped his dick, swallowing him so much deeper than he expected. She bent her head a bit and worked him deeper, sliding her tongue around the bottom of his shaft, stroking him with it. He threw his head back and his fingers tangled in her hair.

He thought of Amanda then, the wife he hadn't seen in over three years. She was the last one who had done this to him, back when he had thought everything was fine, back when he had believed that forever really meant something. The guilt rose up in him but on the heels of it came the anger.

She could have been here, he thought. *She chose not to be.*

Richard then stopped thinking at all, because Rebecca was doing wicked things that demanded attention. She started to bob up and down, sucking him hard at the tip before plunging the length of cock back into her mouth. Soon his manhood was slick, and she was stroking him with her hand as her mouth sucked at his crown. Richard's legs started to tremble. The approaching orgasm promised to be a very, very good one.

"Rebecca," he managed to say. "I'm going to come."

She stopped moving her mouth but her hand kept up that same rhythm, holding him right on the edge. "I'm going to swallow it."

He almost came right then, and probably would have, if she hadn't suddenly squeezed his cock. The orgasm backed away a bit, but came roaring back to life when she lowered her mouth on to him again, this time gliding faster, making her intentions very clear. She grabbed his hips hard as he started to thrust against her, his dick going a little deeper into her mouth each time. He couldn't have stopped her even if he'd tried — she obviously wanted his cum and she was going to get it.

That's what sent him over the edge. He came hard, his cock pumping almost painfully into her, sending warm jets of semen down her throat. She swallowed and he could feel it, a soft spasm around the tip of his dick. He leaned on her and held on to her hair as the last pulses of his orgasm faded away. She swirled her tongue around his dick as she pulled back, leaving him cool and damp in the warm air between them.

"That was…" he began, then laughed instead.

Rebecca laughed too, even as she lay back and hauled him on to the bed with her. "That was just a preview."

She kissed him until they were both breathless. Then she gently put her hand on his chest and pushed him away.

"Give me one minute," she said. "I will definitely be back."

"Where are you going?"

She giggled and kissed his nose. "Just a second."

She rose from the bed and disappeared around out the door. Richard smiled up at the ceiling and tried to catch his breath. Before he could start to think about what had just happened, Rebecca appeared with her small purse. She sat it down next to the bed and crawled onto the mattress beside him.

"So, where were we?" she asked.

Richard rose above her and started working the buttons of her shirt. His hands shook and she laughed again, then pushed his eager fingers away and did the work herself. The shirt came off and so did the jeans, pushed down her legs by Richard before she kicked them to the floor. She was wearing nothing underneath the clothes, and Richard sighed in approval as he looked down at her body for the first time.

Her nipples were hard. Richard touched them gently at first, but when she smiled at him he touched them harder, and finally she arched up under him and made a low sound in her throat. It was an animal growl, nothing like the sweet woman she seemed to be. She blushed even as she told him what she wanted. "Like that."

He pinched her nipples between his fingers and rolled them, sending little shockwaves through her body, as if a direct line connected her nipples to her clit. She was already wet from sucking him off, but the rough treatment of her nipples made her even wetter. It had been over a year since she had got off with anything other than a toy or her own hand, and she wanted nothing more than to lay back and let him do whatever he pleased, so long as she came at the end, and came hard.

Richard hovered over her, watching every reaction. He loved the way her nipples got even harder as he pinched them, and the way her chest flushed red, as if a fever were glowing within. She tried to open her legs but he sat on top of her, trapping her thighs between his knees, forcing her to keep them closed. The restraint, even as gentle as it was, wreaked havoc on her. When he slid a fingertip down between her breasts and headed for her belly, the little muscles there jumped in anticipation.

His tongue swirled around one of her nipples, and Rebecca cried out with the pleasure. That line between pussy and nipple tightened even more, until her body was primed and her emotions were raw.

"Fuck me," she growled, and in answer Richard licked down her belly, finally freeing her thighs as he moved down. She opened her legs and he immediately put his hands on her knees, pushing her legs wider apart, until she was spread open for him.

He sat back and looked at her. Her cheeks blushed scarlet under his gaze, but she didn't try to close her legs. The muscles in her thighs quivered as he looked at her. Her carefully-trimmed pussy was already so wet, it was almost dripping. Her chest heaved as she waited for the touch she wanted so badly.

Richard bent low between her legs and took a deep breath, inhaling her scent. Rebecca reached above her and grabbed the headboard as his mouth hovered closer. When his tongue snaked out and touched the cleft of her pussy, she let out a long cry of desire.

"Please do it," she panted, any inhibitions long gone. "Please, oh, please. It's been too long."

Richard didn't make her wait. He recognised the desperation in her voice, so much like the sound of his own. His tongue dipped into her as he spread the lips of her pussy, the final secret of her body opening like a flower rising to meet the new rain. He pressed his tongue as deeply as he could, tasting the wetness of her before sliding his tongue up to touch the base of her clit. She went perfectly still at the new sensation, waiting for more.

Richard slipped the tip of his tongue against the sensitive nub and pressed, moving slowly up and down, waiting for the reaction that told him he was doing the right thing.

She started to tremble, the delight flooding her from the inside out. Her whole body tingled; her very skin felt alive. "Yes, yes, yes," she chanted, a mantra that kept pace with the stroking of his tongue. When that stroking became too fast, too hard, pushed her too close, she stopped talking and simply closed her eyes, raised her hips up to him, and let it happen.

The orgasm shattered from her centre, a thousand pinpoints of light glistening in her head, the waves of it lifting her body even higher, closer to Richard's talented tongue. She writhed under him but he held her hips, his tongue still working magic even though the goal had been reached. When she would have become too sensitive and stopped touching herself, Richard kept on, intent on driving her to another orgasm right after the first.

She hadn't thought it would happen again, but when it did she let out a wail of pleasure. The waves were higher this time, stronger, and her heart pounded so hard she could hear it in her ears. She let go of the headboard and instead grabbed his head, his hair thick under her fingers. She closed her legs around him, trapping him there until the last of the pleasure trickled away.

When it was over she lay stunned, almost unable to move. Richard climbed on top of her and paused. "Are you sure?"

"Yes."

She reached for the purse she had placed beside the bed. She had been prepared for anything on this trip, but she had thought her preparations would be for Gene, not for this other man she hadn't dreamed she would meet. She found what she was looking for and pushed thoughts of

Gene out of her mind. She was quite happy where she was, thank you very much.

Richard smiled as she held up a shiny condom packet. "I'm on the pill," she explained, "but we haven't had that very important talk about histories, so..."

Richard smiled and took the packet from her. She watched as he rolled the protection on, then opened her arms to welcome him against her.

With one long, smooth stroke, he slid his hard cock into the place his tongue had just worshipped. The stretching, so foreign and so welcome, sent more shockwaves through her body. He held very still, watching her face, waiting.

"More," she murmured.

Richard began to move, his cock inside her hotter than she had imagined, the size of him making her ache. She wrapped her legs around his hips and rocked with him, her hands discovering the muscles in his back. She loved the way they tensed and relaxed with each thrust, the way his buttocks hollowed out as he drove forward, then relaxed as he pulled out. Soon they found a rhythm that melded so easily, it was hard to tell where he ended and she began.

She watched him as he fucked her. When he closed his eyes and lost himself in the pleasure, she relaxed her legs and looked down between them, where she could see his cock slide in and out of her pussy. When it came out, his dick was slick and shiny with her juices; when it slid back in, she noticed how their pubic hair pressed together, the curls tangling in a seductive dance. Soon he was buried deep and not pulling out anymore, stroking hard, and she wrapped her legs tighter.

"You're going to come," she murmured into his ear. "I want you to come so hard. I want to feel your cock throbbing against the walls of my cunt. Give it to me, Richard. Give it to me…"

Richard closed his eyes and threw his head back, gritting his teeth as the sensation spread up his spine. His thrusts became jerky and his knees started to slip on the sheets. She grabbed his ass to pull him harder into her, her calves now riding the small of his back, her body almost bent double. He thrust harder, so hard she couldn't catch her breath.

When he came, it was with a shout that echoed down the hallway of the house. He pushed as deeply into her as he could go, his dick completely buried in her warm, soft body. The orgasm seemed to go on forever. She held him so hard he couldn't have moved away if he'd wanted to, and that alone made the moment last longer — he loved the fact she wanted his cum so badly she would hold him there until she got every last drop.

When the final spasm of his body faded, he collapsed over her. Instead of pushing him off, Rebecca rolled with him, her legs still locked around his middle, his dick still inside her. She pressed her body hard against him, keeping him in, and she stared at his face until he opened his eyes and smiled at her.

"You…" he began to say, and she held a finger to his lips.

"Hush."

He thrust against her once more. The aftermath of the orgasm made his body tingle. He gently pulled out of her and made quick work of getting rid of the condom, then wrapped his arms around her.

Richard kissed her, a slow and lingering exploration. They lay together on the pillow, their bodies still humming with pleasure, and smiled at each other.

Chapter Five

"It's hard to believe you haven't done this in years," she teased as they lay in his bed together, a quilt pulled over their naked bodies. "You gave quite a performance, Mr Paris."

"You did quite a good job yourself," he said. His body still throbbed with the delicious aftermath of what they had done. He could hardly believe he had come twice. He couldn't remember the last time he had done that.

Rebecca's body felt alive in his hands. She watched as he traced a finger down the middle of her chest, going as far down as he could before his hand met the quilt. Then he came back up, trailing that finger over her collarbone and under her neck, pausing to test the pulse at her throat.

"Still pumping hard," he whispered, and she smiled.

"Are you proud of yourself?"

"Why not?"

Rebecca cuddled closer to him. The clock on the bedside table said it was now one o'clock in the afternoon.

Nothing had moved outside. If the phone had rung, neither had heard it. The world seemed to have stopped completely, and all they had was time.

Richard would have been at the newspaper office today, assuming the sheriff wouldn't have yanked him off the streets as soon as he had heard the roar of his snowmobile headed for the town square. He would have worked on a few articles for next week's paper, made small edits to the one going to print tomorrow, and spent time doing unnecessary work just to keep busy. He would have been the only one there, and he would have wavered between going crazy with the silence and being grateful for the solitude.

Now he didn't have to worry about either.

"It's hard to believe you showed up in my life less than a day ago," he said to her now. "I'm not the kind of man who does this."

"I'm not the kind of woman who does this."

"Snow makes people crazy."

They grinned at each other, complete strangers who definitely weren't strangers anymore. She loved the way he looked at her, as if he couldn't get enough of the shape of a woman. When he slid his fingertip down between her breasts again she stretched, her supple body a canvas before his hands. His eyes roamed every inch of her skin and then his fingertip followed. He smiled when his touch brought forth goosebumps, turning her perfect smoothness into perfect roughness.

"I would much rather be with you right now than with Gene," she said.

"Gene is his name?"

"Yeah."

"What happened, anyway? He was your boyfriend last night and today he's not. How did things change so quickly?"

Rebecca sighed and shifted on the pillows. Thinking of Gene made her feel slightly guilty, but when she recalled his words from the night before, the guilt fled just as quickly as it had come. "He called me names," she said. "And told me I was an idiot for not listening to him. It was just confirmation of what I already knew, in the back of my mind. He's not the kind of man who would take kindly to a strong, independent woman."

"You're definitely strong and independent," Richard said.

"You hardly know me," she chided, realising how ridiculous that sounded, considering they were lying together naked in his bed.

"Anybody who runs their own business has to have those qualities, and then some," he said. "Man or woman, doesn't matter."

"Gene seems to think only a man can do things that require such spirit."

Richard was now down at her knee, blowing breath over her skin and making her squirm. "How did you wind up involved with him, anyway? Surely he couldn't hide the way he really felt for long."

"I was lonely, and he gave good phone."

Richard laughed out loud, his belly moving against her toes. She reached down and mussed his hair. "Well, it's true."

"I believe you."

He kissed his way up her belly and peered at her from between her breasts. His hands slid up her arms, pinning her to the pillows, as his body rose over her. He was taller than her, perfect for kissing her while he slid into her. She kissed him back and laughed into his mouth when she felt his cock, hard, ready to go again.

"So," she whispered, "what about your sexual history?"

He grinned. What she wanted was the same thing he wanted, but he had felt it a bit too soon to ask such questions. "I'm clean," he said, dropping small kisses on her face. "I had a complete physical last year. I had never been tested before. I had always been in monogamous relationships. But when the doctor asked about it I thought, well, why not? So I had it done. Clean across the board."

She smiled up at him. "I get tested every year," she admitted. "I mean, you never know, right?"

"So, since we're both clean..."

"And since I'm on the pill," she said with a grin.

She opened her legs and he pressed between them, thrusting forward, filling her again. This time the sensation was more intense, the heat of her more evident. His moan of pleasure echoed hers. He began to move, very slowly at first, then picked up the pace.

"Again?" she teased.

"I can't come again," he admitted. "But there's nothing wrong with making you come, is there?"

She wrapped her legs around his hips and rocked with his thrusts. This time was slow and easy, now that the desperate need of earlier had been sated. There was no rush, only Richard's constant motion and her answering one, rising to meet him when he slid in, angling her body so that her clit got attention, letting the orgasm build. She could have hurried it along by touching herself as he thrust into her, but she chose instead to let her body ride the wave of sensation. The orgasm would happen when it happened.

When it did, it was just like their lovemaking — slow, easy, a full-body tingle that made her sigh with happiness. Richard watched her face as she came, and she found it made her feel even sexier than she already did. When she opened her eyes and smiled at him, he let out a long breath and shook his head in appreciation.

"That was beautiful," he said.

They spent the day in bed, sometimes talking, sometimes watching television, sometimes creeping naked to the kitchen to get a snack from the cupboards. Mostly they touched each other, memorising angles and curves and the things that made goosebumps rise. They finally drifted off when the moon was high in the sky, streaming through the window to fall over the bed that had held only one for so long, but now held two.

The early morning was crisp and cold when they stepped out of the house and confronted the snow. The sun was up and it was bright, but the heat from it did nothing to warm their little corner of Iowa. Richard led her to the garage, where she smiled at the snowmobile. It looked almost alive on the black skis, thrust slightly forward, as if sitting at the starting line of a race and ready to run hard. Richard checked the gauges and added a bit of gas from the container in the corner.

The other vehicle in the garage was a truck, a newer model but well-worn. The tyres were huge and the bed was scratched. The interior lights of the garage glinted off the silver-grey paint. She looked in the window at the wealth of things in the cab — old newspapers, not one, but three travel mugs for coffee, sunglasses and reading glasses on the dash, and a few books with library stickers on the cellophane covers. There was an old blanket thrown on the back of the bench seat. A small rip in the leather showed from under the frayed corner.

"This truck gets a lot of use," she said. "You sure you're a newspaperman?"

He smiled as he got on the snowmobile. "I don't have the patience for farming."

"But your house sits in the middle of all this farmland."

"Most of it is mine." His voice was nonchalant. He turned the key in the ignition and the snowmobile roared before it settled down to a ready hum.

"It's yours?"

"About seven hundred acres of it."

In Miami, land was precious. Seven hundred acres was a priceless commodity. "But you don't farm it?"

"Somebody else does. I lease out the land and by the middle of the summer I'm surrounded by corn and wheat. The newspaper pays peanuts, to be honest. Leasing the land keeps me in the black." He patted the back of the machine and gave her a grin. "Get on."

Rebecca lifted her leg and slid on behind him. Her thighs were sore from a different kind of riding, and she groaned as she settled into the seat. She wrapped her arms around him and the snowmobile started to move forward, inching towards the snow-covered driveway. By the time they were out on what had once been the road, Richard had picked up speed, and Rebecca was glad for her coat and the thick gloves he had loaned her. They were far too big for her, but they kept the wind away from her hands, and she was toasty warm as they rode in ten-degree weather.

"In Miami," she said over his shoulder, "it's about seventy degrees right now."

"But in Miami, you can't do this."

Richard hit the gas. The world whooshed past them, and she hung on tighter. When they reached an open field, Richard suddenly turned the snowmobile, and they did a perfect doughnut on the white surface. Her heart thudded with excitement.

"Wow!" Rebecca hollered. "More!"

Richard accelerated to an impossible speed, then whipped the big machine to the side. It glided effortlessly, as if it were flying on air instead of snow. The whole world spun, and when it slowed down Rebecca laughed hard, so hard her belly hurt. Richard pulled to a stop and turned to grin at her.

"I know what you want," he said.

She gave him an exaggerated leer. "I'll bet you do."

"You want to rev my engine."

"How did you ever guess?"

That's how Rebecca wound up behind the handlebars of her very first snowmobile, plunging through drifts and throwing up rooster tails of white. She slid and shimmied and raced through the snow, revelling when she hit a dip and came up out of it with enough speed to make the machine roar. Richard told her where to stay, far away from the fences and low brush that could be so dangerous to a snowmobile and its rider. Between his safe guidance and her impressive driving skills, they were having the time of their lives.

When they were both winded from the excitement and pumping adrenaline, she slowed the machine and turned to Richard. She pulled up his helmet, yanked down his mask and kissed him, her warm tongue sliding between his cool lips. His hands slipped down between her legs and pulled her back, her ass tight against his open thighs, his hand warm on her pussy. He kissed her back, wanting nothing more than to take her clothes off and have his way with her, no matter how cold it was.

"Wanna fuck?" she murmured into his mouth.

"Here?"

"I've never fucked in the snow."

He pulled her tighter against him. He had never done anything like that, even with all the ample opportunity that living in Iowa provided. The closest he had come to making love in the snow was stealing a kiss or two on a doorstep while the flakes came down around them. To take off his clothes — enough of them, anyway — and have sex in the freezing cold was just as new to him as it was to her.

"Someone could see us," he said, a last-ditch effort at sanity.

"That makes it hotter, doesn't it?"

He grinned. "You're going to get me in such trouble."

She climbed off the machine and turned to face him. Even under all those layers of toboggan and mask, he could make out her wicked grin. "Come get me."

He turned off the ignition as she took a step backwards. She took another step as he swung his leg over the snowmobile and stood up. By the time he took his first step towards her she was trying to run in the snow, sinking in almost to her knees, making a comical sight if he had ever seen one.

"It ain't like running on a beach, sweetheart," he laughed, and started to chase her.

He caught her not far from the snowmobile — his long strides overtook her smaller ones with little effort. As soon as he touched her, she twisted around and fell to the snow, laying back and looking up at him. Her coat was long enough to shield her from the cold wetness, and when she unbuttoned it and opened the sides, it was wide enough to protect him, too.

"Come get me," she said again.

He wasted no time in kneeling beside her and working the zipper of her jeans. She wiggled out of them, sinking deeper into the snow despite the coat underneath her, and she set to work on his pants. She pushed them down to his ankles and then he was on top of her, their legs bare and freezing, the rest of them warm. He pushed into her and she thrust up, the warmth of her core enveloping him. The cold air rushed over his ass as he pumped into her, his cock warmed by her body, the rest of him already shivering with the exposure to a wind chill that was well below zero.

The contradiction of cold and heat turned him on more than he had thought possible. He thrust into her until they were both breathing hard, then he abruptly pulled out and sat back on his knees. Rebecca watched as he slipped off his gloves and dug a hand into the snow beside them. Picking up a handful of it, he grinned at her before he pressed it against her pussy.

The shock of cold almost drowned the passion. "Richard!"

"Trust me."

He pushed snow into her pussy with his nimble fingers, then immediately slid his dick in behind it. The icy cold froze her for an instant before his warmth made the snow melt. He held there, felt the trickles of water slip down his balls, and waited until Rebecca's eyes widened with the surprise of it.

"I'm so sensitive," she murmured.

"You like?"

"Do it some more."

He scooped up another handful of snow. He thrust into her a few times, making her hot inside, then pushed more snow into her. His cock followed the way the snow had gone, and this time he fucked her through it, making the snow melt.

Rebecca was melting, too. She hadn't expected playing in the snow to be so intense. She lifted up her shirt, reached out beside her and grabbed small handfuls of snow, and pressed them to her nipples. They started to melt immediately, even as her nipples hardened under the cold.

"Make me come with it," she begged.

Richard scooped up more snow, this time leaving a handful of it on her clit as he plunged inside her. Her pussy tingled as the cold overtook her nerve endings, then tingled harder as the ice and snow started to melt. Her pussy was suddenly ultra-sensitive, ready enough that the slightest breath might make her come. The heat of Richard's thrusting was the perfect contradiction to the cold.

When he reached between them and squeezed her clit with his fingertips, her scream of pleasure echoed over the fields. Her cunt throbbed hard enough to force him out of her. Along with him went a gush of icy cold water, soaking the coat underneath her. He continued to rub her clit, making it warm again, until she had to push his hand away.

"Can you come?" she panted.

"It's too cold."

"Let's get back to the house so I can take care of you," she said.

Richard wrapped her clothes around her and helped her struggle out of the snow. He pulled up his jeans, his teeth chattering, and led her to the snowmobile. Once on the machine, they couldn't get close enough. The excitement of making love in the snow was quickly wearing off.

"Next time we try that," Rebecca said into his ear, "let's do it with ice cubes while in a nice, warm bed."

Richard laughed. "Next time," he mused, and started up the snowmobile.

They set off with the wind at their back. The sun was high in the sky but they met nothing on the way back to the house, neither animal nor human. It seemed that everyone else had the good sense to stay inside and away from the cold.

In the garage, Rebecca stomped her feet to get rid of the snow that had accumulated around her tennis shoes. Richard carefully took off his coat and hung it on a metal hook to dry, then took Rebecca's coat and carefully laid it out on the hood of his truck. Hers was wet all over, not just on the outside, and he smiled as he remembered the reason why.

When he came into the house Rebecca was already in front of the fire with two mugs of hot chocolate. She was barefoot, her wet shoes and socks sitting on the hearth in front of the flames. Her hair was messed up and her eyes were bright with the memory of what they had just done in the middle of the day in a snow-covered field.

"Drink this," she said. "You need it."

Richard took it gratefully and sat down on the floor. Rebecca did the same, resting her head against his shoulder as they watched the flames dance and let the enjoyment of the morning sink in. Every now and then Richard reached forward with the cast-iron poker and moved a log about, sending up embers and a blast of even more heat. Soon they were more than warm enough but neither of them moved, both happy with the presence and touch of the other.

"I know I should try to go into the office today," he said, "but I like the idea of staying in."

"Me too."

"We need to go to your car sometime soon, though. I'm sure there are things you need."

She nodded, thinking about her cell phone and her clothes. It would be nice to have her things, though Richard had been more than accommodating. He had even given her a new toothbrush, one he had bought to replace his old one, and had given her a package of disposable razors. These things had showed up on the vanity in her bathroom without a word from him.

"Thank you for taking care of me," she said now, meaning so much more than the lodging.

"It's entirely my pleasure."

She gave him a good-natured elbow to the ribs, and he laughed before settling back down to stare at the fire.

"How long until you're supposed to be back in Miami?"

She stretched her legs out in front of the fire, and Richard watched them with more than a little interest. He knew she would have to leave, and he had no illusions about forever with a woman he hardly knew, but he loved the discovery of sex after years of not having any. He hoped she would stay as long as she could.

"I've got an appointment in..." She thought about it, conjuring up a calendar in her head. "Nine days. I think."

"So you've got a week before you have to head back."

"Yes."

The pause was long and comfortable, but the question rode on the silence.

"You're welcome to stay here," he finally said. "I would love to have you."

Rebecca smiled and cuddled closer to him, glad he had said the very thing she was hoping for. "I would love to stay. I'm having the best time."

Richard was amazed that she had agreed so quickly, but he wasn't about to question it. Instead, he was going to make the best of it. "You have your camera with you?"

"It's the one thing I asked you for from the car the night before last. I took my purse and left everything else behind, except my camera."

"There's a camera in that big blue case? I thought it was clothes."

"It's a big camera," she admitted.

"There are dozens of good photo opportunities around here. I'll need to do some work at the newspaper tomorrow morning, but then I can take you around. With the snow on the ground, it's probably a photographer's dream."

She was already thinking of what she might be able to see in her viewfinder. She wondered how agreeable Richard would be to the idea of getting up in the wee hours of the morning to catch the sunrise over the fields of white. "That sounds beautiful."

"Maybe you can get enough shots for a book. Like Robert Kincaid in *The Bridges of Madison County*."

She smiled, thinking of how Richard was so accepting and encouraging of her work, as compared with Gene's constant put-downs and sneers when she mentioned the latest project. Had she really been that lonely that she had been willing to put up with his attitude towards her work? She supposed maybe she spent too much time working, that her insistence on following her dream made a personal life impossible. Other than Richard, she hadn't had an honest-to-God fling since college, and that was ten years ago. Fooling around with some guy after the second or third date didn't exactly count as a good sex life.

"Penny for your thoughts?"

She watched a red flame dance up from between the yellow. "I was thinking about Gene. I must have been very lonely to put up with him."

"Loneliness can make a person do what they shouldn't."

"I work far too much," she admitted. "Sometimes I think that's all I do. I even decided to drive to Iowa instead of flying so I could take more pictures."

"It's your passion," he said.

She smiled. "But it also means that Internet dating is my only hope."

"Not this week."

She laughed, and they watched in content silence as the fire crackled.

"Are you lonely?" she asked.

What a question, and Richard wasn't sure how to answer it. He was always lonely—it had become such a natural state that he didn't really recognise it anymore. At first it was a deep, gut-wrenching dread of going to bed alone, and soon that deepened into a depression that had lasted for more months than he'd cared to count. Now it was just a constant reminder, like an aching tooth. Sometimes it was worse, sometimes it was better, but it never really went away.

"I'm lonely all the time," he said. "Today is an exception to the rule."

He nudged her with an elbow and she nudged him back, grinning.

"I'm surprised you're not taken by now," Rebecca admitted. "A man like you, it seems a woman would be lucky to have you."

Richard took a deep breath, not sure how much he should tell her. If he mentioned his wife, would Rebecca understand? Or would she decide things had gone too far and retreat to the guest bedroom, only to appear again when the snow was cleared enough to pull her car out of it? Why hadn't he said something to her before, when she was standing in his doorway and giving him an invitation he didn't know how to refuse?

"It's complicated," he said instead. When he tried to find more words to explain, Rebecca saved him from it.

"It always is."

She stared at the fire for a moment, thinking about Gene, Internet dating, and all the guys who hadn't worked out; then shook off the doldrums like they were flakes of snow, determined to focus on the here and now. "Let's not think about that. Let's think about the fact that we're snowed in together, and that makes me a very lucky woman, indeed."

"It does?"

She stood up and reached for his hand. "Let's go to bed."

Chapter Six

They were in his bed. The covers and sheets were thrown back and the bedside light was on, the better for Richard to watch Rebecca as she moved over him. Her body was lithe and supple, and she arched like a cat when he hit that particular place she loved so much, the one he had already learned would drive her crazy.

She reached down to touch her clit and, when she did, her whole body responded. He watched in fascination as she shuddered. Her nipples went from hard to harder. Her pussy was suddenly wetter, drenching him with her juices as she moved. Her lips fell open as her eyes drifted closed.

"My vibrator would be perfect right now," she murmured, almost to herself.

"Where is it?"

"In the car. In a suitcase."

She rocked back and forth on him, strumming her clit, bringing herself close but not letting it happen. Every now and then Richard would reach out and touch her. His hand slid over her hip, then disappeared. A moment later it cupped her breast and squeezed gently, testing the weight of it. She kept her eyes closed, enjoying the question of where his touch would land next.

"I have a vibrator," he whispered.

She stopped moving and opened her eyes. For some reason this simple statement was so shocking, it tore her out of her fantasy world. "What did you say?"

"I have a vibrator. If you really want one."

She stared at him for a moment, then laughed out loud. The sound made her pussy tighten around his dick, and he thrust up into her. She started to move again.

"So you have a vibrator," she mused.

"Yeah."

"When was the last time you used it?"

Richard actually blushed as he thought about it. "Last week."

"Oh, really?"

The way she was looking at him sent his passion to a fever pitch. He hadn't seen a look like that before, but he was pretty sure he knew what it meant.

"Yes, really."

"How, exactly, did you use it?"

Richard took a deep breath. His cock got harder as he told her. "I ran it up and down my shaft, then held it against my balls while I stroked. That's how I got off."

Rebecca leaned over him, her breasts touching his chest, her breath on his lips. "Where did you come? All over the vibrator? In your hand? All over the sheets? In a tissue? Where?"

Richard reached up to kiss her but she moved away. "On the sheets. I had to wash them the next day. They had spots on them."

"What other toys do you have?"

Richard grinned at that. The idea of being snowed in for a week was appealing enough already, but it was getting better by the minute. "Enough to do the job."

Rebecca climbed off of Richard and sat on the edge of the bed. She was breathing hard and her eyes were bright with anticipation. "Get them."

Richard did as he was told. He opened the bottom drawer of the chest and pulled out a small, soft-sided box. He sat the box on the bed and flipped open the lid, gratified by Rebecca's gasp of delight. He had a small variety of toys, all bought from the store in Des Moines, where he was just as anonymous as any other man who ventured into the shop. He had two different vibrators, a few cock rings, the usual assortment of lubes and creams, and something the woman at the shop had called, with a wicked gleam in her eye, a 'pocket pussy'.

Rebecca held it up and looked it over, then quirked an eye at him. "Do you like fucking this?"

"Yes."

"How tight is she?"

He grinned at the way Rebecca made the toy sound like a woman. "Tight enough."

She smiled and put it back in the box. After a moment of consideration, she pulled out the smaller vibrator and a cock ring. Motioning to him to come a little closer, she leant forward and sucked his dick between her lips. The sudden and unexpected sensation made Richard shudder with appreciation. His head fell back and he thrust forward, going deeper into the warm, wet cavern of her mouth. She gave him a few moments of bliss before she put her hands on his thighs and pushed him back.

She held up the cock ring.

Richard got even harder at the sight of it. It was the tighter one, and he knew what that would do to him — it would prolong the pleasure until it was almost torture, and when he came it would be with such force he would howl with the delight of it, then collapse in exhaustion.

And that was when he did it himself. How much better would it be with Rebecca riding him?

"Put it on," she murmured. "I want to see."

Richard took the ring from her and slipped it over his dick. He pushed it tight against his balls, making certain it was on as far as it could go, then dropped his hands to his sides.

Rebecca stared at his cock for a moment, then reached out her tongue and gave the underside of his head a delicate lick. His manhood jerked in front of her and she was satisfied to watch it swell even bigger with the aid of that little piece of soft plastic.

"How sensitive is it?"

Richard was breathing hard as he watched her. "More than it was."

She took her fingernail and traced it down the underside of his cock. It jerked harder. "Now?"

"Yes..."

"Good. Lie down."

Richard did as he was told. Rebecca watched as he lay in the middle of the bed, waiting on her to tell him what came next. She knelt beside him and turned on the vibrator.

She pressed it against his chin and he lifted his head a little, his heart pounding harder now that he knew it wasn't just to be used on her. She slipped it down his throat and over to one nipple, where she held it, watching his face.

Richard squirmed under the assault. His dick was so hard it almost hurt, and now his nipples were, too. Rebecca switched the vibrator from one to the other as he moved under her on the bed, trying to get away and trying to push closer at the same time, unsure which one he really wanted.

Rebecca suddenly pulled the vibrator away and gave him a sweet grin. "My turn."

She yanked the pillow out from under his head. He blinked at the ceiling in surprise. Before he could move, Rebecca had climbed on top of him. She straddled his head, her knees pressed against his shoulders. Her pussy was right above him, at perfect eye view. He lifted his head, intent on licking what was presented to him, but she grabbed his hair and kept him right where he was.

"Don't move," she ordered.

She turned on the vibrator and pressed it to her clit. The sudden buzzing motion made her knees weak. She leant forward a little, held on to the headboard, and began to move the vibrator up and down, getting the most from her strokes. She made sure she was right above Richard's face, right where he could see every move she made. She absolutely loved being in control of him.

"How hard is your dick now?" she taunted.

Richard's dick was harder than it had been in recent memory. It poked straight up at the air, so sensitive that even the slightest motion made his balls ache with the need of a release. The pussy he wanted was right there in front of him, but he couldn't have it with his mouth or his dick. The reality of what he wanted, so close but so far away, made him even hotter.

Rebecca's pussy was dripping. She could feel it, the dampness on her thighs, and wondered if he could taste any of her. Had she given him any of her juices? She was so close to an orgasm, one good thrust of that vibrator against her clit would tip her over the edge. She braced her knees and pulled up a bit. She knew exactly what she wanted.

"Take your hand," she instructed. "Take your fingers and spread my pussy lips."

Richard reached up with a trembling hand and did as she asked. He looked right up into her as she kept moving the vibrator. He could see the tiny muscles moving when she touched the right spot, and he could see the wetness of her as it slid down. Unable to resist anymore, he lifted his head and licked at a drop of arousal, revelling in the musky taste of her.

At the touch of his tongue, Rebecca pressed the vibrator to the tip of her clit. The orgasm rocketed through her, leaving weakness in its wake. She collapsed over him but he was ready for it, held her up by her hips and neatly flipped her under him. Before the pleasure had faded he was on top of her, her legs over his shoulder, driving into her with enough force to push her up the bed.

She'd had a few long-drawn-out plans for what to do with that vibrator and cock ring, but Richard was beyond caring what they might have been. He had never before seen a woman come like that, so close he could almost feel it himself, and now his dick was in control of his actions. Rebecca simply opened her legs and braced herself on the headboard while whispering into his ear: "Do it. Come. Come inside me, Richard. Come."

The mantra matched his thrusts, and he came with a hearty shout. The orgasm actually hurt—whether it was from coming so often with Rebecca, or coming so hard, he didn't know, and he really didn't give a damn, either. All he knew was that pain was pleasure, pleasure was pain, and he hadn't come so hard in his whole life.

When he came back down to earth, Rebecca was smiling up at him.

"I simply adore Iowa," she said.

That afternoon, as the sun was dropping in the sky, they were back on the snowmobile, heading for the place where her car was still stuck in a ditch. They could hear the distant rumble of vehicles. Their hideaway would soon rejoin the rest of the world, thanks to the wonders of snowploughs and road salt. Richard knew he had to get back to work at some point, but these last few days with Rebecca had been more than newsworthy for him.

"What are you thinking about?" he asked her as they approached the buried car.

"Wondering if my lenses are okay," she admitted. "Pretty romantic, huh?"

"We've been romantic. Now's the time to be practical."

He slowed to a halt in front of the car and they both sat in silence, staring at it. The red paint shone through the snow, but so did the broken window — the emergency blanket he had used as a makeshift tarp had blown away — and looking in that window made Rebecca realise again how scared she had been, and what would have become of her by now, had Richard not come around when he did and pulled her out of the car that had so quickly become her prison.

Richard was seeing much the same thing, and marvelling at the fact she was so strong in the face of the memories that car had to bring back. He didn't rush her, instinctively knowing Rebecca would have to make the first move towards the car.

When she did, he breathed a sigh of relief and hurried to join her.

Rebecca knelt down beside the broken window and peered into the car. Her cell phone was on the dash, covered with a light dusting of frost. There was one medium-sized bag in the backseat, and her suitcase was in the trunk. She reached in and yanked out the bag, then retrieved her cell phone and her case with the new lenses. The first two she sat haphazardly down on the snow. The last she carefully opened, holding her breath as she peered in at the pristine black lenses, resting comfortably in their velvet cases.

"They look just fine," she said. "I'm not sure what the cold did to them, though."

"They're insured, right?"

"Oh, yes. Definitely."

Richard walked back to the snowmobile and returned with a folding shovel. He started to clear snow from around the trunk, but it was a one-person job, and that left Rebecca with too much time to think. The reality of what had happened settled over her, and tears stung her eyes, spilling over before she could brush them away. She took deep breaths to calm herself down.

Richard knew she was crying. He had seen it out of the corner of his eye. He had wondered when and if a breakdown would come, but, now that it was here, he didn't quite know how to help her. Would it be best to let her handle it on her own? Would she appreciate a hug or would she think he was being too much like her ex-boyfriend, trying to look down on her and make her cheer up?

Finally he turned and stared at her until her eyes met his. "I don't know what to do," he admitted, and she smiled.

"Let me shovel for a while," she said. "I need something to do."

Richard leaned into the driver's window as she started scraping away at the snow. He wiggled in until he could reach the glove compartment and flipped it open. Right on top was what he hoped he would find — her insurance card. He was sure she would need it to get the window fixed. He stuffed it in the pocket of his parka and wiggled back, cutting his hand on the shattered window in the process.

The shock of the pain coursed through him. Blood stained the snow underneath him. Realising what he had just done, he cursed roundly.

"What happened?" Rebecca called.

"Cut myself. It's nothing," he called back, holding snow against the cut to stem the bleeding. It was a little more than nothing. He looked in the backseat for something to wrap his hand in and came up empty, so he trudged back to the snowmobile for the first aid kit, holding his hand close and hiding it from Rebecca. He already knew her well enough to know how his hurt hand would affect her — even though it was his own fault, it was her car, and that would be enough to send her into the land of guilt.

Rebecca watched him go, thinking again how different he was from Gene. Richard had a deep-seeded patience about him. She already knew he was the kind of man who would say nothing unkind, nor would he look down on her. Instead, he had made it clear how much he admired her, and didn't hesitate to praise her strength.

How in the world was a man like Richard alone for so long? She pondered the question as she went back to shovelling snow. He said it had been three years, and she believed him—if there was anything else clear about Richard by now, it was his honesty. But what made him stay away from women for that long? Had someone hurt him, wounded him terribly and left him reeling? Had he not dealt with something from his past, or even worse, was he still pining after a woman who had broken his heart?

Rebecca's shovel scraped against metal. She had reached the trunk. She dug carefully around it, glancing back every now and then at Richard, who had just wrapped his hand in a white bandage and was now securing it with tape. She contemplated what might have gone wrong in his life, what event had caused him to live in that big house all by himself. She found that it really mattered to her, perhaps much more than it should have, and the more she thought about it, the bigger the questions grew.

"Need some help?" he asked from behind her shoulder, cheery now he had staunched the bleeding of his hand. He took the shovel out of her hands, dropped a kiss on her cheek, and started to clear out around the lid of the trunk. "We'll have your clothes out in no time."

"You're wonderful to me," she said.

"I'm glad you're here.

She kissed his cold cheek, and he turned his attention to the shovel.

When the trunk was finally visible, Richard found the can of denatured alcohol he had remembered to bring along. Pouring it on the seam of the trunk and the lock, he melted the ice that lingered there, and soon the trunk was open. Inside it was a spare tyre, a jack and a suitcase.

"All that work for that one little bag," he joked, pulling it out. It was stuffed full but still not as heavy as it looked. He strapped it on to the back of the snowmobile, making sure to leave enough room for Rebecca to sit, and looked back at her when she got settled.

Together they listened to the sound of approaching snowploughs.

"I hate to do this," he said slowly, "but we need to make a detour before we go back to the house."

"Okay?"

"I cut my hand on your window over there, and I might need a stitch or two."

Rebecca's knees went weak, a reaction that caught her completely by surprise. She immediately reached for his hand. "You're hurt?"

"It's not bad, but it's not the kind of thing that will heal on its own."

"Then it's bad."

"No, it's not."

"Yes, it is!"

Richard shook his head. "It isn't bleeding anymore."

Rebecca climbed off of the snowmobile and motioned for him to move. "I'll drive."

He looked up at her for a long moment. "Are you mad?"

"No. I'm worried."

"I'm fine, Rebecca," he soothed. "Really, I am."

"You got hurt on my car," she said, as if that explained everything.

"Don't do the guilt thing. Don't do the worry thing, either. I'm okay. If it was really bad, I would have told you as soon as it happened."

"That sounds suspiciously like a little white lie," she challenged, a grin playing around the corner of her mouth.

Richard blushed. "I'm fine."

She took his bandaged hand in hers and gently turned it over. She lifted the tape a little bit and tried to see under the gauze, but she was afraid to pull it too much. If he said he needed stitches, she believed him. He wasn't the kind to overreact.

"Let's get you to the hospital," she said, reaching for the key.

"Rebecca, honey."

The endearment made her go perfectly still. Jesus Christ, she had known the man for a few days, and under the least ideal circumstances, but already he was getting to her in a way that nobody had in a very, very long time.

"It's a few stitches," he said softly. "That's all. Why are you so upset?"

"Because..." She tried to find the words but was appalled to find only tears instead. She dashed them away with the back of her glove. What had got into her?

"I'm okay," he said. He wrapped his arms around her, even though his bandaged hand hurt like hell. He held her until she looked up into his eyes.

"I'm upset because if it weren't for me, you wouldn't be hurt," she said. "You had to break that window to get me out and now you've hurt yourself on the glass..."

"And if you hadn't bought a car with electric windows, instead of the old-school crank ones, this would never have happened?"

His teasing made her smile. "You know what I mean."

"If you hadn't come along, I wouldn't have just got cut. Okay. I wouldn't have had some of the best sex of my life, either."

That won a broader smile. "Best, huh?"

"Uh-huh."

"Want some more?"

"Once I know I'm not going to bleed to death."

Rebecca smacked him on the shoulder. "I thought you were fine?"

He dropped a kiss on her nose. "You drive."

With his careful directions, they made it to the hospital in less than five minutes, though it normally would have been a fifteen-minute drive. They cut through open fields and backyards, sometimes drawing the attention of the people inside those homes, who looked at them with furrowed brows through frost-edged windows. When they reached the hospital, it was a little jarring to see a perfectly cleared parking lot at the end of a cleared street. Rebecca had almost let herself forget there was asphalt underneath the blanket of white.

She parked the snowmobile beside the parking lot and they walked in together.

Richard took her hand as soon as they started walking, held it as he walked into the hospital, and only let go when he had to sit down and talk to the triage nurse. The nurse glanced at her with interest and might have asked about her, had she not been more interested in what Richard had done to his hand.

Rebecca stood beside him as the nurse carefully removed the bandage. Richard winced, Rebecca stared and the nurse whistled low under her breath when they saw the gash in the palm of his hand.

"I know one newspaper man who isn't going to be typing for a while," the nurse chided. She grabbed more gauze, held it against the wound and motioned to Rebecca to apply pressure. "I'll be right back," she said, and whooshed out of the room on quiet shoes.

"Jesus," Rebecca said, stunned by how deep the cut was.

"A few stitches will take care of it," he said.

"We'll have to be careful not to get lube on it."

He laughed out loud at her teasing.

When the nurse came back with the proper supplies, she led them into a little room and instructed Richard to sit down in a comfortable chair. She sat a metal tray on the desk beside him. On his lap she placed a pillow, then a waterproof mat on top of that, making a comfortable place for his arm to rest. She unpackaged what looked like an enormous needle, and Rebecca turned her head away.

"You can stay if you want to," the nurse said, "but it's not going to be pretty. You might want to wait in the lobby?"

Rebecca met Richard's eyes. There was no expression in them. He was letting her make the decision, and the fact that he wasn't about to ask her to stay made the decision for her. The nurse watched as Rebecca stepped to his side and put her hand on his shoulder.

"I'll be all right," she said.

The nurse gave her a broad smile. "Here we go."

Rebecca stood behind the nurse as Richard got a few shots of numbing medication, then got his stitches. She watched through all fourteen of them, and marvelled at how rarely he flinched. He seemed to be more interested in a story for the paper about the nurses at the hospital. He asked one question after another, and eventually more nurses came into the room, adding their own answers. Richard joked that he needed his tape recorder at a time like this, and more than a few of the nurses offered to answer his questions — anytime. Would he like their phone numbers, so he could call them when he was ready to do the story?

Rebecca reminded herself that she was leaving in about a week, that these women would be here long after she was gone, and that she had no cause to get jealous about things. After all, when they had cast curious looks in her direction, she had told them she was just a friend from out of town. That's what she was, wasn't she? She was a friend who happened to have wild sex with the man they all seemed to lust after, but how well did she really know him?

She watched as Richard collected phone numbers, prescriptions for antibiotics and pain medication. The attending nurse finished wrapping his hand again and pointed a finger at him.

"Take that medicine. Finish the entire antibiotic. Don't hesitate to take those pain pills if you're hurting. And stay away from broken glass, for God's sake."

"Yes, Madam."

The nurse gave Rebecca a final grin and walked out with his chart. Richard shrugged into his coat as Rebecca watched him from across the room. With his good hand he stuck the papers deep in his pocket, and a small twinge of jealousy nagged away in the corner of Rebecca's mind.

"You okay?" he asked, and she nodded.

"Are you?"

"Yeah. But I need to get some of this pain medication in me, because I have a feeling I won't be so okay in an hour or so. That was a big needle."

"That was a big cut."

They walked together down a long hallway and wound up at the pharmacy, where the receptionist knew him by name and didn't ask for his insurance information. The bottles were filled amid banter about the snow and what the paper would have to say about it, and a minute later they were outside in the darkness. The sun had gone down while they were under the fluorescent lights of the hospital, and now the world seemed a bit disorienting.

"What's wrong with you?" he asked when they were out of earshot of the hospital.

"Nothing."

"That's not true."

She didn't answer him, and soon he realised that no answer would be forthcoming.

Rebecca sat on the snowmobile and Richard climbed on behind her, wrapped his arms around her middle, and decided it might be best just to keep his mouth shut until she was ready to talk. Not a word was said between them as she manoeuvred the machine down the hillside and along the same path she had taken a few hours before. Richard laid his chin on her shoulder and watched the world go by while he wondered at the thoughts running through her head.

When they reached the house, Rebecca carefully slid the snowmobile into the garage. She turned off the engine and the silence rushed in, making it clear just how much time had gone by without a single word from her. Finally she sighed and turned in the seat to look at him. Why be anything but perfectly frank and honest?

"I've had so much fun these last few days," she started. "I've enjoyed every moment of being with you. It's almost magical, how it happened—you saved me from the blizzard, we wound up in bed, and it felt like the most natural thing in the world. But I guess when we were at the hospital I started to realise that this isn't a fairy tale, and it's going to end soon. When it does, you'll have your life and I'll have mine, and never the two shall meet," she said, and smiled sadly. "You'll have a lot of nurses waiting for your call."

Richard didn't know what to say. While in the hospital he had acted the same way he always had, and he'd had no designs on any of the women there. He had known most of them for years, and while some of them had made their interest known, he had never returned the favour.

"I don't think I'll be calling any of them for personal reasons," he said carefully.

Rebecca nodded and put on a brave face. "What you do is your business. I just think...well, I think I'm going to miss you."

What else could she say? No matter how magical things might seem, she was a realistic person, and the reality of so many miles between Miami and Crispin was very clear.

"You don't have to miss me yet," he said.

She climbed off of the snowmobile and took off her coat. Outside the garage the moon had drifted behind the clouds and it was almost pitch-black, but they could still hear the roar of snowploughs, so much closer now. The roads would be cleared by morning, and then they could pull her car out of the ditch, and then...

And then?

Rebecca stared at the snow until Richard pushed the button that lowered the garage door. They were left in utter darkness. She listened to him as he moved towards her, the rustling sound of his coat the only indication of his movement. When he wrapped his arms around her from behind, she bit her lip and fought the urge to cry.

"I don't know what's wrong with me," she murmured.

"Maybe there's nothing wrong at all."

She shook her head. "I'm not usually this emotional."

"I knew seeing your car again would be emotional for you. Maybe this is part of it."

"It's not the car," she whispered. She turned in Richard's arms and found his lips in the darkness. "It's not the car."

He kissed her back. "What is it, then?"

"I'm jealous."

The admission was like fuel to a fire. His desire for her blazed brighter than before, something he hadn't thought possible. He grabbed her arm and hauled her to the door of the garage, fumbling with the doorknob until she moved ahead of him and opened it for him.

They burst into the kitchen and immediately he took her down to the floor, where she rolled on top of him and reached for the snap of his jeans. Richard kicked them down, even as she stood above him and stripped out of her clothes. There was the sound of a seam ripping, a zipper opening, a swish of fabric on the tile floor, then she was on top of him, guiding him into her with one deep thrust.

At the now-familiar sensation of his cock impaling her as deeply as it could, Rebecca took a deep breath. She began to rock back and forth. There was no gentleness to her as she rode him, and when Richard reached up to touch her, she yanked his hand away. She looked right into his eyes as she slid her pussy up and down his cock.

"You're mine," she hissed. "For the rest of my time here, I'm going to fuck you so often and so hard that you won't look at another woman for months."

The warmth of her words flooded Richard. It was the balm he had always wanted, but had never really had, even when he'd worn his wedding band. "Show me."

She sat straight up and ground down hard. Her nails found his chest and drew sharp lines, taking away his breath and leaving raised welts on his skin. He thrust up into her from the floor, raising her up on his hips, and she pounded back so hard it hurt them both. The intensity of the physical taking pushed Richard quickly to his limits.

"I'm going to come."

"Good," she said. "Say my name when you do it."

"Rebecca."

"More."

"Rebecca. Rebecca…Becca…"

"Yes."

"I'm going to come…"

When he did come, he didn't hold back. He shouted her name as his cock twitched and spurted into her. She rocked hard on him, getting the most out of it, and when she felt the heat of him flooding her, she reached down between them, touched her swollen clit in just the right way, and came with him. Her pussy tightened on his dick as she threw her head back and cried out, her fingernails bringing blood from his shoulders, her whole body rigid, every muscle tense.

When it was over she sat on him and looked down into his eyes. Neither of them smiled. Neither of them knew what to say.

Finally she stood on shaky legs. He sat up and looked around at the kitchen as though he had never seen it before. He held on to the table as he stood, almost afraid his knees wouldn't hold him, his hand smarting with the motion. As soon as he let go of the polished wood, Rebecca flung her arms around him, almost knocking him back down to the floor.

"Thank you," she murmured, though she had no idea what she was thanking him for.

Chapter Seven

The sun came through the windows the next morning, waking Rebecca first. She lay in bed beside Richard and listened to his light, rhythmic snoring. He was on his belly, the covers pulled up to his shoulders. His bandaged hand rested on the pillow beside his head. He had got up twice in the night for pain pills, and each time he had woken her up just to hold her, kiss her and cradle her until they both fell asleep again. Now she smiled at him in the early morning light, tempted to kiss his temple but not ready to wake him just yet.

If she listened closely, she could hear cars passing slowly on the road in front of the house.

The snowploughs had come through during the night and cleared the snow away. She wondered about her car, if it had been hauled out by some anonymous driver, or if it was still buried in the snowdrifts. Today she would have to make arrangements to have it taken to a shop for repairs.

Then she would have to think about leaving, and getting back home to Miami.

The thought sobered her and her smile disappeared. She tried to imagine what life would be like when she returned to the sunny south. She would go on with her work, keep her appointments, and keep trying to find that perfect shot in the frame of her lens. She would ignore Gene's calls — she knew there would be several, because he wouldn't give up without a fight — and she would eventually contemplate getting involved with someone else.

The idea seemed so distant, almost ludicrous, as she lay in bed beside Richard. She was having the time of her life here in Iowa, and she was in no hurry to see it end. The fact that it *would* end was something she was just now starting to face, and already she didn't like the way it felt. She couldn't remember the last time she had enjoyed herself so much, and the thought of this happy vacation ending was more than she wanted to bear on a bright, sunny morning filled with such promise.

Richard stirred under the blanket and turned his face towards her. He didn't wake up, and Rebecca took her time studying him: the long, black lashes, the curve of his mouth, the two-day stubble on his face. She knew well what that mouth felt like against hers. She knew the roughness of his face and the looks he could shoot her with his eyes. She knew the way his hand trembled when he was close to an orgasm, and the way his voice dropped when he was out of his depth.

Who was to say she didn't know him?

Rebecca watched him until her own eyes became heavy. She fell asleep again and when she awoke the second time Richard was sitting on the edge of the bed, looking at her with a smile on his face. She didn't move, accustomed by now to the way he loved to stare, and let him study her as long as he wanted.

"I want to take pictures of you," he said.

She raised an eyebrow. "What kind of pictures?"

"Naked ones."

She laughed and buried her face in the pillow. Richard kissed the back of her shoulder.

"I have to go to the office. The newspaper must go on, even if I want a week off."

She watched him as he dressed — or tried to, anyway. His hand gave him trouble, and he stopped after he shrugged into his shirt, retreating to the bathroom for more pain pills. When he came back to the bedroom, she was waiting to help him with the buttons on his shirt. He wore slacks, which actually looked better on him than the jeans did, if such a thing were possible. She buttoned those for him, too. He found his watch and couldn't get it on without hurting his hand. So he handed it to Rebecca, who put it on his wrist as casually as if she had done it a thousand times.

They looked at each other after she had done it, and Richard was the first to speak.

"Come to the office with me."

She slowly shook her head. "I don't know that it's a good idea."

"Why not?"

"Because it will raise questions."

"Of course it will. I can handle those."

It wasn't just the questions that would come from the townsfolk who saw them together. It was also the fact that Rebecca wasn't sure she wanted to see another aspect of Richard's life. She already knew it would be easier to let him go at the end of the week if she could convince herself it was nothing but a fling, nothing but sex between two people who needed a touch. The deeper she delved into his life, she more she wanted to learn.

The more she knew about him, the more she had to miss.

"I think I should stay here," she said. "I need to make calls to get the car out of the ditch, first of all, then I need to talk to my insurance company, and then..."

"You can do all that from my office."

She gave him a desperate look, unsure how to explain her fears. "No."

Richard stared at her, dumbfounded by the sudden turn of events.

"Rebecca?"

She held up a hand and shook her head, willing him to stop. She couldn't make him understand without breaking down into tears, and she already knew how that would go over. He would talk her into telling him everything, then he would convince her it would be all right, and she would believe him because she wanted to, not because it made sense.

It was going to hurt so badly when she had to leave.

"I'm not going to shut up," he insisted. "I want to know what's going on with you."

"I'm telling you, I want to stay here."

"Yesterday, you were so interested in everything...and now you're hiding."

She refused to answer. Richard pushed it.

"Why?"

She climbed out of bed and grabbed at her shirt, trying to cover herself. Richard caught her in mid-stride and pushed her back on to the bed, where she bounced once before looking up at him in amazement. "What's wrong with you?"

"Don't turn this around on me," he said.

"You don't understand," she said, wanting to make him see her point, but she didn't know where to begin.

"You're not going to do this. You're not retreating into a shell."

"I'm not."

"You're not the only one who is scared to death," he said.

The roughness of his voice—that almost desperate sound—was enough to take her breath away. Rebecca closed her eyes and listened as his words rained around her.

"Don't you think I wonder what it's going to be like at the end of this week? That I would give anything to be able to ask you to stay for another week, and then maybe another, and get to know you in every way I can, not just while we're naked?"

Rebecca's heart started to pound. Her eyes flew open. "What did you say?"

"You act like I'm taking this casually," he said. "I'm not. I said I don't do this kind of thing, and I meant every word of it. I'm not the kind of man who lets a woman in like I've let you, and then lets her walk away without at least trying to see what could be there."

"It's just sex," she insisted.

"It was never just sex," he shot back.

Rebecca started to tremble. She pulled her knees up to her chest and wrapped her arms around them, hiding her body from him. It was a natural reaction to an emotional upheaval. How had this happened to her? She didn't know him a week ago, and now she was already dreading what it would be like to miss him.

If it wasn't just sex, then what was it, exactly?

"You've had a long-distance boyfriend before," he said. "It's not like it would be new…"

Richard stopped, realising what he had just said. Was he really asking her for a commitment? Was he really pushing that far? And what right did he have, the man who was still married to someone else, even if his wife hadn't been around in years? He hadn't filed divorce papers, and, even worse, he hadn't told Rebecca about the woman who was between them. She was there, just as surely as a physical presence, and until she knew the truth it was entirely unfair to ask her to continue in any sort of relationship, emotional or otherwise.

But he couldn't make the words come. He couldn't tell her.

"Are you serious?" she was asking him now, and he looked into her wide blue eyes.

"Yes."

The word sent shockwaves through both of them. She stared at him, taking in the word and the possibility. How crazy was it that she had wound up in this man's bed in the first place? Nothing could trump that kind of insanity, yet here she was, considering how Richard might fit into her life. Rebecca was never one given to snap decisions, and certainly not decisions on affairs of the heart made within just a few days, but damned if she wasn't thrilled at the prospect of having Richard for more than just her time here in Iowa.

He stood before her with his heart on his sleeve and his secret beating a tattoo of fear across his world. If he told her, he would lose her. He knew that as surely as he knew she would eventually leave his house and go back to her life in Miami. He knew that no matter what kind of distance there was between them when she was over a thousand miles away, it couldn't compare to the distance he put there himself by not telling her the truth.

She thought he was an honest man, didn't she? Once she knew he had hidden something from her, she would never be willing to believe the rest of what she had learned about him. He would lose value in her eyes and he would never be able to regain it.

"You're right," she said, and Richard was startled out of his thoughts.

"What?"

"You're right. I've had no problem with a long-distance relationship before."

Hope flooded Richard, as thick and strong as the guilt that was already there. "You mean..."

"I mean, yes. Yes. Let's see where this goes, Richard."

He crawled into the bed beside her, held her head in his hands, and kissed her until the thoughts of his wife and all the things he hadn't told her were chased away by the passion he felt for Rebecca. When he reached between her legs and tried to entice her into letting him do more, she laughed and pushed his hand away.

"I'm going to make you wait," she teased.

"Why?"

"Because it's fun."

She gave him a mischievous grin, and he couldn't help but wonder what kind of fun would happen after she had made him wait all day long. "Can we get out the toy chest tonight?"

"Now you're reading my mind."

He was hard already, straining against the fabric of his slacks. "I have to try to write stories for the paper while you're right in front of me? And then watch you take pictures while I want you so bad I could bend you over the nearest park bench and ram you in front of God and everybody?"

"Yes."

He almost groaned at the idea of Rebecca spread out over a park bench. "We had better get to the office, then, because I want to get this day over with."

She swung her legs over the bed and stretched, arching her back and showing off her breasts. Richard swallowed hard as he looked at the pert nipples, already hard and taunting. She stepped towards him until those nipples were tugging at the fabric of his shirt. "Let me go get a shower."

He watched her sashay into the bathroom. When the water started, he sank down on the bed and put his head in his hands. His body throbbed for attention. His mind was racing.

His hand ached. His heart was full with happiness and sick with dread.

"It's going to be a very long day," he murmured to the pillows.

For the first time in his life, working was torture. His hand hurt—that was the first thing to become apparent. No amount of painkiller kept it from aching as he tried to type, and that alone put him on edge.

It wasn't just his hand that caused him problems, though. He had to sit at the computer and put together articles while the woman beside him kept whispering naughty things into his ear. When he started to work on the story about the town's annual budget woes, she made a point of counting sexual positions — out loud — and disrupting his ability to make sense of numbers. When he went to upload a file on to the server, she casually asked if he would like to upload a few files into her when the sun went down. She asked him where he would like to upload — her mouth? Her hand? Her pussy? Or the tight ass he had yet to sample?

When she told him how much she had been craving a good ass-fuck, he almost choked on his coffee.

Amanda had never acted this way. The thought of being anything but a lady had never crossed her mind. In the bedroom she had been willing and eager, but had left the adventurousness to him. The first time he had brought home a vibrator she had blushed and hidden under the covers. It had taken weeks to get her to use it, but even then she had never done it when he was around.

The direction of his thoughts made matters worse. The thought of sex with his long-lost wife while Rebecca sat right next to him made him feel all kinds of guilty.

When he was finished with the articles he started working on the layout, and that's when Rebecca stopped teasing and got interested in something other than what was in his pants. She watched as the paper came together on the computer screen, marvelling at the puzzle of articles, pictures and advertisements that formed the *Crispin Tribune*. When she asked about where it printed, and how, he explained that a central server in Des Moines accepted the files and printed them throughout the night. Someone at the processing centre then pulled the papers from the racks, folded them, and had them ready for the delivery van by the wee hours of the morning. One of the three employees of Crispin's paper picked them up, inserted local ads in the middle, put mailing labels on those that went through the postal service, and put the others in clear plastic bags for doorstep delivery. Every week, the same process was repeated, and by now Richard had it all down to an art, if not an exact science.

She watched as he uploaded the files, thrilled to be learning more about what he did every week. The office had been in the same place since the first editor of the *Crispin Tribune* had started it, way back in 1938, and it was obvious that not much more than the computer system had changed. Ancient equipment filled up several of the back rooms and made the large building look smaller than it really was. Dust covered everything in the back storage area and made Rebecca sneeze. Richard laughed at her as he explained how the old printing press worked and showed her the drawers that still held their metal letters. Half-full bottles of old ink lined the shelves.

"This is fascinating," she said, staring at the bottles. Her eyes suddenly widened and she smiled at him with an air of discovery. "I'll be right back."

She disappeared out of the door and Richard chuckled. He knew exactly where she was going. Sure enough, she returned a few moments later with her camera. She had told him she carried a camera everywhere, always, for she never knew when inspiration would strike. Apparently it had struck in the offices of the *Crispin Tribune*.

Richard watched as she framed shot after shot of the back room, zooming in on things he never would have noticed: a mistake in the typeset on an old box, dozens of ancient papers fanned out with their dates showing, a bottle of ink with a perfect fingerprint on the closed lid. Rebecca saw these things with her creative eye and suddenly Richard viewed his office as a lovely place with secrets in every corner, instead of a dust-covered place that needed a good cleaning.

"You're amazing," he said to her, and she grinned at him before she lifted the camera.

She caught her first photograph of him while he stood in front of an old *Crispin Tribune* sign, a worn and faded banner they used to use at sporting events until it was too ragged to be hung with any dignity. He looked into the eye of her camera as she took the picture, completely relaxed under the gaze of her film.

Most people instinctively shied away from her lens, or worried about how the film would record them. She loved that Richard was comfortable enough with himself to allow such things and not bat an eye in embarrassment.

"What a place," she said, turning in a circle on the dusty floor.

"It is great, isn't it?" He had caught the fire from her, and now he was seeing all kinds of things to use in photographs, and even an article or two about the old printing press, the hectograph, and all the things that went together to make a paper run efficiently throughout the decades. He could do a whole series of stories on how the newspaper made it into the hands of readers each week. He was already seeing the headlines.

Rebecca read the thoughts in his eyes and smiled at him. "We make a good pair."

He took her into his arms and kissed her.

No one had come by the offices all day, but, as fate would have it, one of the local police officers chose that moment to walk in the front door with a classified ad. When Officer Watts saw Richard embracing a woman who was definitely not his wife, his surprise was written all over his face. He was even more surprised when Richard didn't immediately spring from the woman's arms. In fact, he took his time in moving away from her before coming to the desk and greeting the young man with a smile, as though nothing was amiss.

"Been a long few days for you boys, hasn't it, Steve?"

Steve blinked at Richard, looked again at the pretty brunette who was standing on the other side of the room, and decided to take the very obvious hint. "Busy doesn't begin to describe it," he said. "Why every fool with a heart condition chooses the same moment to shovel his snow, I'll never know. What happened to your hand?"

"A nice little slice of glass."

"Stitches?"

"More than I care to count."

"Hey, at least it wasn't a heart attack."

Richard grinned. "There's a reason I don't shovel snow."

Steve handed the ad to Richard, who pulled paperwork from under the counter and started putting the information into the form. "I just sent the paper off for printing, so this will have to run next week. I hope that's all right."

Steve nodded, eyeing the young woman as she walked through the back room. As soon as she was out of earshot, Steve leaned over the counter. "Hot damn and shazaam," he whispered. "Who the hell is the chickie?"

"The chickie is named Rebecca. She's here visiting from Miami."

"How the hell did you get a woman from Miami?"

"Mail order," Richard quipped.

The officer rolled his eyes. "I mean...how did you meet her?"

"She had some car trouble and I helped her."

Steve raised an eyebrow. "How's her car now?"

Richard paid attention to the paperwork and didn't answer. Steve looked around the corner at Rebecca then looked back at Richard. "Haven't heard from Amanda, I take it?"

Richard shot him a look that could freeze an ocean. Steve held up his hands and backed away from the counter. "Hey, whoa, okay. Sorry. It's none of my business."

"We can talk about it later," Richard said, smoothing things over. "Just not now, okay?"

"Okay. Man, I'm sorry. Really."

"It's all right." Richard gave him a genuine smile to show him that it really was all right, then handed the paperwork over for Steve's signature. Steve signed it, slid the appropriate amount of money across the counter and stepped towards the door, but not before shooting another look in Rebecca's direction.

When he was gone, Richard sighed and leaned on the desk. Close, so close, and now he knew the word of Rebecca's presence would be all over town by the end of the day. It wasn't that Steve was a gossip of any higher order than anyone else, but Crispin was a small town, and one overheard conversation would make it into every nook and cranny of their little world with surprising speed.

He had to tell her.

Richard looked at her as she walked back through the room, her camera in front of her face, taking shots of things he hadn't noticed before. He watched her as she lost herself in the old articles pinned to the bulletin board, and studied her as she took a good look at his awards on the wall. When she turned back to look at him, her smile was so radiant his whole heart warmed at the sight of it.

He had to tell her, but it didn't have to be right now, did it?

"Come on," he said, pulling the keys out of his pocket. "I know a place your camera will love even more than this."

As they stepped out into the snow and he locked the door behind them, Richard didn't miss the curious eyes looking at them from the diner across the street. Steve Watts stood in the middle of them, talking, and Richard thought he knew exactly what the man was saying.

"This is beyond beautiful," Rebecca said.

They were standing at the end of one of Iowa's famous covered bridges. Richard had told her the name of it but she had hardly heard him. She was too interested in the way the afternoon sun shone through the loose slats at the top of the bridge, the way the inside of it seemed to come alive with dancing light. Rebecca was glad she had brought along extra film. She stared at the bridge as she put the new roll into her camera with one hand. The digital camera was in the truck, but for shots like this she preferred to go old school.

She approached the bridge cautiously, gauging the light with every step. Her heart was pounding but her mind was serene, and that was always a good sign that she was in the right place at the right time. The world narrowed to the focus of her viewfinder, and nothing else around her mattered.

Richard watched silently as she worked, unwilling to disturb her concentration and happy to be able to watch her as she moved in her own creative world. It was like watching someone take a shower, or catching someone dancing when they thought no one was looking. She was so lost in the process, so absorbed with the world through her lens, that disturbing her would be tantamount to committing a crime.

Long minutes passed as she snapped one shot after another. Richard looked out over the creek that ran below the bridge and watched the water flow down the centre, gradually chipping away at the ice near the shore. When spring came the creek would be so swollen with runoff from the snows that the bridge would become almost impassable. He picked up a handful of ice with his good hand, gingerly patted it into a ball with his fingertips, and flung it into the water. The tiny splash was satisfying, so he did it again. On the third snowball he looked up to see Rebecca's camera pointed at him, capturing his every move.

She walked towards him as he threw the next one, sometimes kneeling for a shot, sometimes circling behind him. He let her take the pictures, as many as she wanted, and made a point of not looking at the camera. She cheered him on through a dozen snowballs before she abandoned the pictures and threw her arms around his neck.

"I'm hungry," she said. "Where are we going to eat?"

Richard thought of the diner in town, and the gossip that was already going strong.

"Want to get some things at the store and take them home?"

"No. We wouldn't get around to eating food."

He grinned. "Okay, then...there's a fantastic restaurant just over the river. You like steak?"

"I love steak."

"You like wine, too?"

"I'm not that big a drinker."

"Me, neither."

"But first…"

Rebecca grinned up at him as she dropped down to her knees and carefully set her camera aside. The blood began to sing in Richard's head, a song of desire.

"Becca?"

"You've been such a good boy," she teased. "I figured it was time for a little…reward."

She unbuttoned and unzipped his slacks. They were on the road where anyone could come along, anyone at all, and Richard realised he really didn't give a damn. Everybody knew by now, and not a single one of them mattered a whit. This woman on her knees in front of him was the only person whose opinion mattered. Obviously she didn't mind the whole world seeing her, so who was he to worry?

She opened her mouth and took him in. He was instantly hard and aching. Her tongue was maddening, flickering against his head before pressing against his shaft and rubbing with slow, careful circles. She kept it up until he grabbed her hair and pulled her closer. With a sound he could have sworn was a giggle, she started to bob up and down on his dick, sucking hard on the upstroke. She worked him into a near-frenzy of desire before she abruptly pulled away, leaving his cock wet and straining in the cold air.

"That's a preview," she said. His hand tightened in her hair and he tried to pull her back on to his dick but she resisted, watching him with feline eyes. He shot back a look of such frustration that she almost took pity on him and let him come.

Almost.

"Don't move," she murmured, and reached for the camera.

Richard stood still and let her take those pictures, too. She took shots of his cock from every angle, enjoying the way it moved and twitched as she snapped the pictures, as if it had a mind of its own and wanted to hide from her viewfinder. Richard leant back against the railing and closed his eyes, to better hear the tiny motor in the camera as it took one image after another. Richard had never known what it was like to pose for a sexy picture, but now that his chance was here, he found it even more enjoyable than he thought it would be.

"Can I take pictures of you later?"

"We can take pictures together." Her voice was nonchalant. "It has a timer."

The thought of that made him even harder, and Rebecca noticed. She took one more picture then sat for a moment, looking at his dick. Suddenly she leant forward and sucked it into her mouth again, this time driving him deep with one long thrust. She almost gagged on him. She took a deep breath and slid him deeper, until he brushed the back of her throat. The feeling of that made her go all liquid between her thighs, and when Richard put his hand in her hair, she almost forgot what kind of game she was playing. She started to fuck him with her mouth, keeping her lips tight and her tongue moving. He thrust forward then she did gag, but quickly recovered to take him deeper than she had the first time. She started thinking of angles, of lying back on the bed and letting him slide into her mouth, so she could take the whole length of him. She thought about lying back on the bridge and trying the same thing, but just then Richard tightened his fingers in her hair, and the pain of it brought her back to reality.

She gently pushed him away again, and this time his groan of frustration was more than clear.

"Let's go get dinner," she said as she rose from her knees and kissed his neck. She was breathing hard, the teasing taking its toll on her, too. His cock was still hard and wet. When she wrapped her hand around it she was gratified by another deep groan. She stroked until his eyes went glassy with need, then she slowed down and let him keep some dignity.

"Rebecca," he managed, but wasn't sure what to say after that. Only one word came to mind. "Please."

"Save it for later," she said.

"I don't want to save it for later," he said. "I want you right now. On the bridge."

She raised an eyebrow.

"I want you here, in front of the whole town. I don't give a damn who comes along. Let's give them a good show. I want them to see me fuck you."

Rebecca's eyes were bright with a smile that she fought to keep off her lips. "No."

He sighed, studied her for a moment, and then pulled away. He stuffed his manhood back into his pants and, with a wince that was just as much from the pain in his hand as from frustration, he zipped them up. "You're a very cruel woman, you know that?"

She was already headed towards the truck when she heard his words. She might be a lot of things, but cruel wasn't one of them. Didn't he know that about her by now? She spun and looked him in the eye.

"Do you really want to fuck here?" she asked, walking back towards him. "Because I'm so damn wet, I could let you slide right in, and I swear to God I would come in seconds. Is that what you want? Or do you want to wait until tonight, when I pull out all the toys and do wicked things to you, things you've only imagined, and then let you make me come until I can't breathe, or remember my own name, or think a coherent thought other than…" She pressed her lips to his ear. "Fuck me."

Richard closed his eyes, hardly able to breathe. "Yes."

"Wait?"

"Yes."

"Then let's go torture each other," she whispered, and they headed for the truck.

Chapter Eight

Dinner was indeed torture, as they sat at a little table that allowed their legs to touch and ordered decadent things from a stellar menu: for her the filet mignon with cream and chive sauce, and for him the grilled chicken topped with fruit salsa and grilled pineapples. They ate by lamplight and watched each other over the table, teasing by taking long bites or sucking the juice from a tender slice of meat, dissolving into laughter when the tension got to be too much. She pressed her knee against his and rubbed up and down. That motion alone made him hard again, and now with the pleasure came an ache, the sign of being deprived for a little too long. He shifted in his seat and Rebecca smiled at him with approval.

"I have big plans for tonight," she told him, as casually as she might have described the weather outside.

"Do you?"

"It involves using several items from your toy box."

His mind immediately went to the possibilities. His appetite for the food in front of him was nothing compared to his appetite for what she might use from that box. He resisted the urge to beg her to tell him what her plans were, and they finished their meal in silence, their eyes speaking volumes.

Back at the truck, Rebecca slid over the bench seat and buckled herself into the middle, right beside Richard. She laid her head on his shoulder as he drove and whispered into his ear: "When we get back to the house, I want you to go upstairs and get a few ties out of your closet. I'm going to tie you up with them, and then I'm going to have my way with you."

Richard pressed down harder on the gas pedal and said a silent thanks to the road crews for getting the snow out of the way. They roared down the highway as Rebecca's hand snaked out of her pocket and found its way to Richard's crotch, where she squeezed hard enough to make him draw in a sharp, pained breath. "I'm going to do whatever I want to this, and you won't be able to stop me."

Richard nodded. "Yes."

She watched him as the streetlights cast shadows in the cab of the truck. He was so eager for everything, so ready to do whatever she might want, that she wondered anew why he didn't have a woman in his life until she came along. Three years was a long time to go without, but it was especially long for a man with such a rich, fertile imagination and a sex drive to match. She felt as though she had stumbled on a winning lottery ticket.

They almost skidded into the driveway. Richard didn't bother to put the truck in the garage. He helped Rebecca out and they both ran up the sidewalk. Richard's hands fumbled when he tried to open the door so Rebecca took the keys from him and did it herself. Once inside, Richard turned to her but she stopped him with an upraised hand.

"Upstairs," she reminded him. "Naked, on the bed, with ties."

He went up the stairs to do as she asked. His heart was thudding already, and his cock was hard—God, had it ever gone down since the blowjob at the bridge? He yanked ties out of his closet, not caring whether they were the good ones or not, and flung them on the bed. He stripped out of his clothes, kicked them into the corner, and lay down on the cool sheets.

He looked up at the corners of the bed, the posts that he had never thought of tying anyone to, or much less being tied to himself. He looked down at his cock, standing just as erect and ready as those bedposts.

When Rebecca's shadow fell across the bed, he looked up at her. She was naked too, her body almost shimmering in the dim light from the hallway. She leaned over him and took the ties. He raised his hands above his head. As she wrapped the silk around one wrist and made it tight, he lifted his head and licked at the hard nipple right over his mouth. He groaned when she pulled away.

"Not yet," she said, and turned her attention to his injured hand. She gently wrapped the tie around his wrist and fastened it to the headboard, leaving ample room for him to move for comfort, but not so much that he could get away or touch her without her permission. He smiled at her consideration.

"Thank you," he whispered.

He watched as she picked up the toy box and placed it on the end of the bed. After a moment of thought, she went to his closet and pulled out one more tie. This one she placed carefully around his head and tied it over his eyes, blindfolding him to what she was about to do.

"Rebecca," he began, but she cut his words off with her own.

"You're my fuck toy tonight," she said. "I'm going to do anything I want to do to you, and if that includes blindfolding you then that's my choice. You have no say in the matter."

He lay on the bed, a little stunned by her words but so turned on he wasn't about to argue. He shifted his hips on the bed, the weight of his cock moving with them, and he let out a long sigh of relief as Rebecca wrapped her hand around his shaft and stroked him.

"Yes," he murmured, and then her hand went away. The next thing he felt was the stretching of rubber over his dick, pressing against his balls—the cock ring. Rebecca made it snug on his dick and then stroked him some more, until the throbbing was almost painful.

Rebecca stood back and looked at him. He had no idea how handsome he was there on the bed, with his cock straight up in the air and his hands tied above his head. She considered getting her camera but quickly decided against it. Right now, she had other things in mind.

She pulled the vibrator out of the box and turned it on. Sitting back on the foot of the bed, she started with his feet. The vibrator made him jerk and squirm, but he did an admirable job of holding still. She ran it up his legs, over his hips, down the inside of his thighs. She barely touched his dick with it before she went up to his chest and played with his nipples until they were as hard as hers. Then she turned it off and held it above him, pressed the tip to his lips, and demanded: "Suck."

To her surprise, Richard immediately opened his mouth and sucked in the tip of the vibrator. She thrust it gently in and out. "Have you ever sucked on a dick?" she asked.

He shook his head. No.

"Have you ever wanted to?"

The shake of his head was slower this time, but the answer was the same.

"Have you ever had a threesome?"

He shook his head again.

"Ever wanted one?"

His nod was vigorous and made her smile. She was enjoying her interrogation.

"Have you ever fucked a woman in the ass?"

Yes.

"Has a woman ever fucked you in the ass?"

No.

"Have you ever wanted a woman to fuck you in the ass?"

He hesitated, and Rebecca smiled.

"What if I said I wanted to fuck you with this?" she asked.

Richard slowly nodded.

"You would let me fuck your ass?"

He nodded again. She took the vibrator away.

"Why?"

"Because you can do whatever you want to do to me."

"Would you like it?"

"I don't know."

"Does it scare you?"

"Yes."

"Does it turn you on?"

He swallowed hard. "Yes."

She sat beside him for a moment, studying his face, letting him wonder what was coming next. She knew the images in his mind would drive him crazier than her words would, and she gave him ample time to fuck with his own head. She pressed the vibrator to the centre of his chest and turned it on. He jerked like he had touched electrical current.

Rebecca smiled as she slid the vibrator down his body. When she reached his dick she carefully let the tip of the vibrator brush over the sensitive skin, and was rewarded with his loud groan. She reached into the toy box and found a bottle of lube. She didn't bother to hide the squirting sounds as she covered the tip of the vibrator with the liquid.

"Spread your legs."

Richard's whole body rebelled for a moment, and he was tempted to call the whole thing off. No woman had ever done that, and it wasn't something he had ever imagined he would do. Now that Rebecca wanted to do it—no, seemed determined to do it—he was a little turned on, a little uncertain, and more than a little scared.

"Will it hurt?" he asked.

Rebecca gently pushed his legs apart. After a moment he stopped fighting and let her push them open even farther. "If you want to stop, we will."

"Okay."

His show of trust turned her on more than anything else had, and she was very tempted to take her own pleasure at the same time as she was giving him his. But the thought of what kind of reward she had planned for this little adventure was enough to keep her hands away from her throbbing clit.

She squirted lube into her hand and rubbed it under his balls. The closer she got to the rosebud of his ass, the tenser he became. She encouraged him to relax, and kept rubbing until she needed more lube. This time Richard took a deep breath and forced his body to relent, made himself accept what she was doing. As soon as he did, the pressure of her hand became more and more pleasurable, and he found himself opening his legs wider for her.

Rebecca looked up at his face, and then remembered she couldn't see his eyes. She put more lube on her hand and ran it generously across his ass, then slowly pushed one finger against the tightness. She was surprised when he opened under the pressure and accepted her finger, sucking it in almost to the knuckle. She twisted it around and when she did, Richard let out an animal groan and thrust his hips up to her.

"More," he whispered. "More, please, more."

He had never felt anything like this, but he found that he really did like it, and his request for more wasn't just to please her. Suddenly he wanted to do all the things she wanted to do—he wanted to know what it felt like to do those things he had never really contemplated before.

Rebecca pushed a second finger against his ass. It stung a bit when it slid in but the pain quickly gave way to pleasure, and he wasn't about to tell her to stop.

Rebecca moved those two fingers in his tight passage, sometimes fucking him with them, sometimes twirling them in circles. She slowly spread her fingers, stretching him for the vibrator, and when she thought he was ready she slipped her fingers out of him. Richard protested immediately, and that made her smile.

"You want this dick. Don't you?"

Richard nodded, far beyond playing coy. "Yes."

"You want me to fuck that ass."

"Yes, please..."

"You want to know how it feels to have a cock in there, don't you?"

"Yes. Your cock, Rebecca. Yours."

She pressed the vibrator to the tiny hole. Richard bucked his hips as she started to press it inside. She watched in amazement as the vibrator slipped farther and farther in, until it was filling him and his ass was tight around the smooth metal rod.

"Fuck me," he gasped out, and she realised how turned on he was. She pulled the vibrator out and then pushed it back in, faster this time, and Richard pushed towards her, meeting it with his own thrust. Rebecca watched as he moved slowly up and down on the metal dick, marvelling at how she could stumble upon a man who was so open to trying new things. She pushed it in harder, thrusting as if it really were a dick that wanted to come, and Richard responded with a cry of pleasure.

Richard felt almost outside himself. Was that really him, lying in his own bed and taking a fuck up the ass? He wasn't just taking it, he was encouraging it, sliding up and down on the hard cock she had shoved into him. There was a spot just inside his ass, a place that sent shivers of desire through him every time she hit it, and he wanted more of that. It was the only thought that filled his head as the orgasm built inside him, and somehow he knew this would be a harder one than any he had ever had.

Rebecca knew he was going to come. She knew it, and she considered stopping it before he had a chance to get off, but she wanted to see it happen. She wanted to see him come hard while he had the vibrator buried so deeply in his ass. She thought it was the sexiest thing a man could do in bed, the most exciting and open thing he could possibly give her, and now she wanted to see how much it turned him on, too.

She leaned over his dick, hovering there, watching every twitch and shake. She pushed the vibrator harder into him, almost ramming him with it now, and Richard was pushing back with every thrust. She looked up at him, at the way his mouth had fallen open in pleasure. She looked down at his balls, so tight against his body. Last she looked at the vibrator, and the way he was stretched out around it, the almost painful tightness of his virgin ass around the cold, unyielding metal.

"It's going to come in you," she said.

Richard groaned, long and low.

"You want that?"

"Yes!"

"You're going to come when he does. Aren't you?"

"Yes!

"Fuck that guy's dick, Richard. Make him come in you."

Richard let out a wail of pleasure. Just as he did, Rebecca turned the vibrator on.

The sudden vibration, so deep inside his body, sent Richard over the edge. He cried out as he came. The pleasure of his orgasm was mixed with the throbbing pain of holding back for so long, the burning of it a reward for doing what Rebecca wanted of him. His heart seemed to stop and he found it almost impossible to breathe as his body lost all control.

Rebecca watched as the cum shot out of his dick. It splashed on her chest and slid down between her breasts. She leant forward and caught the second shot in her mouth, some of it dripping down her chin. She sucked his dick into her mouth and drank the rest of what he gave her, licking the underside of his shaft as she carefully slipped the vibrator out of his ass. When he finally collapsed on the bed, she swallowed as much of his dick as she could, sucking him dry with one last upward stroke.

When Richard could breathe again, he lay stunned on the bed. His ass throbbed with his heartbeat. His balls were aching with the intensity of the release. His heart was pounding so hard it almost frightened him. Rebecca was lying beside him, her head on his chest.

"Did you..." He started to ask her something and promptly forgot what it was.

Several other sentences started in his head but he was able to finish none of them. He simply lay in the bed, steeped in a dozen new sensations, and wished he could be untied so he could hold Rebecca tighter against him.

"Untie me," he whispered, and she smiled.

"Not yet."

"But...you haven't?"

"Not yet."

Richard was certain he couldn't come again. Hell, he might not come again for days after that little experiment. If Rebecca hadn't come yet, shouldn't she untie him so he could return the favour?

"Let me get you off," he said.

"We're not done yet."

Richard had no idea what would be better than what she had just done, but he was suddenly too tired to ask. The aftermath of the orgasm swept over him and it was hard to keep a coherent thought. Rebecca whispered into his ear.

"Sleep now...we'll get to the rest later."

Richard slipped into dreamland as Rebecca watched. She was smiling...and planning.

Richard woke the next morning to a feeling of suffocation. He struggled to get out from whatever was covering his face, and was rewarded with Rebecca's mischievous giggle. He tried to see but suddenly the events of the night came back to him, and he remembered that he was blindfolded.

"You don't want to lick pussy?" she asked, and lowered her cunt down on his face again.

Richard took in the smell of her, musky and sweet, then stretched out his tongue and buried it between her folds. Her moan was loud and rewarding. His hands were no longer tied, and he reached for her, but she stopped him with a very stern, "No."

Richard rested his hands on the pillows on either side of his head. His injured hand throbbed. But then Rebecca moved, reminding him of what she wanted, and the painful throbbing retreated to the background of his mind.

He pushed his tongue deeper into her.

He had never been awakened like *this* before.

Rebecca moved on him, getting the most from his tongue. Her juices coated his face as he licked and licked. She pushed back a bit farther and let him find her clit, then squirmed as he worried it between his lips and lashed it with his tongue.

"Don't you stop," she warned him. "No matter what happens to you, don't you stop."

That made Richard stop, just as she had known it would. She rose up a bit. "What are you doing?" he asked her, and she just lowered her pussy back down on his face.

"You'll like it."

He had already taken a vibrator up the ass for her. What more did she expect?

"You've wanted to be with two women. Haven't you?"

Richard grinned against her cunt.

"I'll bet you never imagined such a thing could happen to you so soon," she cooed, and Richard closed his eyes as he went at her cunt again. She was going to give him a blowjob while he got her off? Or a handjob? She was doing something to his dick, he knew — the smooth, cold sensation of lube ran down his shaft and made him hard.

"He likes it hard," she said, confusing him completely. She giggled. "He likes it good and deep, too. But don't make him come. I'm saving that for me."

Richard froze as a warm, soft something brushed over the head of his dick. Rebecca giggled again and wiggled her hips, urging him to get back to work.

"Give it to him," Rebecca whispered, and suddenly that softness was back, this time sliding down the tiniest bit and enveloping the head of his dick. At first it was cool but then it was warm, almost too warm, and he realised with a shock that it felt just like a woman's pussy.

"Rebecca," he called, and she lifted her hips again. Was there someone in the bed with them? He moved his legs to see if there was, and touched nothing but the cool sheets and blankets.

"You want it, don't you, Richard?"

He didn't know what to say or what to do. The softness was back, this time going farther down his cock, taking him in halfway. Then it slid back up, leaving him wanting more. He groaned as the softness came down again, this time taking him in all the way, mercilessly fucking him as Rebecca rode over his face. It felt just like a woman, and even as he moved his legs again and found no one else in bed with them, he let himself fall into the fantasy. He let himself believe what he was feeling was absolutely real, and thrust his hips up to meet the woman in his dreams.

"That's it," Rebecca encouraged, her own breath short and hard. "Fuck her."

Richard tried to focus on Rebecca's clit but was terribly distracted by the things happening below his waist. The woman was riding him hard, touching him only with the sweet softness of her cunt, and her juices were dripping down on him. His dick throbbed as she slid up and down on it. He reached down with his good hand to figure out what was going on, but Rebecca grabbed it in mid-air. He wished he wasn't blindfolded so he could see, but the best he could do was try to picture what was happening.

Rebecca slid back and forth on his face. She was close to an orgasm, and her body was determined to get it. Her motion became jerky as Richard started to suck on her clit, his moans humming through her like a natural vibrator, his tongue licking the most sensitive spot every now and then, keeping her on the edge but not letting her go over it. Finally she called out to him, "Make me come, Richard. Make me come, then make her come, too."

The pussy riding him suddenly tightened, and he almost shot off right then. He lifted his head a bit and got a better hold on Rebecca's clit. He began to suck mercilessly, almost too hard, driving her to the edge of that orgasm she wanted so badly. As it roared over her, she had the presence of mind to cry out something that would get him off, too:

"Fuck him until he comes. Make him come in you, and then I'll lick it out of your pussy."

Richard didn't need any further urging. The orgasm slammed him at the same time Rebecca began to convulse in pleasure and pulled away from him. He thrust up and came.

The wetness around his dick got even wetter, but the stroking of that soft pussy didn't stop. She milked him for what he had left, and when it was over she moved softly on him, working him until he was soft and slipped out of her.

Rebecca sat on the bed beside him and grinned, pleased with the orgasm that still thrummed in her veins, happy with her ingenuity. Richard lay stunned on the bed, still unsure of what had happened but pretty damn convinced that Rebecca was the naughtiest woman on the planet.

Richard sat up. He took off the blindfold and the dim light from the hallway immediately showed him that there was no one in the bedroom but the two of them. Rebecca was watching him with a wide smile.

"Those pocket pussies are great," she said, and Richard suddenly laughed as he realised what she had done.

"You little vixen!"

He grabbed her and pulled her down beside him, kissing her. She tasted herself on his tongue. She licked at him, trying to get more of it, then whispered in his ear, "Tell me. Was she a redhead, or a brunette, or a blonde?"

Richard chuckled. "Redhead."

"That's what I thought."

They lay down together and he ran his fingers through her hair, pulling out the tangles there. She stared up at him with wide, happy eyes.

"I wish you never had to leave," he said softly. He watched the tenderness creep into her eyes.

"Me too."

Chapter Nine

When Rebecca woke up the next morning, Richard wasn't in bed, but she could hear him singing along with a radio somewhere in the house. When the scent of bacon and sausage wafted up the stairs, she knew exactly where he was. With a smile she tossed back the covers and stood up, her body protesting a little from all the attention Richard had given it over the last few days. She had sore muscles in places that had never been sore before, but she was sure that was a good thing.

The more she thought about the fact that things could progress past this one week — that they could try to sustain a long-distance relationship and see where it led — the more Rebecca felt happier than she had been in a very long time. From time to time she marvelled at the way they had met, but after all, didn't everyone have a story to tell? Theirs was just a little more unusual than most. She wasn't one to put much stock in fate, but she did believe that ultimately things happened for a reason — and maybe someone, somewhere, was trying to tell her something when her car slid off into that ditch and Richard was the one that happened to find her there.

The object of her thoughts was waiting for her in the kitchen, drinking coffee and reading the morning paper. He casually flipped a slice of bacon in the pan and grinned at her as she walked through the door. She kissed him, stole a piece of sausage from the plate, and sat down at the table to watch him cook.

"You look good in my shirt," he said, and she did. She was wearing one of his button-down dress shirts from his closet. It came almost to her knees, a dark blue colour that set off her pretty eyes. She had rolled the sleeves up around her elbows. Wrapping herself in one of his shirts made her feel small and vulnerable, and the smell of him caught in the fabric made her heart sing.

"I want to take one home with me," she said.

"Only if you leave something of yours here with me."

"Deal."

She watched as he took the bacon out of the pan and pulled the eggs out of the refrigerator. His pyjama pants had little bottles of Tabasco sauce printed all over them. His shoulders were broad and strong, but what she noticed more than anything were the marks of her nails on his skin. The marks were still red and long, the sign of the passionate time they had spent over the last several days. The trip certainly hadn't been what she had planned, but as she smiled at the eight parallel lines on Richard's back she thought it was most assuredly better.

Eggs splattered in the pan as Richard cracked them open, then worried them a bit with the spatula. He shot the egg shells towards the garbage can and grinned as they went neatly inside. "Two-point shot!" he exclaimed, and watched as the eggs cooked to a clean, fresh white. He flipped them over and counted to twenty, then scooped them on to plates and brought them to the table. He poured another cup of coffee for himself and one for Rebecca as he sat down across from her.

"You know, it's funny," she said, looking down at her plate. "We've already fallen into a kind of routine. You cook breakfast every morning."

"I'm just trying to impress you. Once I know I have you hooked, it will be doughnuts every day."

She laughed and took a bite of her bacon.

"I was thinking this morning about getting that car pulled out," he said. "We can call the tow truck after breakfast."

"It doesn't seem so melancholy now," she admitted, cutting into her eggs and watching the yolk run out to mix with the bits of sausage on her plate. "Before yesterday, getting the car repaired seemed like a death knell to my time here, but now it just seems like...well, getting a car repaired."

"Because you're going to see me after you go back to Miami?"

"I'll be making this trip again, that's for sure."

"Are you going to fly next time?" he asked, and grinned at her. It was his first overt jab at Gene, and the sweet delivery made Rebecca smile.

"Yes, smartass. I don't think I'll be driving back through Iowa anytime soon."

"Snows like this don't come often, you know. During the summer it's hot as hell."

"It seems like it could never warm up that much." She looked out the window at the snow that was still piled up on either side of the road and covering the yard. She had never imagined so much snow could exist anywhere but the Arctic.

"Rebecca," Richard said slowly. "There's something I need to tell you."

She grinned at him, expecting some sort of tease, but at the serious look in his eyes her smile melted away.

"What is it?"

"It's nothing bad. At least, I don't think it's bad."

Rebecca lost all interest in her food. She laid her fork down on the edge of the plate. Her stomach turned into a cold, hard knot. "Tell me."

Richard took a deep breath. He was going to tell her everything, and then deal with the fallout. He thought maybe he had figured out a way to do it, a way that she would understand. Ironically, the reasons he was going to give her were the honest truth about the situation.

"When we first started this…it was a fling. You agree?"

She nodded. "Yes."

"So there were things I didn't think I needed to tell you, because they didn't matter. Like a few things in my past, things that wouldn't make any difference to you if I was just a week-long affair, but things that might make a difference if you were looking at a long-term thing, like I think we are."

"I understand that. Go on."

Richard looked at his plate for a moment. "I got married when I was thirty-five. Her name was Amanda, a pretty little farmer's daughter from Dubuque. I met her at a writing conference there."

Rebecca studied him as he told her this. She wasn't surprised at all—she had known there was something in his past that had turned him into a loner, and she had guessed that it might be a woman. She had even suspected there might be an ex-wife lurking in his past. Richard was the kind of man any woman would be lucky to have, and if he had been single for three years there had to have been a very good reason.

"I thought everything was good in our marriage...I really did. I didn't think I was one of those clueless guys who comes home one day and finds his wife has headed for the hills. I thought those men were reserved for talk shows and sitcoms, you know? That happens to men who ignore and neglect their wives, not for somebody like me, who tried so hard to do everything right."

Rebecca stared at him. "You came home one day and she was gone?"

"She left a letter. She told me she needed to find herself." Richard shook his head and let out a wry, pained laugh. "I'm still trying to figure out what that means. Does anybody ever know what that really means?"

Rebecca reached over the table and took his hand. She tightened her fingers almost painfully over his. Whatever she had imagined had happened to him, she hadn't expected a story like that. "I'm sorry she did that to you."

"Maybe I should have told you earlier. I don't know. I was so afraid you would walk away from me if you knew."

"Why in the world would I do that?"

He raised frightened eyes to hers. "Because I'm still married, Rebecca."

The shockwave of that statement rushed through her, turning her first cold, then impossibly hot. She slowly pulled her hand away from his. Her cheeks flooded with the shock of his announcement, with the fear of all the things she didn't know. She touched them and felt the burn through her fingertips, all the way down to her heart. She stared at him, her eyes wide.

"You never filed for divorce?"

"I never had a reason to file. I never wanted another relationship."

Rebecca sat very still, absorbing this news. Her boyfriend—the man she hoped she could call her boyfriend, the one she was well on her way to maybe, just maybe, falling in love with—was married to someone else?

"But then you came along. And it made me realise that I've waited long enough. I guess I knew a long time ago that she wasn't going to come back, but having that failure hanging over my head, and never knowing what I did wrong…well, that was the part I couldn't accept. That's the part I still haven't accepted, to be honest. Her leaving is not so hard to handle as the questions of why she did it, and what part I might have played in her decision."

Rebecca looked out of the window at the snow, unsure what to say. Part of her wanted to run, while another part of her wanted to throw her arms around him and tell him it was okay. She thought she might cry, but the shock was too immense, and she found herself taking deep breaths instead.

Richard watched as the emotions flickered across her face, but he didn't say anything else. He wanted to let her decide what to say and do, and didn't want to try to convince her to say anything that wasn't in her heart.

Finally Rebecca sighed and looked back at him. Her eyes were sad. "I understand why you didn't tell me earlier. If it was just a fling, why would you?"

He nodded.

"But it's not a fling, and the fact that you are telling me this makes that very, very clear. I appreciate that, not only for your honesty, but for knowing you really do want to see where this leads."

Relief flooded Richard. He lifted her hand to his lips and kissed it.

"What happens if she comes back, Richard? What then?"

He shook his head. "I don't think she will."

"But what if she does?"

What if she did? It was a question Richard had thought about long and hard for many nights before Rebecca had fallen into his life. He had never come up with any answers then, but he certainly had a few now.

"I would tell her to leave."

"But she's still your wife."

Richard leant back in his chair. "Part of the reason I haven't filed for divorce is my family. They are very traditional, sometimes far too traditional, and they see divorce as the equivalent of living on another planet. My mother has made it very clear how she feels about the situation, and has told me over and over to wait on Amanda to come back. She's even gone so far as to ask what I did to make her leave."

"Your family won't be very open to a new woman in your life," she pointed out.

"No. But after wasting three years waiting for a woman who obviously doesn't want to be married to me, I think my family will just have to deal with it."

Rebecca played with the food on her plate, not certain how to say what was on her mind. Finally she decided that blunt honesty was the way to go.

"Are you going to file for divorce now?"

Richard knew this question might come, and he had thought long and hard about what he would say if it did. Now that the words were on the tip of his tongue, he knew it was the right decision. "I think three years is enough time to make her intentions clear, and it's probably time to respond in kind."

Rebecca gave him a tentative smile and reached for his hand again.

At that moment a long, sleek Cadillac roared into the driveway, sending up a flurry of snow in its wake. The car slid on the surface, almost clipped the corner of the truck, and settled at an angle to the sidewalk. An older, stately woman got out of the car, wrapped her coat tightly around her, and marched towards the front door, her face drawn into a frown.

"Shit," Richard murmured, and stood up. The pounding on the door was hard and long. Rebecca stood up too, and looked at Richard for an explanation.

"Speak of the devil," he said.

"That's your mother?" Rebecca asked, incredulous.

"Yeah."

The pounding hadn't stopped. Richard started for the door and Rebecca went towards the stairs, but Richard called her back. "No. There's no need to hide. She's heard the rumours, and that's why she's here. I'm not going to lie to her."

Rebecca stood at the base of the stairs, trying to decide whether to listen to Richard or whether to run and hide. She was still reeling from the news of his wife, and now she had to face his mother?

Richard swung open the door. Janette Paris stepped into the house as if she owned it, pushed her son to the side with one hand, and peered at the woman hovering by the stairs.

She took in the dishevelled hair, the clothes and lack thereof, and summed the situation up in an instant.

"Well, this just figures," she said, and turned to glare at Richard. "First you send your wife packing, then you cheat on her. If the two aren't bad enough, you had to go for the third strike by bedding a woman young enough to be your daughter!"

Rebecca's face burned with anger.

"I'm not cheating on my wife," Richard said reasonably, his quiet voice a sharp contrast to the loud bellowing of his angry mother. "It's impossible to cheat on a woman who took leave of me over three years ago, Ma."

"You're still married to her!"

"In name only," Richard said, and this seemed to infuriate the woman even more.

"You!" She pointed at Rebecca, who stood rooted to her spot at the bottom of the stairs. "You know he's married! That makes you a lying, cheating whore, and a whore isn't good enough for my son!"

"That's enough!" Richard finally raised his voice. The shock of that made both women look at him instead of at each other. "Her name is Rebecca, and she's my girlfriend."

"She's the other woman!"

"She understands the circumstances, and, no, she is not the other woman. I'm not hiding her. She's my girlfriend, and anybody who knows my history will understand and accept that."

"She's a whore," his mother spat again, her face a mottled red. She stared at him as if she were determined her point would get across and bully his into oblivion. She had always disciplined with a firm hand, even when her kids were grown, and she wasn't the kind to let a differing opinion get in her way.

Richard stepped towards her, forcing her back to the door. "She's not a whore. If you call her that again, you can remember this is my home, and I won't tolerate it here."

"Don't you mean your home with Amanda? Your wife's name is still on the deed, isn't it?"

The sneering tone of voice sent fury through Rebecca. This was his mother? How did Richard manage to grow into such a gentle, non-judgemental man if this was the example he had?

"Get out of my house."

The order was delivered with such quiet fury that Janette took a step back from her son and stared at him, seeing a totally different person. Rebecca stared at him too, surprised at the amount of fury he conveyed in a few short words.

"What has she done to you?" she demanded, glaring at Rebecca.

"She's shown me what I've been missing," he said, and started to swing the door shut.

"You're not throwing me out!"

Richard looked at the woman in front of him. He loved her, but she was so filled with anger and self-righteousness that he felt as though he had no idea who she was. His heart softened towards her, but he wasn't the same pushover anymore. He had done a lot of thinking, and he had decided long before Rebecca came along that it was time to move on with his life. Rebecca had been the final push in getting that process started.

"I love you, Ma," he said, and Janette's chin quivered. "But this is my life, and I'm going to live it how I see fit. I'm sorry if that way doesn't agree with you."

"But you can't do this. You're married, Richard! I raised you better than this!"

"I'm sure Amanda's parents are thinking the same thing about her."

Janette's mouth dropped open. Richard stood in the doorway, unmoving. His mother finally moved back on to the sidewalk and shot him one last glare.

"You're doing something wrong, Richard. The laws of both God and man say so."

"Be careful going home, Ma. I love you."

With that, Richard shut the door. He leaned his forehead against it for a moment, trying to get his emotions under control. Jesus Christ, how much upheaval could one day hold? It wasn't even noon yet.

He turned to look at Rebecca, who yet stood by the bottom of the stairs. Their eyes met and for a moment they stood perfectly still. Rebecca was the first to break, and when she did she ran towards him, needing his touch more than anything else. He scooped her into his arms as they listened to his mother's car navigate out of the driveway and roar away.

"That went well," Rebecca murmured, fighting tears. She held on to him as hard as she could, realising what a chance he was taking with her, and how much resistance he would encounter from those who loved him most. Amanda might be alive and well, but her ghost was very clearly haunting those she had left behind.

"You're not what she said," he told her, unable to repeat the words his mother had used. The thought of applying them to someone like Rebecca, a woman who had done absolutely nothing wrong, was out of his realm of belief.

"I know."

"Do you?"

"Three years is long enough. It's not possible to be a home-wrecker when there's no marriage left to destroy, is there?"

Richard kissed her. They were both shaking from the aftermath of the confrontation. Richard could feel the fine tremors of her body as she fought to keep her emotions under control. In a sudden decision, he led her to the living room. Her thighs bumped the back of the couch in front of the fireplace. Richard slipped his hand up her back, under her shirt, until he reached her neck.

He bent her over the back of the couch.

Rebecca had no idea what he was doing until she was draped over his couch, naked ass up in the air, her hands on the cushions to steady herself. The ready pose immediately set passion afire, and she spread her legs, bracing her feet on the floor. Richard pushed down his pyjamas and pressed his hard cock against her pussy.

"Fuck me," she said over her shoulder, and before the words were out, he was buried to the hilt inside her.

He slammed into her with the second stroke, lifting her feet from the floor. His good hand on her hip and his bandaged one resting on the small of her back, he pulled her closer to him with every thrust. She couldn't push back against him. With all her weight resting on her hands and the back of the couch, she couldn't thrust at him, and she couldn't reach back to touch him, either. She could only ride on the wave of his motion and let the sensations come as they would. It was a curious feeling, not having any control, and she found that she liked it much more than she had thought she would.

"Fuck me harder," she called out. "Please, fuck me harder."

Richard let go on her, thrusting viciously, hitting bottom every time and making her cry out in both pain and pleasure. He reached forward and yanked her hair. Rebecca let out a howl of pain and he would have stopped, but her next word was very clear: "Yes!"

Richard moved closer to the couch, so that his thrusts were angled upward a bit, and rammed her again. This time she hollered in approval but then stopped, because every thrust was taking the breath from her. When Richard's hand let go of her hip and that same hand came down on her ass, spanking her hard, she almost came with the shock of it.

"Do it," she growled, and he began to spank her with a rhythm that matched his strokes. Thrust in, pull out, spank. Thrust in, pull out...spank harder. Every slap of his hand stoked the fire in her pussy and made her clit jump with the thrill. She hovered on the edge of an orgasm for what seemed an eternity, until Richard reached underneath her and stroked her clit with two fingers.

The blood rushed out of her head and almost made her faint. The orgasm rushed up from the middle of her, making her cry out. The heat of him rushed out of his dick and into her, spreading within her as he groaned. Rebecca's hands finally gave way and she fell forward on to the couch, landing on her side, the juices of his orgasm painting the inside of her thighs. She lay on the couch and looked up at him, breathing hard, her eyes wide with discovery.

"You spanked me," she said, when she could breathe again.

"You wanted it."

She grinned and reached back to touch her ass. The skin there was burning hot. She could only imagine what it looked like. Richard reached down and gave her another playful swat, but this time she arched away from him — only to tumble off of the couch and on to the floor with a resounding thud.

"Owww!" she hollered, and Richard was immediately kneeling beside her, laughing hard. Rebecca started to laugh too, and soon they were both howling. They lay on the floor in front of the fireplace and laughed until tears ran down their cheeks and they once again lost their breath.

When the fit of giggles was finally over, they sat back against the couch and grinned at each other. "Breakfast is still on the table," Richard reminded her.

"My car is still in the ditch."

"We've got all kinds of things to do today."

"You just fucked me and spanked me and made me fall over the back of your couch."

"I did not make you fall!"

"You think I would have done all that on my own?"

They went off into a fit of laughter again.

"Come on," he said when he could speak. "Let's go eat cold eggs."

Chapter Ten

Word in Crispin travelled fast. By the time the tow truck got to Rebecca's car, the driver already knew her name, where she was from and who she was with during her stay. He cast an interested eye in her direction and kept looking at her legs, even as he talked about where she wanted him to take the car and who would cover the bill for the tow. When the tow driver craned his neck to check out her ass as she turned away, Richard loudly cleared his throat and raised an eyebrow.

"Gonna get on it right now," the driver said, and headed for the back of the truck, still staring at Rebecca's legs a little longer than was appropriate.

The car was still half buried in snow, but now that everything was melting it was easier to get it out. Snow had sifted in through the broken window, ruining the leather seats. The front of the car was almost nose first in the ditch, and as Rebecca walked around it she marvelled at how far off the road she had travelled. In the snow it had been hard to tell which way was the right direction, and now she realised she had been trying to get out of the ditch by going deeper into it. She now knew firsthand how tricky a blizzard could be.

Richard came to stand beside her and put his hand on her arm. "You okay?"

"I'm all right."

"Really?"

"I'm going to have to rent a car. There's no way those seats can be replaced in a few days."

"You could always fly back to Miami," he said.

"There's time for figuring all that out."

"Or you could just ditch everything and stay right here."

She shot him an indulgent smile.

The tow truck roared as the cable tightened, and soon her car was moving out of the snow like a snake shedding its skin. Now that it was out of the ditch, the damage to the front bumper was clear. She winced as it was pulled up on to the back of the flatbed truck, more snow shaking off the car with every bump and shimmy. Glass made tinkling sounds as it fell from the doorframe and bounced on the cold asphalt.

"You did her up good, hon," the driver said as he secured the wheels of her car to the flatbed. "You want to ride with me in the cab to the shop?"

"She's riding with me," Richard said, annoyed.

"Suit yourself."

They followed the tow truck and its cloud of billowing black smoke. Her Florida plates looked forlorn and lost as they peeked over the snow-covered bumper. Richard reached over and took her hand as they pulled into town, where it seemed everyone had to stop and stare at the shiny red car. At the mechanic's shop, the tow driver put the car down in a corner of the lot and took off for another call, but he didn't fail to try one last look at Rebecca's ass.

The mechanic looked the car over and gave a list of things to be done. "The window. The dents in the front, I think I can knock those out, no problem. I can set up a paint job for you in Florida if you want. I'm not sure what's wrong with the engine, guess it depends on how much of a good bang you took into that ditch. The seats are all kinds of a problem, and I can't fix those. That's a factory issue." He kicked the tyre on the driver's side. "And you've got a flat."

"My insurance will cover anything but that."

"Ah, no worries. I've got an old tyre that will fit. It will get you to Florida and then some."

Rebecca smiled at the young man. "Thank you."

"You're welcome. You take good care of our Richard, you hear?"

Her smile grew broader as he popped the hood and peered underneath. It was the first overtly kind word she had heard about her relationship with Richard, and it had a soothing effect, like balm to the soul.

Climbing back in the truck, she told Richard about it. "He wants me to take good care of you."

"You've been doing a good job of that already."

At the offices of the newspaper, many townsfolk made a point of stopping in just to chat. The place hadn't been that busy since the local election night, and Richard was more than fed up with it by noon. It didn't help that curious faces were staring at the office from the windows of the diner across the street. Rebecca stayed hidden away in the back room, pretending to look at the old equipment. Richard was uncomfortable with the attention, so he could only imagine how she felt.

When they went out to lunch, he suggested what had been on his mind all morning.

"How would you feel about getting out of town for a few days?"

She smiled. "I was thinking it might be nice, but I know you've got work to do."

"I've got staff. They can handle things for a while."

"Where would we go?"

Richard shrugged. "Wherever the truck happens to take us."

"That sounds good."

"Do you like Chinese?"

"Oh, yeah."

"There's a great Chinese place in Clinton. Let's go there."

She had no idea where Clinton was, and she didn't care, so long as she got to spend time with him there. "Okay."

Back at his house, they packed one small overnight bag, her clothes nestling in right beside his, and they made sure not to forget her cameras. Richard switched the home phone so it would ring to his cell, and watching him reminded Rebecca of her own cell phone. It had sat on the kitchen counter for days, drying out from the snow. She knew better than to turn it on before the parts inside had had a chance to dry, because the slightest bit of moisture would fry every circuit in the little gadget. Now she wandered into the kitchen and picked it up, studied it for a moment, and decided to try it.

The screen came up and her greeting appeared. So far, so good. She waited another few seconds and watched as the address book appeared, then the listing of missed calls. She was grateful the phone was working, but shocked at the number of messages waiting for her.

Forty-four? Forty-four messages in just a few days?

She scrolled through them, and her shock turned to annoyance. Gene had left her messages forty-two times. Of the other two messages, there was one from someone wanting a photo taken, and also one from her friend Lisa, wanting to go to lunch when she got back into town. She stared at the missed calls from Gene. There were plenty more than forty-two, and she wondered what she would find when she listened to his messages. Begging and pleading, most likely, and when that didn't work he would have resorted to an angry defence of the way he had acted.

She listened to the first one. Sure enough, it was filled with apologies. Gene actually sounded sorry for the way he had acted, and for a moment she let herself feel badly about the whole situation. She could almost believe he meant what he said. The second message and the third were much the same, but with the fourth they got more heated. By the time she reached message number ten, he was yelling into the phone, cursing at her for being such a bitch, for making him worry and not returning his calls. According to Gene she was a childish brat who had gone off on a fit of pique when her boyfriend dared to question her actions, and she could just hang with the little boys until she grew up and wanted a real man.

She stopped listening at message number twenty, and deleted the rest. She had heard more than enough to know her decision had been the right one.

Richard stood in the doorway and watched her going through the messages. She had no idea he was there, and he studied her reactions with every one. Her shoulders slumped, she gestured in the air, then she started to get mad. She punched the air with her fist then, and said more than once into the phone, "Yeah, well, fuck you, too."

When she hung up the phone, she turned and saw him standing there. She blushed hard and shrugged.

"Gene had a lot to say," she explained.

"Anything worth listening to?"

"Not a single word."

Richard smiled and held out his hand. "Your chariot awaits, darling."

Driving out of Crispin that afternoon, Rebecca felt like she could breathe again. The scrutiny of the town had got to her, no matter how much reassurance Richard had given, and she was sure it had got to him too. The word of his fight with his mother had spread, no doubt told over and over by Janette herself, and now the town was abuzz with what might happen next. Rebecca was happy to be leaving the microscope. She squeezed Richard's hand as he drove, hoping her gratitude was clear.

Richard felt liberated, too. He was going to another town, a place where he was not likely to be noticed. They would be just happy faces in the crowd, not the objects of speculation. He was looking forward to feeling like a normal man in a normal relationship, not someone with a wife hidden away God-knew-where and a girlfriend his whole family wouldn't accept.

They pulled into Clinton and found the first hotel that looked good. The room was simple but clean, with a huge bed and a view of a snow-ringed parking lot. Richard took advantage of the bed as soon as they arrived, pulling her down on it with him and unbuttoning her jeans.

"What are you doing?" she giggled.

"I'm making you happy."

Her words slipped away when his hand pushed between the denim and her skin, heading straight for her pussy. She had had plenty of time to get revved up during the ride, and now she was soaked with desire. He found her clit and twisted it gently between his thumb and forefinger. She lifted her hips to him and looked into his eyes as he played with her. His smile was content and his eyes calm as he worked magic between her legs. Finally the orgasm came upon her and she closed her eyes, bit her lip and let out a long moan of surrender.

When she opened her eyes, he was licking his fingers. She blushed at the sight of it.

"You're much better than Chinese," he said, "but I've got to get some real food in me before I perform sexual acts of any kind."

She eased off the bed and headed to the bathroom to clean up. Twenty minutes later they were in the restaurant, their waitress a demure Chinese woman who walked with tiny steps and bowed with every other word, and Rebecca wondered if the woman could see any of their secrets. Could strangers tell she had just come? Could they see it in her eyes or feel it in her very presence, like a vibration of passion around her? Could any of them see the way she looked at Richard and tell that she was falling in love with the man in front of her?

That thought made Rebecca's heart pound. She looked at him over the steaming hot cups of tea and wondered how he felt. Was it possible to fall in love with someone over the span of a few glorious days? Was she really capable of giving her heart so freely to someone she had just met? But it felt absolutely right, perfectly sane, as though she had known him forever and was just waiting for the chance to make a go of a relationship with him.

Richard stared at her, having the same thoughts of his own. She was so beautiful sitting there, with her cheeks flushed and her hair not quite right and her lips swollen from his kisses. Her eyes were wide as she looked back at him, as though she had just seen something beautiful and delightful, and was on the cusp of sharing it with the rest of the world. He wanted to know every thought that was flowing through her pretty head.

"Penny for your thoughts?" he asked, and she shook her head, then reconsidered.

Hadn't he been honest with her this morning? Hadn't he made his feelings clear every step of the way? It was her turn to take that leap.

"I was just wondering how long it takes to fall in love."

Richard blinked at her. He was stunned by the words but even more stunned by the fact that he knew the answer. There was no doubt in his mind, none at all.

"A week in the snow," he said.

Tears sprang to her eyes. She reached across the table and his hand was waiting there, palm up, inviting her. She placed her fingers gingerly on the bandage, the place where glass from her vehicle had marred his skin. The cut wasn't even close to healed yet, and already she was in love?

"A week," she mused.

"Snow makes people do crazy things," he whispered.

They didn't say another word until their dinner arrived, piping hot plates of chicken and seafood on beds of noodles and rice. They sipped tea and soup, ate small bites of fiery hot food and didn't take their eyes from each other. Rebecca was already thinking of the hotel room a few miles away. Richard was thinking about flight schedules, and when he could visit Miami. She was right here in front of him and already the thought of her being so far away made him feel almost sick.

When the dinner was over they walked hand in hand into the cold night. Before Rebecca got in the truck, Richard pulled her back to him and cradled her against his chest like a fragile prize he had just won. She went willingly, tipping her head back for a kiss, and instead just breathed in the scent of him. Together they stood until the wind became too strong and the cold became too much.

In the truck, neither of them spoke. The drive to the hotel seemed to take forever, and they hit every red light on the way. Rebecca rested her hand lightly on his thigh, feeling the muscles move under his jeans every time he hit the gas. His arm was around her shoulder, pulling her tight against him while he drove with one hand and cursed the traffic.

At the door of the hotel room, her hand shook when she tried to use the keycard. He stepped forward and took it from her hand, gave her an indulgent smile, and opened the door on the first try.

Once that door closed behind them, all the words they hadn't said in the restaurant tumbled out of them, a frenzy of talking, even as they undressed each other with impatient hands.

"I'm falling in love with you. I had no idea..."

"I knew I loved you the moment I kicked my mother out."

"I think it was the night at the hospital..."

"I don't want any of those nurses."

"I want you right now."

"Hurry."

Soon they were naked and their hands everywhere, their lips following, and then he was on bottom and she was above him. The bedside light was on, and her skin glowed under it. She moved like a cat, scratching his chest with her nails, staring seductively at him through dark, feral eyes. Her hair fell in disarray around her face and her cheeks were flushed with heat. Her nipples were hard as little rocks and her chest heaved with every tortured breath. Richard lay underneath her and wished he could capture that moment forever, the sheer beauty of her.

She smiled down at him and bent low to give him a kiss. As she did, he took the very breath from her, breathing the air she breathed out. "I love you," she said into his mouth.

"I love you, too."

She sat back up and started to ride him hard, a punctuation mark on what she had just said. He grabbed her hips and held her tight against him, making her grind instead of thrust. The emotion and the angle made it quick. Rebecca came with a scream, and Richard pushed his hand against her mouth, lest she send the hotel staff running to see if he was fucking her or killing her.

Rebecca slumped over him for a moment, but when his cock twitched inside her, she realised he hadn't come with her. She ground lazily on him, slowly picking up speed. When he was on the edge of an orgasm, she climbed off and gave him a grin.

She crawled between his thighs and sucked his cock into her mouth. Richard exploded into her, arching his hips as she pushed her hands underneath them. She held him where he was until the last of his cum had disappeared down her throat. She crawled up beside him and was surprised when he grabbed her face between his hands, kissed her deeply, and then murmured in complaint, "Why didn't you save some for me?"

"Next time, I will."

"I need a shower," he said. "After I get some sleep."

"Wake me up when you get in there. I'm going, too."

"Ever made love in the shower?"

She thought of the first night at his house, when he was sleeping upstairs and she was under the water, thinking of a fantasy man who would do all the wicked things she wanted. She smiled now as she realised that fantasy man had been upstairs above her that whole time.

"I've never made love in the shower with anyone else."

Richard grinned against her forehead. "Me, neither."

"Let's go, then."

"Sleep first." His voice was so tired; she didn't have the heart to tell him she was wide awake. She lay on his shoulder as he slept. She was used to the rhythmic snoring by now, and she liked the way he looked when he was asleep, so trusting and almost innocent. Soon her eyes were heavy too, and though she had been sure sleep wouldn't come, it did.

Chapter Eleven

An hour later Richard woke to see Rebecca lying sprawled out on her side of the king-size bed. The bedside lamp was off and she was sound asleep, breathing so lightly that he had to press a hand to her ribs to make sure she was breathing at all. He got up and padded to the bathroom with a grin.

"Wake up." His voice came low into her ear, invading a good dream about a beach. "Your shower is nice and hot, Rebecca. Wake up and get in there with me."

The good dream of a beach turned into a very real, very good dream of Richard when she opened her eyes. She stretched hard, then sat up on the edge of the bed and looked around, disoriented.

"Hotel room," he said helpfully. "Clinton, Iowa. Just fucked me an hour ago and about to fuck me again."

"Oh."

"You told me you love me."

"I remember that part." She smiled and ran a hand through his hair. She could hear the pounding of the water in the shower, beckoning her to get underneath it and get dirty.

She stretched again, revelling in the little aches and pains of a body well loved, and followed him to the bathroom.

The shower was small, but it fit both of them. Richard reached for the little bar of hotel soap and had a hell of a time unwrapping it, especially with one hand not quite up to par yet. "It's not Fort Knox," he murmured, and Rebecca laughed as she took the tiny bar from him.

With deft fingers she freed it from the wrapping and turned it over and over in her hand, working up a thin lather. She put that lather on his chest and started to make circles with it, washing his body with slow hands.

"That first night," she mused.

"Yeah?"

"I got off while I was in the shower."

Richard threw his head back and laughed, the sound bouncing from the close walls of the shower. "I got off, too. You interrupted me that night."

"I did?"

"You came up to knock on the door and ask if you could use the phone," he reminded her, and she looked at him with wide, surprised eyes.

"You were jacking off?"

"I was almost at the finish line."

"Oh, God," she laughed. "If only we had known then..."

"I fantasised about you," he admitted.

"Did you really?"

"It started out with fantasising about a woman at a sex toy store. Just some random chick who ran the counter.

My fantasy was being the hottest stud she'd ever seen and she just had to have a piece of me among the dildos."

Rebecca rolled her eyes. "Uh-huh."

"Well, I was in the midst of that when you came to the door, and after that the woman in my head was you."

"In a sex toy store?"

"Why not?"

She knelt in front of him, and Richard gave her a rakish grin. She grinned back and didn't touch his dick. She set about washing his legs instead.

"Was I good?"

"You were really good."

"How were you having me?"

Richard's cock was getting hard at the memory. "You were bent over a display of something. I don't remember what now."

"I fantasised about a man watching me as I took a shower, then coming up behind me and fucking me silly while I played with my clit and made myself come."

"Want to?"

"What?

"Want to let me watch you?"

Rebecca stood up and smiled. "Turn around."

Richard did so, pressing his hands against the back wall of the shower. She worked her way down his back with the small sliver of soap, paying special attention to his ass.

When she dipped a finger between his cheeks, he let out an embarrassed laugh.

"Are you sore?" she asked sweetly, and he could feel himself blushing.

"Yeah."

"Do you like it?"

"Yes."

Rebecca worked her way down his legs. On her way back up, she slid her fingertips between his ass cheeks. He turned around and gave her a mock glare. "Your turn, smarty."

Rebecca lifted her arms above her head. Richard started with her chin, an excuse to kiss her again, and then started washing her body from top to bottom. He could use only his good, uninjured hand, so the washing took a deliciously long time. When she turned around for him to wash her back, she pressed one hand to the wall, and the other hand snaked down between her legs.

Richard watched as she spread her legs wide, bracing them almost to the edges of the shower, and leant forward. She pressed two fingers into her pussy and let out a long, low growl.

"Watch me," she ordered.

Richard leant back against the opposite wall, his eyes glued to her hand. She was stroking her fingers in and out, playing with her pussy the way he loved to do, but she was focusing on one particular spot — something on the inside, towards the front. He watched in fascination as her legs began to tremble the slightest bit, as her breathing got harder and her moans got louder.

He reached down with his own hand and cupped his dick. The soap was very small by now, but it fit perfectly under his shaft as he closed his fingers around his manhood and started to pump his hand. The slickness of the soap made motion easy, and soon he was in a rhythm that matched hers.

"In my fantasy," she panted, "my dream lover came up behind me and rammed me with his cock."

Richard stepped forward, but she shot him a warning glance over her shoulder.

"In this new fantasy," she said, "my lover wants something else."

Richard watched as she bent lower, until her forehead was almost touching the wall. She slid her hand back until her fingers were covering her ass. The water rushed over her back and made a vee where the cheeks of her ass met. She played with the water for a moment, then slid one finger down her crack, until she was touching the tight rosebud between her cheeks.

Richard stared as she teased herself with that finger, then slowly pushed it inside. He tightened his hand on his dick, watching as her finger sank deeper.

Rebecca arched her back and rocked against her hand. She loved the stretching, the feeling of being full, and she loved doing it in front of him. She had never let anyone else see her do such a thing, but it seemed anything with Richard was more than okay. She pulled her finger out and pushed it back in, taking her time, making sure he was watching every move she made. When she looked back at him, the sheer lust in his eyes spoke volumes about what he wanted to do.

"In my fantasy," she said, "my lover wants to fuck my ass."

Richard's dick jumped at the words. Rebecca pulled her finger out and then slid two inside, working a bit to get them in, stretching herself while he watched. She looked impossibly tight, as though she would never be able to get his cock in there. She pulled her fingers out, stretching her ass as she went, and then pushed them back in, harder this time. She moaned with the thrust and braced her legs wider against the shower walls.

"My lover wants to fuck my ass," she said. "Doesn't he?"

Richard stroked his dick, the soap working into a lather around it. He wondered if it would be enough, but the way Rebecca was moving against her hand, he wasn't sure she would care. She was ramming her fingers into herself, moaning with every thrust. When she looked over her shoulder at him, her eyes were dark.

"Fuck me there," she ordered.

Richard stepped up behind her and pressed his cock against her fingers. She grabbed him, stroked him once, and pushed the head of his dick against her ass. Richard watched as the tiny hole opened a little under the pressure, almost as if it were sucking at the tip of his dick. He swivelled his hips and the hole opened wider. Rebecca kept her hand on his cock, holding him tight while she guided him into her.

"I don't want to hurt you," he said over the roar of the shower.

"The hurt is good," she insisted, and pushed back against him. The sting and burn told her the head of his cock was almost in. Rebecca bit her lip and wiggled her hips. With just a little more pressure, the pain suddenly flared across her hips, making her gasp for breath. Then just as suddenly as it came, it was gone, replaced by a sweet, dull ache and the delightful feeling of fullness.

Oh, God. It was perfect.

"All the way," she said.

Richard pushed into her with one smooth, long stroke. He moved slowly, giving her time to adjust. Her ass was stretched tight around him, and he remembered the way it felt when she pushed the vibrator into him, the incredible pleasure that built and built until it overwhelmed him. He pulled out a little and pushed right back in. He grunted with satisfaction as his cock buried itself to the root in her ass. She suddenly braced both hands against the wall of the shower and thrust back at him, almost knocking him off his feet.

"Turn off the water," she panted.

Richard reached behind him and did as she asked. The steady drip of the faucet kept pace with his thrusts, until the desire became too much and he went at her harder, faster. Her ass was a tight ring around his dick, deep and warm, holding him captive as he fucked her. His balls slapped against her cunt with every thrust, and soon the sound of their fucking was loud in the small space. The soap began to wear away and the thrusting wasn't as easy, but still he kept on, unwilling to stop until she told him to. He reached under her, grabbed at her breasts and caught her nipples between his fingers.

"Pinch them harder," she hissed, and he did as he was told. Suddenly she yanked his hands away and murmured, "I can't come this way."

"What do you need?"

"More lube."

"Soap?"

"No. I packed toys in our bag."

Richard slowly pulled out of her. She opened the door of the shower, her body still throbbing from the stretching invasion of his cock, and she stumbled to the bed. The overnight bag was beside it. She fumbled with shaky fingers until the side compartment opened, and she pulled out the bottle of lube. Handing it to him, she climbed on to the bed and spread her knees on the rumpled sheets.

"Put it on me. Then fuck me, Richard. Hurry."

Richard took a moment to look at her. Her body was tense, tight, every muscle ready for pleasure. Her whole body was still wet from the shower but her pussy was the wettest part of all, glistening in the light of the bedside lamp. Her hair was wet and tangled, her cheeks were flushed, and her hands shook as she reached back and spread her cheeks with them. "Fuck me," she said again.

Richard spread lube on his cock, then on her. For a moment he wondered what other toys she had stashed away in that bag, but before the thought got all that far, he was standing behind her, staring at her ass as his dick pressed against it again.

"Ram me," she hissed at him. "Ram me, you fucker."

Richard thrust into her. The stretching of her ass around his dick was exquisite. She shrieked like a fireball as he buried himself deep. Never before had he been so rough, but when he grabbed her hips and gave her a second thrust, the way she slammed back at him said rough was exactly what she wanted.

Rebecca's ass burned like fire as Richard impaled her on his cock. She cried out with the pain, even as her pussy throbbed hard, wanting more. She thrust at him, taking some control back, and that made the sensations more pleasure than anything else. She had wanted this for a long time, and now that she had it she was determined to wring the last drop of pleasure from it. She bit her lip and concentrated hard as he rode her, milking the most from the sensation of his dick stretching her, every nerve ending alive and begging for more.

She reached under herself, touched her wet clit, and growled one last command:

"Come in me."

Richard closed his eyes and rode her hard. Her body rocked with every thrust. Her fingers played underneath them and every now and then she slid her hand even farther back to caress his balls. The wet slapping sounds of their fucking filled the room, and Richard thought nothing in the world had ever turned him on more.

"Fuck, fuck, fuck!" Rebecca screamed out, and Richard pushed deep. The throbbing of her orgasm was clear, her ass pulsing around him as she collapsed on to the bed and cried out incoherent things. Richard was right behind her, the tight grip of her orgasm finally pushing him over the edge, and he emptied himself into her, the feeling so intense he could hardly breathe.

After a long, silent moment, Richard carefully pulled out of her. She crawled into the centre of the bed and he followed, cradling her in his arms. Much to his surprise, she had begun to cry — deep, hard sobs that seemed so at odds with the pleasure of only a moment before.

"Rebecca, what's wrong? Did I hurt you?"

"No…"

She buried her face in his shoulder. He held her and thought about what he might have done wrong, how he might have moved the wrong way, and tried to figure out if there was something he missed. Had she told him to stop? What if she had, and he had been too far gone into pleasure to hear the words? What if this was all his fault?

"What have I done?" he asked.

"You made me feel so good," she whispered, and started to cry again.

Rebecca had no idea how to explain why she was crying. She had certainly had anal sex before, and it wasn't like this time was anything new or even all that different from the times before, with other men. But something about the way he treated her, even in the middle of an all-out fuck, touched her on a level that nobody else had reached. There was something about him that made their lovemaking, no matter how rough or kinky it got, feel like it was absolutely right. Maybe it was the tenderness and constant respect she had from Richard. Even if she was taking it up the ass, she always felt like she had her dignity.

"If I hurt you, I'm so sorry," he was saying now, and she reached up to touch his lips, shushing him with her fingertips.

"You didn't hurt me." The tears were gone just as suddenly as they had come, but now she had a case of the giggles that threatened to overtake anything she might want to say. She bit her lip and struggled to keep the laughter under control. "You made me feel so good, and I don't know how else to explain it..."

The laughter took over, and suddenly she was howling with it, the chuckles as deep as the tears had been and just as uncontrollable. Richard stared at her for a moment, then smiled and relaxed into the pillows. The woman was acting completely nuts, and he loved it. He laughed with her and ran his fingers along her back until the mirth wore itself out.

Rebecca hiccupped once and then lay down beside him, giggling.

"That was a good cry, then?"

She nodded. "A good cry."

"I've never understood women who cry after sex. I've never seen a woman cry after rough sex."

"I don't understand it, either."

"Men don't cry after sex, do they?"

"Some do."

"I don't think I ever have."

She gave him a wicked grin. "Then I just haven't fucked your ass hard enough."

Richard blushed, which sent Rebecca off into another round of giggles. When they wore themselves down to a smile, she looked into his eyes and said, "I love you."

"I love you, too."

"Will you come see me? In Miami?"

"Of course."

"When?"

Richard smiled at her eagerness. "Give me a few weeks to make sure the paper is up to speed, and then I'll come see you for a weekend."

She cuddled into his side. She would have to leave soon, and she didn't want to go. She tried to imagine facing all the mundane parts of her life in Miami, but she reminded herself that she still had him — it was no longer a fling that would end with a kiss and a hug as she left town, but a long-distance relationship that would give them time to nurture it and find out where it might lead.

"Let's not leave this room until we have to," she said, and Richard kissed her forehead.

"That sounds perfect," he said.

Chapter Twelve

When the call came from the mechanic, Richard was lying in bed and Rebecca was in the shower, humming along to some tune in her head. Takeout boxes littered the little table in the hotel room. The television was on, turned to a news channel that neither one of them had bothered to watch. Richard was dozing off when his cell phone rang. Though he knew the call would come, his heart still fell a bit when he saw the number on the caller ID.

"The car's ready," the mechanic said. "The seats will have to be replaced but they're good to get her home, for sure. Turns out she needed two replacement tyres instead of one, so I used her new spare and put an old one in the trunk, just in case. No electrical problems, so she got off lucky."

"Thank you," Richard said. "Can we pick it up this afternoon?"

"If it's after four. I'll leave the keys up on the visor."

"That sounds great."

"You and the lady take care."

Richard hung up the phone just as Rebecca came out of the shower. Her hair was wrapped in a towel but her body was completely naked. "Who was that?"

"Mechanic."

Rebecca's lip suddenly quivered, but she got it together fast. "It's time, then."

"You sure you have to be back? You can't make it one more day?"

She thought about the calendar on her desk, and how carefully she had planned her schedule in order to take this vacation time. One more day would mean rearranging a dozen different appointments, and that meant inconvenience at best, lost business at worst.

"I do have to go," she said, her voice filled with regret.

"Then I guess I need to start planning which weekend I'm coming to see you," he teased, trying to lighten the mood.

Rebecca smiled at him as she pulled clothes from the overnight bag. "Good."

Richard pulled himself from the bed with real effort. One of the realisations he had come to during their week together was that forty-four was no longer as young as it used to be. When he stretched, every muscle ached and his back creaked. He stretched his arms over his head, yawned wide enough to hurt his jaws, and joined her in getting dressed.

As they were leaving the room, Richard turned to look at it one last time. He looked at the bed, the rumpled sheets, the pillows on the floor, and the blankets twisted into knots. The lampshade on the bedside lamp was tilted. "Hey, honey?"

"Yeah?" she called from the truck.

"Get your camera."

Rebecca brought it to the door, looked in and laughed. She took a few shots of their love nest, then put the cover on the lens and smiled up at him. "I'll send them to you."

"Thank you."

The door closed locked behind them. Richard laced his fingers through hers as they drove out of the parking lot and headed for Crispin.

She drove her car from the mechanic's shop to Richard's house, where she parked in the driveway and watched the garage door go down behind his truck. She looked around, at the wide porch and the rocker there, the big trees in the front yard still covered with snow, and thought about how much she was going to miss this place.

Richard was waiting for her at the front door. Together they went into the guest room and gathered her things, then made their way through the house, picking up items that had been left here and there during the course of the week. Finally they put her suitcase on the kitchen table and started packing everything.

"Something's missing," Richard said, and Rebecca smiled when he returned a minute later with one of his dress shirts. He carefully folded it and put it in her suitcase. Rebecca reached over and touched his hand.

"How long?" she asked, fighting back tears.

"A few weeks," he promised. "The time will fly. You'll see."

She held it together as he put her suitcase in the car. She was stoic when he talked about the work he had to do at the paper throughout the week, and she laughed when he joked about how his report on the snow would be read very carefully by the townspeople who knew what he had been doing during the blizzard. She smiled as he walked around her car, pretending to look at the body work but really checking out the tyres.

When he pushed his hands into his pockets as she opened her door, a man out of his depth and unsure what to say, she finally lost it. She threw herself at him and he met her halfway, catching her in his arms and crushing her against his chest.

His voice was rough with the need to cry. "You call me every step of the way. I don't care if you call me twenty times a day. I want to know where you are, and I want to hear your voice."

"I'll annoy you as often as possible," she joked, then they held each other so tight it was hard to breathe. Neither of them knew how to let go.

"A few weeks," he said again, and finally she loosened her grip on him. There were tears in her eyes as she got in the car and closed the door. The sound of the door closing was so final, so complete, that it broke her heart. She looked at the interior of the little car and wished she could invite him to take a ride with her, so the smell of him would be in there when she finally did have to leave, but she knew the realities of time. If she was going to get back to Florida to keep her schedule, she had to leave now.

She rolled the window down and looked up at him.

Richard reached into the car and touched her face with the back of his hand. She closed her eyes for a moment and soaked up the feeling of his skin against hers. "Be careful," he said. "I want you safe and sound when I come to Florida."

"I love you," she murmured, and watched the tears turn his eyes bright.

"I love you, Rebecca."

She put the car in reverse and backed out of the driveway. They looked at each other for a long moment before she stepped on the gas. As the car started to pull away, Richard moved into the road behind it, watching the taillights all the way to the end of the long street.

When she turned the corner, he stood a while longer, watching for any sign of her, knowing she was already on her way out of town. He dreaded going back into that empty house, the one that had been so full of life during her time with him.

As he walked into the house, his cell phone rang. "Hello?"

"I miss you already."

The sound of her voice made his knees weak. He let them give way and sat down on the couch in front of the cold fireplace. The tears stung his eyes again but this time he wasn't brave and didn't try to blink them away. "God, this is hard."

"A few weeks, right?"

"Right. Yes. I'm going to book plane tickets as soon as you call me about your schedule."

"That's the first call I will make when I pull into my driveway."

"You don't have to wait that long to call me."

Her laughter was happy, almost as clear as if she were there with him, and with a start he realised this was the first time he had heard her voice on a phone line. Long after she said goodbye Richard stared at the phone, both happy for the direct line to her, but frustrated that it would be the closest he could get to her for the next few weeks.

In the car, Rebecca put the phone down on the passenger seat and pulled over to the side of the road. All the tears she had held back finally came in a flood, and she cried hard while trucks and cars whipped past her. She went over every word in her head, every touch and every look he had given her. She finally laid her head back against the seat and took deep breaths, reminding herself that he would be in Miami before she knew it, and she had a lot of obligations to take care of before he got there.

But he would be there. He would get on a plane and fly to where she was, he would see her apartment, he would touch her and kiss her and tell her he loved her, over and over again. Now, instead of wishing time would crawl, she hoped it would fly.

The tears gone and the hope firmly in place, Rebecca pulled back out on the road and pointed her car towards Miami.

"I've never done this before," he admitted.

He was lying on the couch in the living room, the fire roaring in front of him, Rebecca's voice on the phone line. She was in a hotel in southern Illinois, the first one that had looked good when she had decided she was too tired to drive any farther.

"It's just like masturbating," she said. "Only the fantasy isn't just in your head. It's delivered by a real, live woman whispering into your ear."

Richard unzipped his jeans. He had missed her all damn day, no matter how many times she had called, and the farther away her car got the more lonely he felt. He was tired of the quiet house and he hated the fact that he would go to bed alone. If this was the only way he could have her, he would take it and be grateful.

"What do I do?" he asked, slightly abashed at being so clueless. At his age, shouldn't he have known something about phone sex?

"You talk," she said. "You tell me what you're thinking. Your fantasies. Memories of us together. Things you want to do when you see me again. And while you're talking, you picture it…and you stroke yourself."

"Are you going to be talking, too?"

"Yeah. Either together, or one of us goes first. You want to come together?"

"Don't I always?"

She smiled against the phone, thinking about how well she knew him already.

"I'm willing to bet your dick is hard. It is, isn't it?"

"It's getting there."

"I bet if you think about fucking me in the ass, it will get there faster."

She was right. Richard looked at his dick, silhouetted by the firelight. Sometimes it ached, and now there was a raw spot on it, just below the head on the right side. He touched it with a careful fingertip and winced.

"You worked me raw, woman."

"I'm not exactly smooth down there anymore, either."

"Oh, yeah?"

"You left a sore spot on my clit. I have to get off by touching myself inside, which takes longer." She sighed into the phone, an unmistakable sound of pleasure. "But if I get that G-spot just right, it might take longer, but it's better."

"Is that the spot you showed me yesterday?" They had done all sorts of exploring in the hotel, and she had taught him things he hadn't known existed.

"That's it."

"That's the place that almost makes you pass out when you come."

She blushed on her end of the phone line. Her legs were open, and she was stroking her inner thighs, letting the feeling build. She wanted more than anything to be there with him, showing him exactly how to have phone sex, but this would have to do.

"Yeah...that's the spot."

"I like the G-spot. I think everybody should have one."

She laughed hard. "Everybody does. It's just a matter of finding it."

"I have a G-spot," he said proudly.

"You do?"

"Yeah. It's that place inside me that you hit with the vibrator. The one that made me scream." He paused, stroking his dick slowly with his left hand. "Remember that, baby?"

She definitely remembered. "You're good at this phone sex thing."

"It's all about a story, right?"

"Right."

"Honey, I'm a newspaper man. You want a story? I can give you a story."

She laughed out loud again, and marvelled at how easily he could make her happy.

"Tell me."

"I've been thinking," he said. "With as much as you like cock and all..."

She lay back on the pillows and grinned, her hand sliding to her pussy. She touched herself carefully — she was even sorer than she had let him believe — and soon the pleasure started to flow.

"Yeah?"

"I was thinking how much you need to have all your holes filled. How one dick isn't enough for a woman who loves dick so much. You would love to have three men at once, wouldn't you?"

It was the fantasy that had got her off more than any other, but there was no way Richard could have known that. Her heart started to kick against her ribs as she slipped a finger inside herself.

"Can you imagine it? You, in the middle of a bed. Not tied up, because you don't have to be forced into anything at all. You want dick. You're hungry for it. When the first guy walks into the room, all you have to decide is which hole he gets."

Richard was stroking his dick, not turned on so much by the fantasy than by what he knew it was doing to her. He could hardly hear her breathing, but he knew she was already well on her way to an orgasm at the idea of having so many horny men in one room.

"Let's say he wants your pussy. But when you look at his dick, you're not sure you can take all of it. He's huge, baby. His dick is thick and long and hard. You want it, don't you?"

"Yes," she murmured into the phone, pushing two fingers in and out of her pussy.

"Good. Because the other guys? They're just as big and just as hard. They are complete strangers, but that's all right. I've checked them out for you. I'm going to sit over here in the corner and watch while they ravage my woman and make her come. I'm going to stroke my dick while I watch you take all the cock you can stand. I'm going to sit right here while that first big one slides into you. Where do you want it, baby? You going to give him your pussy first?"

"Yes…"

"No. No, you don't want to do that. You want to have your mouth stuffed full of cock first. You know why?"

"Why?" she panted.

"Because when that big dick impales your ass, that cock in your mouth will keep you quiet. You don't want to wake the neighbours with the screaming."

Rebecca arched into her own touch, moaning at the visions in her head.

"So suck him down, honey. Let me see you take that cock. That's it...I love watching it disappear into your mouth. You're such a good little cocksucker."

Richard moved his hand away from his dick. He was on the verge already, but he wanted to bring her all the way through his fantasy. "You're ready to go, aren't you, honey? I can see how wet your pussy is. I can see it from here in the corner. Spread those legs, baby, and let that other guy underneath you. You're on your hands and knees...the better to take three dicks in three holes."

She gasped as she touched her clit. A hot flash of pain went through her, but she slipped her fingers into her pussy and found the pleasure again.

"He's right there under you now, his dick is waiting...slide down on it, honey. Show him you want it. Let his dick fill up your pussy. Do you know how hot that looks? The way it is swallowed up by your cunt? No, don't move, baby...don't ride him. Not yet. You have to be full of dick before the fucking starts."

Rebecca was walking the fine line of restraint before the orgasm. She stopped moving her hand, but it took a massive effort. "I want to come."

"You'll come when he's in your ass."

Rebecca moaned and stroked her pussy again. The orgasm was closer now, right there on the horizon, waiting.

"Can you feel the bed move, honey? That's the last guy. He's coming up behind you. And that dick, it's the biggest one of them all. He's lubed it up already, so it's going to slide right into your ass. Since you've already got a dick in your pussy, it's going to feel incredible, isn't it? It's going to stretch you hard and fill you up and make you come. Go ahead, suck hard on that dick in your mouth. Maybe you can get him to shoot in you at the same time that dick is sliding into your back door."

"Jesus, Richard, I need to come..."

"Then let him spread your cheeks, baby. That's it. I'm going to come, too. I'm going to come right now while I watch him slide into your ass. Feel him, baby? Feel him going into you? Look over at me and watch, my dick is going to explode while another guy ploughs my girlfriend's ass."

Rebecca squealed when the orgasm slammed into her. It hit her like a speeding truck, her body convulsing hard. The only thought in her head was a dick sliding into her and Richard coming at the same time, his cum spurting out as he let someone else ride her.

Richard came when Rebecca did. His cock did spurt out—all over his hand, his leg and the couch. He came for a long time, milking every last drop, feeling naughtier than he ever had in all his years. Had he really just come while thinking about another man banging his girlfriend? Holy shit, what had got into him?

Rebecca was laughing on the other end of the line, that low and satisfied laugh that said her orgasm was good, very good, and now she was exhausted.

"See?" he asked. "We can still be just as naughty."

"Even naughtier," she corrected, and whistled under her breath. "Are these the kind of fantasies that go through your head?"

"Yeah. Is that bad?"

"Noooo…it's very good."

Richard smiled at the fireplace. He was a mess and needed to clean up, but talking with her made him so content he wasn't ready to move yet. Just then she yawned, and he knew their conversation was going to be over soon.

"You need to go to bed," he said. "You've got to drive tomorrow."

"You've got to work overtime so you can take some time off," she said.

Richard smiled. "Goodnight, honey."

"Goodnight, love."

This time when they hung up the phone, they were both smiling.

Chapter Thirteen

Richard stared at the front of his mother's house. His father wasn't home, which wasn't a surprise — he usually started his delivery run long before daybreak. His mother's car was parked in the driveway and he knew she was in the kitchen, cooking. The woman never seemed to stop cooking, but everything she made got eaten by the hungry farmhands that always found their way home with her husband. Though the dairy farm ran on more technology than manpower, the farmhands always had something to do and not nearly enough time to do it.

He walked up the sidewalk, thinking about the last time he had seen her and the argument they had had. He had been taught to never walk away without saying he loved someone, and he had told her that he did, but now he wanted to tell her again and make sure she heard him. He was afraid that after this morning's talk she was going to hate him all over again.

She looked up when he walked into the kitchen. Her smile was quickly followed by pursed lips and a disappointed shake of the head. "Is that chickie gone for good?"

Richard smiled wryly. "You always do get to the point, Ma."

"Is she?"

Richard poured himself a cup of coffee. His mother slid the creamer across the counter and went back to washing dishes without missing a beat.

"I need to talk to you about all this, Ma."

"Ah, great. Here we go."

Richard sat down at the kitchen table. His mother stood and glared at him while he calmly drank his coffee, looking up at her with all the time in the world. Finally she sighed and sat down at the table across from him.

"Can I talk to you, Ma?"

Her eyes softened. She reached over the table and patted her son's hand. "I don't know," she said, and, though the words stung, he respected her for the honesty.

"She's been gone over three years," he said softly. "She's not coming back."

His mother looked at him, her expression carefully guarded.

"I'm tired of being alone, Ma. I shouldn't have to be alone. If I had done something wrong, I would understand. But I haven't, and I think I've done enough penance for something I didn't do."

His mother nodded and looked at the refrigerator. There was a magnet with Richard and Amanda's wedding picture in it. The two of them looked so happy, as if nothing could ever come between them.

"Ma?"

Janette sighed and looked back at him, her eyes wet. "You're giving up, then?"

He took a deep breath before he dropped the bombshell. "I filed for divorce today."

"Richard, no!"

"I'm sorry, Ma."

"But did you have to do that?"

"I feel like she divorced me a long time ago."

Janette got up from the chair and walked around the kitchen, flapping her dishtowel at the counter. "But it's not right, Richard."

"It's not right that she left me, Ma. Why don't you ever say such things about her actions?"

Janette shook her head hard. "Women have reasons for running, son."

"Like what?"

She sighed and looked out of the window. "Did you do anything to her?"

"Like what? Hit her? Step out on her?"

Janette shot him a look. He glared right back. "No. I haven't done a single thing to deserve this. I was the perfect husband, Ma. Maybe that was the problem. Maybe she wanted more adventure and passion than I was giving her."

Janette eyed him carefully. "More passion?"

"You know what I mean. She always seemed to want to be somewhere else. Well, now she is, and I hope she's happy. I want to be happy, too."

"You could get a private investigator and find her."

"I could, but I won't. I'm not going to chase a woman who doesn't want me to catch her."

"What if something has happened to her? Something bad?"

"It hasn't." He shook his head. "Her family knows where she is. They just won't tell me. They seem to think it's my fault, just like you do."

Janette stared at him with hard eyes. "Nobody in our family has ever divorced. We're the only family around who hasn't. Marriages have lasted until death, for over ten generations."

"That's the problem, isn't it, Ma? You having the upper hand on everybody else?"

Janette's face flooded with heat, and he knew he was right.

"Well, the family tradition ends here. I'm getting divorced. If you want to kick me out of the Paris family for it, then go right ahead. It won't be the first time I was abandoned."

Janette's mouth dropped open. "You're always a part of this family!"

Richard stood up and walked around the table. He put his arms around his mother, and she leaned into them with no reservation. She might not be happy with him, but she loved him, and he knew it.

"I'm sorry, Ma."

"I'm sorry too, son."

"Are any of your good biscuits left?"

She rolled her eyes and smiled. "Look in the microwave."

There they were. Richard grinned as he pulled the plate of leftovers out of the microwave. That's where breakfast leftovers went, for as long as he could remember. He stuck a piece of bacon in a cold biscuit and took a bite, the flavour reminding him of being a kid and sneaking leftovers because he had slept in a little too long.

Some things were changing, but other things would always be the same.

Rebecca had been almost too busy to breathe from the moment she arrived back in Miami. She hadn't even found time to get the car to the body shop for a paint job — the shop kept calling, but she hadn't been able to find the time when they were open. She was too busy filling obligations. Now that her name was getting out there and she was building up a reputation for quality and good prices, her schedule was booked solid. She had juggled like crazy to get away for the week she had spent in Iowa, and now she was paying the price.

Standing in her darkroom in Richard's dress shirt, she hung another 8x10 on the line. Anyone who took a look at her darkroom was surprised at how simple it really was. Since most of her creative work was taken on black and white film, she didn't have to worry about keeping the room completely dark. The safelight cast an amber glow over everything, a soothing light that made the tiny space seem like another world. There were five pans situated on a narrow table in front of her, each of them for a separate chemical. Across the top of the room was a thin cotton line, hung just like a clothesline from one corner to the other, where she hung her pictures to dry.

She looked at the latest photograph and smiled. It was part of a series, pictures of the covered bridge in Iowa, and more than a few pictures of Richard throwing snowballs. He had told her over the phone last night that almost all the snow was gone, and she had found that hard to believe. It seemed there was so much snow, it could never possibly all disappear.

She held her hand up to her face and looked at her watch in the dim light. She had a few more hours before she needed to head to the airport. She had developed the pictures from her trip a few rolls at a time, stretching out the memories during those long weeks before she would see Richard again. Now that he was on his way to Miami, she was developing the last roll. She had every intention of taking another dozen rolls of film, this time all of him and her, and maybe even a few pictures that would never be shared with anybody — the kind of pictures she would keep in her bedside table for erotic inspiration.

She grinned and put up another picture. This one was of Richard looking directly into the camera, his eyes filled with such happiness that it made Rebecca stop and stare. She reached out and touched the picture, ran a fingertip delicately across his shadowed jaw, and stared at those eyes for a long moment. Then she turned back to the trays and brought another few prints to light. When she hung those up, her grin turned saucy. The vision of her lover's dick filled the paper, and she licked her lips.

"I'll have that in a few hours," she said to the room.

She cleaned up in the darkroom, humming all the while. When she came out of the space the bright Miami sunlight was bursting through her windows, almost blinding her. She squinted and blinked as she walked to the closet and tried to decide what to wear. All he had seen her in were long sweaters and jeans, so now she chose a pretty sundress with criss-cross straps across the shoulder and a full skirt. She pulled her hair into an upsweep and put on bright red lipstick, the colour that brought out the pout of her lips and the smile in her eyes.

She stepped into sandals and grabbed a small purse on her way to the car. She stopped once to twirl in front of the mirror, casting a critical eye over her body.

In the car, her hands shook with anticipation as she turned the key.

Richard stared out of the window as the plane circled over Miami. He had travelled quite a bit but he had never seen Miami before, and now he stared out at the skyscrapers underneath him and the blue water in the distance. From up here, it looked like paradise. He knew there was a woman down there waiting for him who would make sure paradise was exactly what he got.

Phone sex was good, but it wasn't the same as having her there in bed with him. He had masturbated more in the last few weeks than he ever had before in his life, and he was sure that trend would continue as long as they were in a long-distance relationship. They had begun mentioning the long-term future and what might come for them, and so far no decisions had been made, or even really discussed on a deep level. What they knew for certain was that, eventually, someone would have to move. Richard saw this trip to Miami not only as a visit to see Rebecca, but as an audition of the city that he might live in one day.

He buckled up when he was told to do so and watched out of the window as the plane began its descent. He always liked the way the world looked when the plane was landing, the buildings that were once little dots now big structures, the cars in the parking lot coming into focus, the signs and lights of businesses making themselves clear. He stared out of the window until the gentle bump, and then the lights of the runway were flashing past the windows, heralding their arrival.

It seemed to take forever to get off the plane. It had been so long since anyone had been there to meet him at the end of a long trip that he had almost forgotten how good it felt to look for that face in the terminal. He had never experienced the thrill of a long-distance lover throwing herself into his arms when he arrived, but that was something he couldn't wait to feel.

When she did spot him in the throng of passengers, she started to run. Dodging bags and strollers and weary travellers, she danced through the crowd in a beautiful yellow dress, her eyes pinned on him. He dropped his carry-on bag and opened his arms. When she threw herself into his embrace, passersby stopped for a moment to stare, smiling at the pretty young lady and the man who held her like she was the only thing in the world that mattered.

She was crying when they pulled apart, but she was smiling.

"I love you," he whispered into her ear.

She laughed out loud and kissed him.

Waiting on the baggage claim was an excuse to hold hands and look at each other. He had never seen a woman so pretty, and he told her so. She blushed becomingly and Richard didn't miss the interested glances of the men around them, or the envious smiles as they caught him watching. She shone like a bright star, standing out in a sea of people. Richard was proud to be with her.

As they walked to the car, she laced her arm with his and laid her head on his shoulder. The warmth of the Miami sun beat down on them, so different from the chilly days in Iowa. He lifted his face to it, soaking it up, and she watched him enjoy what she usually took for granted.

"Hard to believe it's warm here," he said. "I'm so used to the cold."

"It's warmer in my apartment," she teased.

"Yeah?"

"Yeah."

"Show me."

He watched as she drove through traffic, her hands confident on the wheel. She deftly steered between eighteen-wheelers and SUVs, speeding into the empty spaces and making headway in the bumper-to-bumper lineup. She shot into an exit, swerved around a slow-moving truck, and went under a light just before it turned red. Richard was both impressed and frightened.

"Are you this confident with everything?" he asked. She reached over, squeezed his knee, and shaved ten miles per hour off her speed.

"You big baby," she teased.

"I'm used to driving behind tractors and combines," he explained.

"Want to give it a shot here?"

"No way!"

She grinned and pushed down harder on the gas pedal.

In her apartment, Richard was the one in control. As soon as they walked into the front door he gave the room a cursory glance, then pinned her against the wall. His lips found her neck, his tongue tasting her skin, bringing to life the scent of the perfume she had sprayed there. When she put her arms around his shoulders, he took her wrists in his hands and held them against the wall behind her.

"I brought some toys," he murmured against her mouth.

"Which ones?"

"The ones you really want."

He kissed her hard, until they were both short of breath. He abruptly pulled her away from the wall. "Where's the bedroom?"

Rebecca wasn't offended that he hadn't looked at the apartment. There would be time for that later, when the need in both of them was sated. She took his hand and walked through the tiny space to the bedroom, where the Miami sun streamed in through the windows. She was gratified by his look of surprise and awe as he stood in the beams of light and basked in the glow.

"Strip for me and get on the bed," he ordered.

She had missed those words. Rebecca lifted the dress slowly over her head, revealing nothing but bare skin under the fabric, and turned to the bed, certain his eyes were on her the whole time. She listened to him feeling around in his carry-on bag, then listened to his low moan as he watched her move across the floor. Without being told, she got on her knees in the middle of the bed, arched her back and spread her legs.

Richard stared at the way she displayed her body for him, inviting him to take whatever he wanted. The weeks of separation fell away and she was still his Rebecca, the woman who had opened him up in such a sexual frenzy that he knew he would never be the same again.

"Do you remember what we talked about the night you left?" he asked, his voice hoarse with desire as he looked at her.

She remembered very well. "Remind me."

Richard stepped to the bed. He took a moment to look around the room, at the photographs on the walls and the old-fashioned dresser in the corner. The bed was huge, the centrepiece of the room, and for a moment he wondered what other men had been there, and what she had looked like while she fucked them. The thought made him curiously jealous and turned him on all at once.

He touched the small of her back with his fingertips. She jerked and lowered her head to the blanket. He watched her sway against his touch.

He pressed the dildo to her pussy.

Rebecca tensed, immediately aware of what he had in his hand but not quite ready to take it inside her. She held perfectly still as he twisted it against her, not entering her but making her think he might. He waited until she pushed back against it the slightest bit, then pulled it away.

He pressed the dildo to her ass.

Rebecca let out a low, animal sound. She swivelled her hips slowly, trying to get him to push it harder, but he pulled it away from there, too. She knelt on the bed, panting, waiting.

"You wanted more than one man," he said, his tone accusing. "You wanted more than one dick in you. Remember that, Rebecca? How you wanted to be the fuck-toy centrepiece of a gangbang?"

Rebecca's pussy melted with desire. She thrust her hips into the air, offering him any hole he wanted. He watched as she writhed on the bed, her whole body afire with the idea he had just put in her head. She wasn't playing coy and he wasn't about to deny how much it turned him on.

He pressed the dildo to her pussy and began to push.

Rebecca groaned as the dildo went all the way in without pause. Richard held it there, pressing it hard into her, well aware it was hitting bottom and might be hurting her. He twisted it and she hissed as the spirals of pain went through her, but she wasn't about to move away. He played with her, sliding it in and out a few times before pushing it all the way in again. She cried out, once, the sound loud in the bedroom.

"Hold it there," he ordered.

Rebecca reached under her body and pressed her hand to his. He made sure the dildo was where he wanted it, then slowly moved his hand away, leaving her in control. She immediately began to ride it. Richard's eyes were riveted between her thighs as she fucked herself. He watched the dildo, now slick with her juices, as it slid out of her. He enjoyed the way her cunt swallowed it, as though it were hungry for the thick, hard toy.

He spread lube all over the vibrator as she rode the dildo.

She knew what was coming, and the thought of it turned her on more than she had thought it would. She had had her share of lovers, but never had she felt all her holes filled at one time, and that's what she wanted more than anything. It might not be real, live male bodies, but it would be just as good — especially when she had Richard's cock deep in one of those holes, pumping into her and driving them both to an orgasm on the strength of their shared fantasy.

"More than one man," he mused, and pressed the vibrator to her ass.

She shuddered, her whole body primed and ready for what he was going to do to her. She was a little afraid of what it would feel like, and she didn't think for a moment it wouldn't hurt, but she thought the orgasm would be harder if there were a little hurt involved. No pain, no gain.

"Keep fucking him," he told her, watching the dildo go in and out of her. "Make his dick happy, honey. Don't let him come, though. He needs to wait until the other men are coming. Three hot loads of cum in your body all at once...don't you want that, Rebecca?"

"Yes," she murmured. "Yes."

"Then hold still," he said. "Hold still. This other man wants to ride up your back door, and you're going to open your cheeks and invite him in, aren't you?"

She nodded and pressed her forehead to the bed below her. She looked between her legs. Richard's pants were unzipped and his dick was in his hand. She kept fucking herself with the dildo and imagined a man on the bed behind her, his cock lubed and ready. She pictured Richard standing nearby while that man pressed hard against her ass and began to inch his way inside.

Richard was pushing the vibrator in a little at a time. He watched with rapt attention as her sphincter opened under the pressure. She whimpered and he pulled the vibrator back, but she protested loudly. "No! Don't stop. Fuck me."

Richard pushed the vibrator back in. He kept pushing as she opened, this time ignoring her small cries and whimpers. Sliding it in wasn't nearly as easy as he thought it would be, and he knew that was because of the dildo filling her pussy. When the vibrator was in as far as it could go, Rebecca let out a long wail of satisfaction. Richard pushed it harder, just for good measure, and began to fuck her with it.

"They are both fucking you," he said. "Both of them in you. One below, one on top, making you take it. Filling you with cock. And you know what?"

She didn't hear him at first. She was too busy fucking the dildo, fucking the vibrator, feeling both hard fantasy men filling her. Richard had to repeat himself twice before she answered him.

"What?" she panted.

"You're going to suck me off while those men fuck you."

She was on the verge of an orgasm. She tried to hold back but the vibrator was fucking her ass without mercy, going as hard as he pleased, and she was being dragged to the edge of pleasure whether she liked it or not.

"He's going to make me come!" she wailed, completely lost in the fantasy.

"You're going to let another man make you come?" he asked her, his voice a mastery of mock surprise, his dick harder than ever in his hand. "You're going to do that while your boyfriend watches?"

She couldn't hold back anymore, and Richard knew it. Her hand trembled on the dildo and her knees started to give way. He reached under her, grabbed the dildo with his other hand, and pressed both toys deep into her body.

Rebecca came, convulsing on the toys, squeezing them so hard she almost pushed them out. Richard pressed hard against the bases of them, holding them in, making the orgasm so much more intense. He held the toys as she rode hard against them, her eyes closed, lost in the fantasy of fucking two men in her bed while her boyfriend watched every sensation that ran through her body.

Richard enjoyed the view. He saw her toes curl, her calves tighten, her whole body shudder, and her pussy get wetter. He watched as her nipples got hard, as the flush ran from her chest to her face, as her lips fell open and her eyes closed. His cock was rock hard as she collapsed on the bed, the toys still in her, breathing hard.

Richard came around the other side of the bed, careful to hold the toys in her as he moved. "Get up," he ordered her, and after looking at him for a moment with dazed eyes, she got up on her knees. When he wiggled the dildos she reached under her and pressed her shaky hand against his. "Hold those there. We're not done yet."

Rebecca panted as he pushed down his pants, grabbed a handful of her hair, and pushed his dick in her mouth. Immediately, the tiny zings of pleasure shot through her again, pulses that made her pussy clench hard on the dildo inside it. She rocked back and forth, first taking in his cock then taking in the toys, until she built up a steady rhythm. Her body felt liquid, melting from the inside out, a vessel of pleasure.

Richard watched his girlfriend, her hair in disarray and her face red, as his cock disappeared into her mouth. She took him in all the way and gagged once, but quickly got her rhythm back and kept the motion smooth. He resisted the urge to thrust into her and make himself come as quickly as he could. This was her fantasy, and he wanted her to come hard while all three holes were busy.

He knew when she started to lose it again. Her motion became jerky and for a moment, she forgot to suck his cock. Her eyes went distant and her moans became constant. Richard reached down and grabbed her hair, forcing her to look at him.

"Suck me off," he ordered. "Fuck them both, and make them come, and suck me off. Take cum down every one of your holes."

She stared up at him as her body started to shake. When he thrust his cock deep into her mouth, it was like flipping a switch. She came hard enough to push the toys out of her.

They dropped to the bed, wet and glistening. She moaned on his dick, and that final vibration, mixed with the way she looked there on that bed in front of him, pushed him over the edge, too.

Richard came in her mouth. She swallowed him at first, but somehow she had the presence of mind to pull away for the second shot, so it landed all over her lips. The third came when she sucked him back into her mouth, intent on getting the rest of it from him. She looked up at him, his cock buried and his cum on her face, and he could have sworn the look in her eye was a laugh.

When she collapsed on the bed this time, he let her go. She rolled over and looked at the toys, then looked at him, and burst out laughing. She sat up slowly, cleaned the cum from her face with her fingers, and slowly licked it away, savouring it like candy. Richard watched her until it was all gone, then he crawled into the bed beside her, pushing the toys out of the way.

"Three men," he whispered, still trying to catch his breath.

"You were the best out of all of them," she said.

"I was the only one with a pulse."

She cuddled under his chin and he held her with one strong arm. She took his hand, the one that had been bandaged the last time she saw him, and turned it over in hers. There was a straight, even scar there. She kissed it and ran the tip of her tongue across it. "Does it hurt?"

"It twinges if I lift something heavy," he said. "But soon it won't hurt at all."

"Good."

They lay in silence for a while, and for the first time Richard took in the beauty of the room, the tiny space that looked so much bigger with the addition of the sunlight glowing through the wide and high windows. The pictures on the wall were simple, matted in white, skylines of the city they were now in. There was one of a covered bridge, and he knew exactly when it had been taken. That made him smile.

Rebecca lay against him and listened to his heartbeat under her ear. How many nights had she lain on her pillow and wished she could hear this sound instead? Now he was here, strong and solid in her bed, and she had never been happier.

"I have something to tell you," he said.

She sat up in bed, waiting for it. Her hair was tangled, and the makeup she had carefully applied before coming to see him was long gone. He could still smell her perfume, though, something light and airy, so much like that yellow dress she had worn to the airport.

She looked into his eyes and saw happiness there.

"Tell me."

He smiled at her. "I filed for divorce."

Rebecca's eyes grew wide. She had tried hard not to think about the future because she knew his personal life wasn't settled, no matter how confident they were in their relationship. But now he had taken a definite, legal step towards settling all the issues that held them back from a real discussion about what would come next. The word 'divorce' seemed to open up a brand new horizon and made the world look entirely different.

Richard watched the emotions flood her face. First there was surprise, then elation, then a gradual dawning of reality as she thought about what it all meant. Finally there was a calm acceptance, but one that didn't hide the joy she felt.

"How will they find her to serve the papers?" she asked.

"I have no idea, but I'm sure a legal team can find her. I've just never tried."

"You never sent an investigator after her?"

"Why? She didn't want to be with me, so why would I track her down?"

Rebecca nodded. If she had been the one in that situation, she probably wouldn't have hired an investigator, either. "How do you think she will react?"

"I doubt she will care," he mused. "Or she will be stunned that I actually did it."

"She has to expect it."

"Well, it doesn't matter. I've done it, and now she can respond to it if she likes, but the fact remains: I'm moving on. And I want to move on with you."

Her radiant smile was all the answer he needed.

Chapter Fourteen

Their weekend in Miami was blissful. They spent most of their time in her apartment, getting reacquainted and doing their best to wear each other out. When they weren't exploring things between the sheets, they were out on the streets of Miami, exploring all the things that were so different from Richard's life in Iowa. Around every corner he heard the colourful sounds of Spanish. The sun shone down on bodies that were scantily clad, even though it was supposed to be winter. The water was blue, so blue it hurt his eyes, and the skyscrapers looked more like works of art than buildings. He took it all in while Rebecca watched the discovery in his eyes, and did her best to capture it with her camera.

Richard went to the studio with her and looked at everything, remembering how she looked through the back rooms of the *Crispin Tribune*. He now understood the novelty of soaking up the atmosphere in which she spent so much of her time, and he tried to remember everything, so he could take it back to Iowa with him until the next time he came to see her.

He looked through her portfolio, impressed anew at her talent. He scanned her schedule book and was secretly delighted to see how busy she was. It might keep her from coming to Iowa as often as he would have liked, but it was also the mark of her burgeoning success, and that made him happy.

Rebecca kept her camera on him all weekend, taking pictures of him when he was aware of it and even more when he was not. She loved having him there, loved the way her apartment seemed different now, as though the space had been changed by his presence. She knew she would never walk the streets of Miami again without seeing him on the sidewalk, on the street corner, in the little shops. The thought filled her with a peace that was almost startling in its force.

The last night in her apartment, she set up a camera with a timer, and every twenty seconds a picture flashed, capturing their lovemaking on film. They kept going even after the memory card was full, and greeted the morning sun with moans and sighs.

When Rebecca took him to the airport, there were still tears, but not nearly as many as there had been when she had to leave Iowa. Now they knew they were committed to making the long-distance relationship work, and they had handled the separation without losing their attraction for one another. There was also the added element of having a future to discuss, where once there had been no discussion to be had. They kissed at the terminal and let people walk around them, ignoring both the indulgent smiles and the impatient scowls, until the final call for his plane came over the loudspeaker.

"I'll call you in a few hours," he said, and she touched his face as he moved away.

"I'll see you in a few weeks," she promised, and with one final wave he was gone.

Richard fell into a dark, sullen mood when he landed at the airport in Des Moines.

There was no pretty woman in a yellow dress to meet him, the weather was cold as hell, and he had to drive his truck back to his lonely house all by himself. Now that he knew what it was like to be happy again, he wanted her around all the time.

He called her as soon as he was out of the airport, and they talked as he drove home, both of them excited about the weekend they had just enjoyed. They discussed plans for her next trip to Iowa. This time she would fly, and he could already imagine what they would do with those beautiful days.

When he pulled into his driveway, the light in the kitchen was on. Strange, he thought, then remembered that his mother had grudgingly agreed to watch over the house while he was gone. He grinned at the thought of having something good and homemade to eat when he walked in the door, and, though it wasn't the same as greeting Rebecca in the kitchen, it was still a good welcome home.

"Ma is in my house," he said into the phone. "I've got to go."

"Call me tomorrow," she said.

Richard walked through the door, announcing his arrival. "Thanks for watching over the house, Ma," he called. "I'm back, I'm hungry and I'm tired."

He stopped short in the kitchen doorway, staring at the table. The woman sitting there looked right back at him, her smile tight and fake, her eyes blank.

"Hello, Richard," Amanda said.

Richard thought he was going to be sick. He grabbed the doorframe until the world settled down again. When he looked back up at the table, she was still there, as real as anything. Her smile was no longer fake—now it was slightly amused.

"Aren't you going to welcome me home?" she asked.

It was the same voice he was so familiar with, the one he had thought he would never hear again. "Amanda?"

"Don't you remember your wife?"

He stared at her, letting the reality sink in. He had filed for divorce only a few days ago, but he had felt divorced for so long that it seemed like just a formality to the situation.

Now she was here, and there underneath her coffee cup were the divorce papers.

"That was fast," he said, finally finding some equilibrium.

"I wasn't far away." She was still smiling, as if this were a discussion on the weather, not a wife confronting her husband after disappearing from his life for three solid years.

Richard took off his coat and carefully pulled off his gloves. He kicked his boots into the garage and shut the door behind him, careful not to face her. He wasn't sure what there was to say. He wasn't sure why she was even there. It had been over for a long time, and her presence felt like an unnecessary slap in the face. Was she just coming back to rub things in, to make him remember how helpless he had felt way back then?

She watched him, her expression unreadable. He finally turned to her and put his hands on the back of a kitchen chair. For years he had thought about what he would say when she came back, if she ever did, and he had even rehearsed a speech or two. He had a carefully-worded response to everything she might come up with, but now that she was sitting in front of him again, all those rehearsed words disappeared like a puff of smoke. He had no idea what to say, so he just said what was in his heart—the most honest truth he had.

"I don't know where you've been, and I don't much care anymore, Amanda. You made the decision to leave me, and I licked my wounds for years. Now I've made the decision to leave you. It's pretty simple to me, and it should be simple to you, too. I don't know why you're here."

She suddenly glared at him, and her words were filled with venom. "You were the one who drove me away," she hissed. "You were the one who was too interested in your paper and your precious community and your farmland to pay attention to the wife you had at home. You were the one who came home late at night with no explanation, and you were the one who spent every weekend running that damn paper! You were the one who left me here alone." There were tears of anger in her eyes as she looked at him. "What was I supposed to do? I figured when I ran you would come after me, but you didn't care enough to do that. Did you even love me in the first place?"

Richard shook his head slowly. "I didn't make you leave."

"You've spent so much time convincing yourself of that, I'm sure," she spat. "But you always were good at writing your own stories, Richard. You created a story that made you look better, rather than worse, and now you're trying to tell me it was my fault? Spare me, sweetheart."

Richard stared at the table, unsure what to say. The first little questions started creeping in on the weight of her words. Had he ignored her? Had he worked too much? Why hadn't he gone after her when she left, instead of thinking she was the one who wanted out?

Had he really missed all the signs?

When he raised his eyes back to her, he was shocked to see the tears running down her face. She picked up the divorce papers and flung them at him. They hit his chest, some of them ripping loose from the staple, falling to the floor at his feet like a perverse kind of offering.

"You filed for divorce and now you're blaming me for it? I gave you three years to see the error of your ways, which was about three years too long. I should have been the one to file, but I still had hope you would really love me, Richard." She was sobbing now, in a way he hadn't seen before. "I still had hope that one day you would come to find me and show up on my doorstep and tell me how sorry you were."

He shook his head, not knowing whether to laugh or cry. Was all this really happening? None of it made any sense. He needed time to back away, to process all she had said, to get a handle on all those questions he had harboured for so long. Now that she was here, he was more confused than ever.

"Amanda, if you felt this way, you should have said so a long time ago. You should have tried to get through to me. You never said a word. I thought everything was fine."

She raised her hands in frustration. "You never noticed me leaving our bed when you were too tired for sex? Or crying in the kitchen while I cooked breakfast? Or the way

I stopped waiting up for you at night, and how sometimes I would be crying when you came home?"

Richard shook his head. He didn't remember those things. But what if she was right? What if he had just missed them? Under her barrage of questions and accusations, his head was spinning.

"If you felt that badly about our marriage, you should have told me," he said.

She pushed her chair back so hard it screeched on the tile and fell over with a clatter. She leaned over the table and screamed, "You should have noticed me!"

The aftermath of her anger echoed through the house. Richard took a step away from the table. Amanda glared at him with cold, hard eyes, the tears on her face the only thing soft about her. They stared at each other in silence, and when Richard dropped his eyes to the table, he noticed she was still wearing her wedding ring.

Something about that wedding ring finally broke him free of the paralysis. He had just filed for divorce after she had been gone for three long years—after he had dealt with the pain of being abandoned, the hurt, the disappointment, and yes, the fear that crept into the middle of his dreams from time to time—and now she was back, all this time later, and wearing that wedding band? The same one she had accepted when she said her vows?

For richer or poorer. In sickness and in health.

Until death do us part?

He slammed his hands down on the table, startling her so much that she was the one to take a step back. He pinned a glare on her that was furious enough to wither steel, and his voice was cold as ice.

"You spineless bitch."

Amanda blinked at him. "What did you say?"

He didn't take his eyes from her. "You. Spineless. Bitch."

"How dare you!"

"No, how dare *you*! You walked away from this marriage and everything was fine and dandy until I called you on that bullshit, wasn't it, Mandy? Then you had to come running back and make yourself look like the good little girl when the truth is that you ran out on your husband. Where have you been these last three years, anyway? Where did you go? Better yet, who were you with?"

She shrank back with every question, and finally the hardness in her eyes was gone, replaced by sadness and fear. "Who was I with?"

"That's what I said."

"How could you think such things?"

"Answer me."

"I don't have to answer to you!" She straightened her back and met his glare head-on. "From what I hear, you're the one who has some answering to do."

Richard refused to back down. "Funny how it took me moving on to get you back here, isn't it? I'll have you know I didn't even look at another woman for years. I was faithful to you until I knew you weren't coming back."

"Well, now I'm back, so who was wrong?"

Richard flinched inwardly, but was determined not to show it. "You came back after I filed."

"But I came back," she said, pleading now. "I came back and I want to make it work. Richard...I'm your wife. We're still married. Give me a chance to make up for things, and meet me halfway?"

Richard shook his head. "I want a divorce."

"But don't you remember how it was?" she asked, coming around the table towards him. "Don't you remember how good it was once?"

Richard nodded. Why lie to her? "I remember. I held on to that for three years."

"Hold on to it now," she coaxed, and put her hand on his arm. Her familiar touch sent all kinds of emotions tumbling through him, from every corner of the spectrum. This was the woman he had loved for so long, the one he had promised to love forever, the one who had broken his heart. She was both the woman he married and the bitch he couldn't stand. The two aspects of her collided as she stood in front of him, her lips puffy from crying, the tears still making silver trails down her cheeks, her eyes wide and questioning.

"Hold on to it," she said again, and he closed his eyes to her voice. It was too much to handle. He wasn't equipped for this.

Amanda slid her hand across his chest. She rested it on his heart and he thought of all the times she had done that before, when they were lying in bed together. She claimed the beat of his heart helped her go to sleep, and sure enough, her hand would seek his chest even when she was out cold and dreaming.

He was thinking of that when she pressed her lips to his ear. "Hold on to me," she implored, and he reached up to put his hand over hers. Her fingers were cool, like they always were—she was never warm, even in the middle of summer. He pressed her hand to his heart while she stood beside him, her body so close he could smell her shampoo, the same brand she had always used.

When she brushed her lips against his cheek, it was as natural as breathing to turn his head to her. She kissed him gently, not much more than a kiss between two old friends.

When he suddenly began to pull away, she ran her hand into his hair and pulled him to her, kissing him harder.

Richard forgot where he was. Was this a winter day in Iowa, three years after his wife left, or was this before she was gone, when things were good and her kisses were the most welcome thing in the world? Had he really been without that touch for so long, and had he really decided he didn't want it, ever again?

Amanda kissed him the way he liked best, taking control of his mouth, stealing his breath. She held his head as she kissed him, her body pressing against him like it belonged there. Her hands stole to the front of his shirt and she unbuttoned it with practised hands, opening it like she had done a thousand times before. She kissed down his neck and found the pulse at the base of his throat. Her tongue played there as he put his hands in her hair.

"That's it," she whispered, and the words jerked him back to reality.

That voice was not Rebecca's.

Richard pushed her away. She was unprepared for such a thing and she lost her balance, falling gracelessly into one of the kitchen chairs. She looked at him in surprise, but he watched the dawning realisation in her eyes, followed by the furious anger.

"I'm in love with someone else," he told her.

"You son of a bitch!" she shouted.

She came up from the chair so fast he had no time to react. Her hand landed against the side of his face. She slapped him hard enough to rock his head back on his shoulders. Her fists slammed into his chest and he took a few steps back before he caught her arms and held her still. She was beyond listening to reason, and when her foot connected with his shin, he let out a yelp of surprise. She tried to knee him where it counted, and he moved to the side just in time to avoid the blow. She lunged towards him, and for one terrifying moment he thought she might actually bite him.

He shoved her back into the chair and yelled into her face.

"Stop it, Amanda! Stop it right now!"

She stopped. She gave him another of those withering glares. He stepped away from her, his chest smarting, his shin hurting even worse. He could feel the redness of her handprint on his face.

"You come here," he said, breathing hard, "and you think you can get me into bed, and that will make everything okay? Are you out of your fucking mind?"

All the tenderness in her was gone. "Is she really half your age?"

He couldn't resist the comeback. "She's half of yours."

Amanda drew back as if he had slapped her. Richard was immediately sorry for what he had said, but he wasn't going to take it back. He wasn't going to give her the slightest bit of hope for reconciliation.

"You wanted to know why I left," she said, and he nodded, still wary.

"Tell me why."

"I left you for another man."

Though he had thought of the possibility more times than he cared to admit, he was not prepared for the reality of hearing it from her lips. She was entirely cold as she delivered the news, as if she had finally decided to play hardball and had turned on some inner robot.

"I left you for a man who fucked me in all the ways you didn't even think about. His dick was bigger, he could last longer, and he could come more often." Her eyes actually twinkled as she looked at him. "He taught me that there's more to sex than the missionary position."

Richard looked away.

Amanda stood up and slowly put the chair back under the table. She picked up the divorce papers and righted the second chair, the one she had knocked over when she had first risen from her seat. Had that been only a few minutes ago? Time no longer seemed accurate, whether it was minutes or years.

"This is still my house," she said calmly. "I'm staying here for as long as I'm in town, and I'll sleep in the guest room. I won't darken your door, and I know you won't darken mine. I'll pack up what belongs to me over the next few days, and then I'll go after you for this house. I'll get half the bank account. After that, I'll get half your business, and I'll shut your little rag down."

With that, she turned and walked into the darkened living room. He listened as she went down the hallway and firmly shut the door to the guest room behind her.

Richard sat down at the table and put his head in his hands, trying to make the world stop spinning, so he could make sense of it all.

Chapter Fifteen

Rebecca woke up early the next morning and stretched. Her body was warm with sleep and sore with the memory of Richard's hands. It was a delicious kind of soreness, the kind that said she had been loved thoroughly and often, and she had the sudden thought that everyone, at some point in their lives, should have that kind of wake-up call in the morning.

She smiled at the sunlight coming through her window as she reached for the telephone. She had fallen into the custom of calling Richard every morning as soon as she woke. He was usually getting dressed, and they talked while he got in the truck and went to the office for another day of detailing the events and lives in Crispin. She would hang up the phone and jump into the shower, refreshed and renewed, ready to face the day. She was certain that her work lately had been so much better because of his influence—simply because he made her happy—and her customers were appreciative.

She was still smiling as the phone rang, but that smile faded fast when the phone was answered.

"Hello?"

It was a woman's voice. Rebecca shook her head, confused. "I'm sorry," she said. "I must have the wrong number."

She was just about to hang up when the woman said, "Are you calling for Richard?"

Rebecca didn't answer for a moment, too surprised to think of what to say. She was still convinced she had the wrong number, but wasn't this odd?

"I'm calling for Richard Paris," she said.

"He's in the shower."

The woman's voice was lower now, sultry, as though she had just woken up. Rebecca took in the words, but still they didn't quite register.

"He's what?" she asked.

The woman laughed. Rebecca's body went cold. "He's in the shower," she repeated, slowly, as if Rebecca hadn't heard properly the first time. "We're both running a bit late this morning."

The familiarity slammed Rebecca in the gut. She rolled over in bed, unable to let go of the phone, unable to break the connection. The confusion was still there but now the edge of shock was setting in, the realisation that things were not what they seemed. Something was different, something sinister, something very bad.

In the back of Rebecca's mind, she already knew things would never be the same again.

The woman sighed on the other end of the line.

"You must be his girlfriend," she said.

Rebecca wiped a tear from her face. Her cheek was hot, and her hand was shaking.

Her body was already rebelling. "Yes."

"My name is Amanda," the woman said. "I'm his wife."

The world started to spin. "You're..."

"I'm the woman who is married to him," Amanda spat, and Rebecca could feel the contempt in her voice. "I'm Mrs Paris, the woman with his last name and his wedding ring. I'm the one who married him before you were even a blip on the radar, and you were wrong to think you could ever change that. I'm back to claim my husband, and you're history."

The woman hung up. Rebecca stared at the phone, then dropped it on to the bed as if it had stung her. She buried her face in her hands then she was in limbo, uncertain of what to think, not knowing what to do. She lay there for an eternity before the reality of what just happened hit her, and when the pain sank in she rolled on to her belly and screamed into the pillow. It smelt like Richard, and that just made her cry harder.

How could this happen? How could this woman come back? She knew Richard, knew he had never lied to her, but she also knew he was an honourable man, and that damned honourability was the reason why his wife was in his house right now.

His wife.

Richard was a married man. She had known that, hadn't she?

She curled into a ball, her whole body hurting, and wailed while the sun spilled through her windows and the man she loved was in the same house as his long-lost wife.

Richard came down the stairs and stared at Amanda. She was sitting on the couch, the phone in her hand and a self-satisfied smile on her face. When Amanda waggled the phone at him, he realised what had happened.

"How dare you?" he said.

"Good morning to you, too."

He pointed a finger at her. "You are not staying here any longer."

"It's my house."

"Then I'm staying at a hotel." He marched to the kitchen and grabbed his coat from the hook by the door. She followed him to the kitchen and leaned against the doorway.

"Coffee's hot," she offered.

"It's probably poisoned."

She gave him one of those patented glares. He slammed the door on it.

On the way to the office, he dialled Rebecca's number and got no answer. He called her studio and got no answer there either. As he was walking into the back room of the *Crispin Tribune*, she finally answered the phone.

"Rebecca," he started, but she cut him off.

"I talked to her."

He sighed and dropped his coat on the chair. "She appeared out of nowhere last night. She got the divorce papers and finally decided to have it out, I guess."

Rebecca's voice was distant. "And she spent the night there?"

Richard suddenly realised how it all sounded, and he was sure Amanda had done her best to make it seem like a happy reunion instead of the battle it had really been. He sank into the chair. "It's her house, too. I couldn't make her leave."

Silence came from Rebecca's side of the phone. Richard started to explain the fight they had had, but she was having none of it. "I don't care."

"What...what? You don't care?"

"Your wife came back. You're not divorced. She spent the night in your house."

"That's all true, but, Rebecca, you're making it sound like I slept with her..."

"Did you?"

He suddenly thought of the kiss in the kitchen. His face flooded with shame. His pause was a little too long, and Rebecca's answer was crystal clear.

"Fuck you, Richard," she said. "Fuck you and your wife."

Rebecca hung up the phone and turned off the ringer. She rolled over and pulled the sheet over her body. Every little ache and pain from her weekend with Richard was now a source of heartbreak. She wasn't sure what had happened in Iowa, and she didn't want to know. All she knew was that he had been with her, but now he was with his wife, and wasn't that where he had wanted to be in the first place? Why else would a man wait three years for a woman who had left him?

How could she have been so stupid?

She thought of the words Gene had said the night she wound up stranded at Richard's house. *You're a fucking idiot, Rebecca.*

She pulled a pillow to her belly, wrapped her body around it, and willed her love for Richard to disappear as easily as his wife once had. She had thought it was real, and, by God, it had been—she would never be able to believe otherwise. But she knew better than to get involved with a married man, even if his wife had flown the coop and he had seen fit to remove his wedding band.

She had been playing with fire. How had she let herself forget that?

After a long hour of falling apart, Rebecca started to build herself back up. She made herself get out of bed and she found her appointment book. She cancelled all her appointments that day — with all the crying she had been doing, her story of having a terrible cold was accepted with sympathy and without question. She made all the calls to clear her schedule, then sat in her lonely apartment, trying not to think.

By noon, she had decided that she needed some help in making the love disappear. She put on an old T-shirt and jeans, stuffed her hair under a ball cap, and left her building. She walked a few blocks down from her high-rise and ducked into a little bar. She stood for a moment, letting her eyes adjust to the dim light, and thought about how she was fulfilling every cliché in the book. She was going to start drinking before she even ate lunch — before she ate breakfast, truth be told. She was going to drink away the married man she loved, get hungover, maybe find somebody to fuck for revenge, and feel just as bad about everything tomorrow — if not worse.

She picked out a bar stool and planted herself on it.

The bartender eyed her from beside the rack of wine glasses. "What will it be?"

"Something strong, straight up."

The bartender poured black label whisky. She took a sip of it and winced at the burn, then took a bigger sip. She looked at the television above the bar and watched as a reporter talked about the latest bombing in a country whose name she couldn't pronounce. She looked down the bar at the only other person there, a middle-aged man having a beer while he worked on some paperwork at a side table. She watched him for a while then went back to the television. It seemed more interesting.

She downed the whisky and the bartender whipped another shot into its place. He ran a clean white rag around the inside of a cordial glass, eyeing her as she took another sip.

"Broken heart?" he asked, and she looked up at him with a wary gaze.

"Why?"

"That's the only reason a pretty girl drinks alone in the middle of the day."

She stared at the television, hoping he would get the hint.

"He's probably not worth it, honey."

"How would you know?"

The bartender raised an eyebrow at her. "Men never are."

"Maybe this one is."

"Then why aren't you going after him?"

"He's sleeping with his wife."

The bartender nodded. "That's a good reason to back off."

She gave him a dirty look and downed the rest of the shot. The bartender brought her a double and retreated to the other side of the bar. The whisky was spreading warmth in her belly, a burning ember right underneath her breastbone. She watched a news story about a house fire, then another one about a traffic pileup in California. Nothing but bad news on the television, and she remembered why she never watched it.

An hour later, she was spilling out her story to the bartender, who nodded from time to time. He topped off her shot glass once more, then urged her to give it a rest for a bit. "Let it settle," he said. "Or you'll be hurting in a way you'll wish you could forget."

"Like I'm hurting now?" she asked.

The bartender shook his head and went to serve a beer to someone in the corner.

An hour after that she was talking to a man on the next barstool, listening to him bitch about work. He didn't have a wedding band, but she knew to be wary of men without rings. She told him about Richard and he told her about a woman back in Boston, one who had broken his heart and left him for another woman. This made her giggle, and though the man looked offended at first, he was soon laughing with her.

By the time another hour had passed, she knew she was probably too drunk to make good choices, but when the handsome businessman slipped his phone number underneath her hand she took the card. When he asked her what she was doing that night, she gave him her best grin and suggested that *he* might be what she was doing.

Why not? It would serve Richard right, even if he would never know it.

The businessman — his name was Mark, wasn't it? — leaned over to kiss her. His tongue was thick with liquor and he smelt like a beer keg. She fought against the urge to push him away and did a fine job of it, until she thought of Richard and wondered how long it had taken before he had kissed his wife. Immediately? Five minutes? Ten?

"Slow down," she said, but Mark kept kissing her, whether she liked it or not. She pushed him and apparently did it a little too hard, because he stumbled off his bar stool, landed against the opposite table, stood up and cursed her.

"I'm sorry," she said.

"Fucking tease."

Rebecca leaned heavily on the bar as Mark walked away. The bartender shot a concerned look in her direction. She stumbled to the bathroom and looked at herself in the mirror. The woman there was more than a little drunk, heartbroken and looked like hell. She tried to brush her hair as best she could with her fingers. She smelt like alcohol, which she hated. When was the last time she had got drunk? College?

She came out of the bathroom and the bartender caught her eye, motioning her over. A cup of steaming coffee sat in front of her barstool. She slipped on to the stool with some effort and took a deep sip of the black liquid. It reminded her of Richard, and without warning the tears started again.

"Listen," the bartender said, leaning over the bar and whispering to her. "I heard what you said to that jerk. About that guy, Richard. Your boyfriend."

She nodded. Of course the bartender had heard. Bartenders had a talent for hearing everything. Why did this one have to be so nosy?

"If his wife came back after fucking with his head for that long, don't you think she would fuck with your head, too?"

Rebecca stared at him, trying to absorb this. "What do you mean?"

"She said they slept together, right?"

"He didn't deny it."

"But do you know for sure if they really did?"

"She's back," Rebecca said, as if that answered everything. "He slept with her."

"Okay, maybe he did. But put yourself in his position..."

"I would never do that," she said quietly.

"How do you know?"

She took another sip of coffee.

"He filed for divorce, right?"

"He waited three years!"

"He didn't file until *you* came along, right?"

"Yeah."

The bartender held up his hands in mock surprise. "So maybe he didn't file for divorce before because he didn't have a reason," he said. "Maybe you're the reason he finally did it."

She drank her coffee and looked at the television, trying to tune him out. The bartender sighed. "I'm just saying — he did all this for you. Now you should get your ass on a plane and get up there and give that bitch what-for."

Rebecca looked at him, her mind finally clearing a bit. "You're saying she lied to me?"

"Girl, I'm willing to bet you've been burned real good before he came along."

"What's that supposed to mean?"

"You automatically think Mr Wonderful is fucking around. Has he given you any indication that he's stuck his dick where it doesn't belong?"

Rebecca stared at her coffee cup as the bartender topped it off.

"I asked if he'd slept with her," she said. "He was utterly silent."

"Maybe he was shocked you didn't trust him," he said.

Rebecca thought about that. Would Richard have been stunned that she didn't trust him? He had made his feelings on his wife very clear, and if she hadn't believed his words, then she had to believe the divorce papers, didn't she?

"But she sounded so smug," she said, and the bartender nodded.

"Of course she did. She was getting one-up on the new chick. Wouldn't you sound that way? Want to give a nice little jab to the woman who had taken your place?"

Rebecca shook her head.

"Bullshit, sweetie. Ain't nothing cattier than a woman scorned."

The coffee was working, and now her emotions were toning down while her reasoning was kicking in. The bartender wiped down the bar while Rebecca thought things over, and she suddenly reached into her pocket for her cell phone. She had to squint to see the little letters on the screen.

Twenty-three calls.

She held the phone to her ear and listened to every one of them. Richard was asking her to please pick up the phone. Amanda had tried to seduce him, he said. It didn't work. He had slept in his room and she had slept in the guest room. He had told her about Rebecca and he had got a slap across the face for his trouble. Would she please pick up the phone? He wanted to explain. He loved her, and only her, and would she please stop avoiding him and answer?

Rebecca listened to all the messages then sat quietly for a moment, trying to wrap her mind around everything that had happened over the last several hours. She wouldn't put it past Richard's wife to try to seduce him.

It didn't work, he said — but how far did it go?

She thought again of the woman's smug voice. She had sounded as though she owned Richard, as if he was just another piece of property. She had taken a perverse pleasure in telling Rebecca that she was his wife. But where had that pleasure been for the last three years?

Strangely, Rebecca thought of Gene. She hadn't let his words sway her. Was she really going to let go of the man she loved more than anything, just because a woman who happened to be married to him—in name only—said he belonged to her? Or was she going to fight for the man she loved?

Rebecca stood up from the barstool. The bartender proved he was one of the best in Miami when he handed her a travel cup of coffee. She slid a good amount of money over the counter and saluted him with the cup. "I'm going to Iowa," she said.

He clapped, getting the attention of everyone in the bar. "Good for you, honey" he said. "Haul that wifey out in front of God and everybody, then kick her ass."

Chapter Sixteen

The plane touched down right on time, and Rebecca pulled her carry-on from the seat beside her. She had been lucky to get a flight out on such short notice, even if it was the red-eye. The snow in Des Moines was gone, and she assumed the snow in Crispin was gone, too.

The temperature was a balmy forty degrees, practically a heatwave, and she had remembered to wear her jacket. She had packed only for the day, since she didn't think her mission would take very long.

She got a rental car at the counter and pulled on to the road at a little past seven. She took a glance at the map and pointed the car towards Crispin. She was going to stop at the *Tribune* office first and try to find him there before going to the house. She would be more than happy to confront that conniving bitch – if she really was conniving, and if Richard hadn't had a change of heart.

Her phone rang as she was coming into the edge of town. She crossed the covered bridge and looked down at the caller ID. She almost answered it when she saw Richard's number, but decided not to do that just yet. She would know what he really thought when she saw him in person, when she could read the answers in his eyes. Hearing it wouldn't be good enough.

She pressed down hard on the gas pedal as the phone beeped. He had left a message. She flipped the phone open, pressed the button and put it on speaker.

"Rebecca, listen. Just listen. I know you aren't happy with me right now, and I think I can guess why. But please, don't do anything crazy yet. Let me come to Miami and talk to you. I'm getting the first plane out, and if you're not at the airport to meet me, I'll come find you. I'm not letting you go without a fight, Rebecca. I will not make that mistake."

The message ended. Rebecca stared at the phone, amazed. At the sound of an angry horn, she looked up and realised she had drifted to the other side of the road. She jerked the wheel, got back between the lines, and weathered a furious look and a flip of the bird from the other driver.

She pulled up in front of the newspaper office and breathed a sigh of relief when she saw Richard's truck. She hesitated for a moment, looking through the windows. What if the wife was there? But Richard had just called and said he was coming to find her, and surely he wouldn't have done that if his heart was torn between two women.

She barged into the office and was met by a startled young man. He had a stack of papers in his hand and looked like he had just been handed his ass on a silver platter.

"Where's Richard?" she demanded, and the young man jerked his head towards the back room.

"Back there. But you might want to come back later. He's mighty pissed off."

She started in that direction, but the young man stopped her. "Ma'am?"

"What?"

"I mean, he's *mighty* pissed off. Really. He's..." The boy looked at the doorway as if he were afraid a bear would charge through it. "He's throwing things."

"Throwing things?

"Uh-huh."

She turned back to the door. They both heard the cursing from the direction of the editor's office. Rebecca turned back to the young man. "Is there anybody with him?"

"Lord, I hope not."

Rebecca walked into the rear section of the office. There was Richard, standing in front of his desk, staring at the computer screen. He bent low to touch a few keys, and the screen changed. He studied it, scowling. He abruptly picked up a paperweight and flung it across the office, where it banged hard against the back wall.

Rebecca blinked at the space where the paperweight had been. "Richard."

He spun around, fury written all over his face. Maybe it was the kind of fury that had scared his employee, but to her he was sexier than he had ever been.

It took a moment for the shock of her presence to sink in. He stared at her and forgot all about plane schedules, runaway wives and annoying mothers. He forgot about divorces and battles over bank accounts and almost falling into bed with a wicked witch who didn't know how to accept defeat. For the first time since he had come back from Miami, he felt nothing but relief.

"Baby," he said, already choked up. "Come here."

Rebecca walked into his arms and laid her head on his chest. He held her so tightly she could hardly breathe, but she didn't try to move away. She let him hold her as long as he wanted.

"I was just getting a ticket to come see you," he said, his voice rough. "The travel agent put me on hold so I was trying to get something online, but the damn computer system keeps going down, and I have no idea if I just bought a ticket for Miami or a ticket for Maine."

Rebecca laughed.

"Are you here to tell me goodbye?" he asked her, and she tightened her arms around him.

"I'm here to make sure I don't have to."

Richard pressed his nose to her hair and inhaled the sweet scent. He wanted more than anything to cry. He hadn't done this much crying since he was a baby. The emotional rollercoaster was wearing him out, and his emotions were raw.

"I love you," he whispered. "When you didn't answer your phone, I was so scared…"

"I know. I know. It's all right now."

"Rebecca, I didn't sleep with her."

"I believe you."

"But you need to know…"

"I already do."

He pulled away from her and looked into her calm, happy face. "You do?"

"I'm not naïve, Richard. You're human, and you're confused."

"My confusion lasted for two minutes."

She nodded. The thought of him with someone else hurt, and the thought of him with his wife hurt even more, but she did understand. Emotional pain could make a person do almost anything. Hadn't she been contemplating some stupid things of her own as she sat beside some drunken guy at a bar?

They looked at each other for a moment, both of them coming to terms with what had happened in the last several weeks. Had it only been a month since he pulled her from that car in the blizzard?

"Where is she?" Rebecca asked, her voice quiet and hard.

"She's at the house, I think. Packing."

"Good."

"Rebecca..."

She pinned him with the look he already knew so well, the determination that he knew could not be swayed. "Are you going to stop me?"

"I don't think stopping you is possible," he said carefully. "But you have to understand...she's vicious. She will say anything to hurt you, and she can make you believe it."

Rebecca saw the wariness in his eyes. "What did she say to you?"

"It doesn't matter."

"What kind of story did she give you?"

Richard shook his head, the pain of Amanda's bombshell still alive and well, clawing into his conscience and making him doubt everything about himself. "I said it doesn't matter."

Rebecca nodded. "If you won't tell me, I'll get it out of her."

"She left me for someone else."

The words, now they were out in the open, damn near shattered whatever composure he had left. All through the night he had wondered if it was true. He was pretty sure it was. The fact that she had run off with someone else was something he could handle. What he couldn't handle was the way she had looked at him when she had told him, as if he really was that terrible in bed, as if every intimate moment they had ever had was up for laughs when she was with someone who was so much better at the act than he was.

Rebecca watched the emotions flicker over his face. She saw the moment he started to question himself, and that infuriated her.

"She really slammed you, didn't she?"

Richard looked into her eyes. "Rebecca, I'm scared."

"Scared of what?"

He swallowed hard and looked away. "I'm scared you will leave me, too."

She had heard enough. She stepped out of his arms and gave him what she hoped was a charming, reassuring smile, though her body was close to shaking with fury. "I'm leaving you only long enough to put that bitch in her place."

Rebecca turned on her heel and marched into the front room. The young man behind the counter had obviously heard it all, and he watched her with appreciation in his eyes. She nodded calmly, flung open the door so hard it slammed against the wall, and left rubber on the street when she took off.

Richard stood in the middle of his office, still trying to get his bearings in the midst of the hurricane. Amanda was at the house, but given the events of the last twenty-four hours, he wasn't sure she was really packing. She seemed to have her mind and heart set on making sure he gave them a fair shot, which was as hypocritical a notion as he could imagine. When Rebecca showed up, sparks would fly—and from Amanda's physical attack on him last night, he was sure things wouldn't be pretty.

It took a while for the situation to sink in, but once it did he hoped he would get there in time. He flipped open his cell phone as he headed for the door, dialling one of the many community numbers he knew by heart.

"Steve? I have a situation. Meet me at my house, will you?"

He ran from the office. His assistant watched him as he went by, and listened to the second set of squealing tyres headed in the direction of Richard's house.

"Good luck, boss," he said, and started typing invoices.

Rebecca pulled into the driveway at a very sedate pace, belying the fact that she had raced well over the speed limit to get there. She took her time getting out of the car. She fixed her hair and applied lipstick, all the while knowing Amanda Paris was probably watching through the front windows. If she was crazy enough to come back here, she was probably paranoid, too.

Rebecca closed the door firmly and made her way up the sidewalk to the front door. She tried the knob and, sure enough, it was locked. She made a point of trying it again, rattling the door to make her intentions clear, and finally knocked with an impatient air.

Amanda opened the door with a wide smile.

Rebecca looked at her for a moment. She was in her mid-forties, short blonde hair and blue eyes, with fine lines under them. The tiny wrinkles actually looked good on her. She was not drop-dead gorgeous, but she was definitely pretty enough to turn a man's head. She had an athletic body and wore a cross around her neck. It caught the sunlight and winked at Rebecca.

"Can I help you?" she asked.

Rebecca returned her smile, determined to be just as friendly. "I'm Rebecca Connors. I was hoping to fix some lunch for Richard before he got home from the office. Thanks for opening the door—I forgot my key. You must be Amanda."

Rebecca stepped right in, and the cheery look on Amanda's face turned dark. "Excuse me, but this is my house," she said, as if that settled everything.

"How's the packing going?"

"This is my house," Amanda repeated.

"Just like Richard is your husband?"

Amanda stood very still, staring at this new arrival. Rebecca gave her a benevolent smile as she pulled off her gloves and shrugged out of her jacket. She tossed them on to the couch as if she had done it a thousand times. "I figure you've got quite a bit of boxing up done by now."

"I'm not packing," Amanda said, an incredulous look on her face. "I'm staying right here. Richard and I are trying to work things out."

"Are you, now?"

Rebecca sauntered to the kitchen as if she were the one who owned the house. She grabbed the apron from the nail on the wall and pulled a coffee cup from the cabinet. She sniffed of the coffee already in the pot, made a face, dumped it in the sink, and set about making a new pot. "Richard likes it stronger than that," she said. "I hope you don't mind."

"I know what he likes," Amanda said coolly, inching towards Rebecca. She was obviously nonplussed and had no idea what to do, which suited Rebecca just fine.

"You used to, I'm sure."

Rebecca opened the refrigerator. Amanda's hand slammed down on the door, holding it halfway open. She pointed a finger at Rebecca, her wedding band glittering in the sunlight through the windows.

"You're a little hothouse pansy, aren't you? Thinking you can come right in here and take away a woman's husband. Well, I've got news for you, honey. The moment I walked through that door, Richard was falling apart with relief, and last night we slept in our marital bed. Together. So you can just pack your saucy little ass back to that car of yours and hit the road, you arrogant little bitch. We don't need you here."

Rebecca looked Amanda right in the eye. "Are you planning on moving your boyfriend into Richard's house when the divorce is final? Is that why you're making yourself at home?"

Rebecca could see the wheels turning in Amanda's head as she tried to figure out how much the younger woman really knew. Rebecca made it easier for her. "Yes, I've been with Richard this morning. I went down to the office and he told me the whole story."

"The whole story, huh?" Amanda's grin turned wicked. "He told you about our reunion, then?"

Rebecca shook her head, as if the whole thing were terribly shameful. If Amanda wanted to keep up the charade, let her. It would all come to a head soon enough, and Rebecca was determined she would have the upper hand when it did. "Rejection always hurts, doesn't it, Amanda?"

Amanda closed the refrigerator door with a slam that rattled everything inside it. She pointed a finger again at

Rebecca. Her voice was a screech, the sound of a woman losing her composure. "He did not reject me!"

"He rejected you because he's in love with me. He was confused at first, seeing you after so long, but he came to his senses pretty quickly, didn't he?"

Amanda's finger was shaking. "Get out of my house."

"It's Richard's house, and I'm an invited guest."

"You are my husband's whore, is that it?"

Rebecca gave her a genuine smile. Paybacks were hell — Amanda was losing it, and losing it fast. "Takes one to know one, sweetheart."

Amanda lunged. Rebecca let her come, ready for it, almost hungry for it. She hadn't wanted to give anyone their comeuppance in a long time, but now the quiet and demure part of her was gone, and Rebecca was more than ready to do battle. It would have shocked her, had she taken the time to think about it.

The older woman landed against her and they both fell to the floor. Amanda grabbed handfuls of Rebecca's hair with one hand and scratched at her face with the other. Rebecca twisted away but didn't fight back, and this infuriated Amanda. She began to pummel Rebecca with her fists, hitting her everywhere she could reach. Rebecca lay on the floor and counted to twenty, then abruptly rolled back over and slammed the back of her hand into Amanda's face.

The shock of Rebecca suddenly fighting back was enough to send Amanda flat to the floor. Rebecca quickly got to her feet, her shoulders and arm aching from the blows, and stood over the enraged woman. Amanda grabbed at her legs. Rebecca could feel the tiny drips of blood coming from her temple, and realised Amanda had scratched her after all.

At that moment, Rebecca heard the faint sound of siren, and she knew what she had to do.

Rebecca ran into the living room, where she grabbed the cordless phone. She kept running down the hallway to the guest room, where she slammed the door behind her. She could hear Amanda coming after her, and she had just enough time to dial the number before Amanda hit the door with her full weight, making the lock creak.

"Yes," Rebecca said, speaking quickly. "I'm at one-one-two Dearborn Lane. Amanda Paris has just attacked me. I think she's gone crazy."

Amanda kicked open the door. The lock screamed and splinters flew.

Jesus Christ, Rebecca thought. *She's going to kill me.*

Amanda came towards Rebecca with fists flying. The next good punch sent Rebecca to the floor, knocking the breath out of her.

"I'm going to kill you, you fucking whore bitch!" Amanda screamed.

Rebecca turned and lifted her legs, planted one of her feet against Amanda's hip, and shoved as hard as she could. The woman stumbled back and hit the wall with a grunt, then barrelled towards her rival again. Rebecca realised she was in the midst of an all-out catfight, and she could accept that — but the look in Amanda's eyes, the totally unhinged look that seemed almost unreal, was what frightened her more than anything else.

Amanda was crazy.

And she was beyond pissed off.

The sirens were loud now, right outside the windows. Amanda reared back to kick her, and Rebecca grabbed her foot in mid-air. She pushed upwards, hard, and Amanda screeched as she fell back on to the floor with a thud.

Amanda kicked out at her again and caught her anyway, a glancing blow to the side, and the pain seared through Rebecca.

Amanda landed one more kick before a deep voice came from the doorway. "That's enough!"

Rebecca looked up from the floor. Though he was in plain clothes, she recognised the man instantly — it was the young police officer who had eyed her so curiously the first time she went to Richard's office. Now he was standing behind Amanda, trying to get her under control. Amanda turned her fury on him and slammed her fist into the side of his face so hard Rebecca could hear his teeth clatter.

"Oh, hell, you did *not* just do that," he growled, and pinned Amanda against the wall while she called him every name in the book. Rebecca watched as he pulled handcuffs from his jeans pocket, breathing hard and struggling to keep Amanda under control.

Then Amanda froze, and the sound that came from her was a wail of pain. Rebecca sat up and saw why — Richard was standing in the doorway, staring at all of them.

"Amanda?" he said, his voice small and scared.

The young officer hauled Amanda out of the room before she could say a word.

Richard reached down for Rebecca's hand. Her hair was a mess, her lipstick smeared, and fine lines of blood were trickling down the side of her face. She had a bruise blooming under one eye. But when she wrapped her arms around his neck and pulled him down to her, she whispered into his ear, "Something is wrong with her, Richard. What's wrong with her?"

Amanda was dragged from the house, kicking and screaming. "He's my husband!" she hollered back at

Rebecca, who had come to the doorway. "He's my husband, this is my house. It's mine, not yours, not yours, not yours!" She spat in Richard's direction as the police officers tried to get her into the back of a car without hurting her. "He's shacking up with somebody and they both deserve to pay!"

Richard watched as his wife was loaded into the back of a police car. The young officer came to Rebecca, introduced himself as Steve, and took her arm gently, leading her to the porch. The ambulance arrived and, after a bit of tense discussion, the officers and the paramedics approached the police car. Amanda screamed curse words as she was led to the ambulance and strapped to the gurney. The doors closed on her tirade and the ambulance began to move slowly back towards town, carrying a very angry woman in the back.

Richard watched every move. As the ambulance drove away, he looked back at Rebecca. She was talking to Steve and nodding at something he said. He watched as she signed the paperwork he handed her. When she turned to look back at the ambulance, Steve put his hand on her shoulder and whispered into her ear. She nodded and gave him a grateful smile.

Richard looked back at the ambulance and watched until it was nothing but lights in the distance. He wondered again at Amanda's reasons for leaving, but this time he thought he might have the real answer.

Chapter Seventeen

Rebecca sat at the kitchen table and dabbed at her eye with a cool washcloth. It was swelling up and her vision was getting blurry. Her side hurt something fierce, and she knew the bruises there would look terrible in a few days. What hurt most of all was the realisation that she hadn't been involved in a fair fight. There was something wrong with Amanda, something she couldn't put her finger on, and she felt an enormous amount of guilt for pushing her over some edge she hadn't even known was there.

Richard sat on the chair in front of her, gently washing the cuts on her face. She had refused help from the paramedics and they had let her go, assured she was in good hands with Richard. After all, everyone knew him, and they knew he would take care of her.

"I had no idea," she said as he put a Band-Aid over one of the worst scratches. "She's really crazy, Richard. I could see it in her eyes. Batshit crazy."

He nodded sadly. He was upset for a multitude of reasons, and now he had a new one. He had never seen Amanda like that before; she had been kicking, screaming and glaring at them like they were the spawn of Satan himself, and that was something his wife had never done. It was something she never would have dreamed of doing, and he couldn't make himself believe it was all Rebecca's fault. There was something more there, and the thought of what it might be scared him.

"I need to check on her," he said, and Rebecca immediately nodded.

"She needs you," she agreed.

Richard looked into Rebecca's eyes and touched her face. She had taken a real beating.

"Are you going to be okay?"

Rebecca shrugged. "I didn't mean for it to go as far as it did," she said.

"You provoked her?"

"Yes. But I didn't hit her until I had no choice, Richard. I didn't want to hurt her."

"You didn't do it with the intention of getting a restraining order and having her kicked out of the house...did you?"

Rebecca blushed. "It crossed my mind. But then I saw that look in her eyes."

Richard put another Band-Aid on the scratch on her face. She looked like hell.

"She's sick," she said softly, and Richard nodded.

"I think she is."

"Do you think that's why she left?"

Now Amanda had come back and fallen apart, things from the past started to make sense. He did remember her crying as she did the dishes, and he remembered the times she would stare off into space, seemingly in another world. He remembered her sleepwalking, waking up in the kitchen and once in the backyard, naked in the moonlight. She always started crying after those episodes, claiming she was just really tired or there were things on her mind. He had tried to get her to open up but she had refused, saying it was nothing, but now he knew it had been much more than that.

Before she had disappeared, she had taken a trip with her mother. They had driven to Chicago and spent several days shopping, but when Amanda had come back she hadn't had anything new to show him, not even a little souvenir. "There was nothing I wanted," she had said.

Now he thought back on that day and wondered if she had really gone to Chicago.

"I need to see her," he said. "I need to see her family, too."

Rebecca nodded.

"It might be best if you stay here," he said, and she nodded again.

"I will do more harm than good," she agreed. "Do what you have to do."

"Will you be here when I get back?"

She leant forward and kissed him, though her lips were swollen and it hurt her mouth. "I'm not going anywhere."

At the hospital, Richard leaned over the information desk. "I'm looking for Amanda Paris," he said. The attendant gave him a slip of paper with a room number. He recognised it as the seventh floor, and the realisation of that seemed to suck all the breath out of the room.

The seventh floor was the psychiatric ward.

"Mr Paris?" the young woman asked, standing from her desk to hold on to his arm.

"I'm all right."

He got on the elevator and closed his eyes while the floors flashed by. He had been on the seventh floor only once before, when his grandmother had been diagnosed with dementia at the age of eighty. He had hated the place, with the bars on some doors and rubber walls in some rooms. He supposed it had to look that way, but it still made him think of old movies and procedures that were more like torture than medicine.

When the doors opened, he came face to face with his mother-in-law. Grace was a small, compact woman with a dark complexion, so different from the fair skin of her daughter. Her hair was almost black and the curls clung close to her head. Her dark eyes studied him warily as he stepped from the elevator.

"Why didn't you tell me?" he asked immediately, and Grace shook her head.

"You didn't need to see her like that."

So there it was, the real reason Amanda had disappeared. Richard looked down the hallway at the closed doors with their tiny windows and wondered which one held his wife.

"I would have helped her," he said to Grace now. "I would have done whatever I could to help her. You knew that."

"She made us promise not to tell you."

Somehow Richard suspected this wasn't true, but he let it go. What good would an argument do at this point? The last three years could never be taken back, and, though he was sad about the way things had turned out, he wasn't about to rehash the bad memories.

"What happened to her?"

Grace sighed and her whole body seemed to get smaller. Richard felt sorry for her—no matter how she had lied to him, or what she had hidden, her daughter was very sick. He couldn't imagine what that must be like, and he hoped he would never find out. He reached out and touched Grace's shoulder, and that simple human connection seemed to break something in her. She began to sob there in the hallway, and Richard pulled her into a warm hug.

"Let's go get something to drink," he said to her, leading her into the elevator. "You can tell me over some coffee, okay?"

The doors closed behind them. Richard would come back to see Amanda later. Right now, Amanda's mother was the one who needed him more.

"She was always a flighty kid," Grace said, stirring cream into her coffee. The tears had worn themselves out for the time being, and now she sat at the cafeteria table with the kind of dignity Richard had always seen in her. "She had big dreams. Big fantasies. She would spend weeks on end playing princess...she would be in perfect character when she woke up and still in character when she went to bed. At first it was annoying, then it was eerie, but after a while it became a part of who she was, and we just didn't notice it anymore." Grace shrugged. "It was just a quirk."

Richard nodded and sipped his own coffee.

"She had her first breakdown when she was sixteen. Some high school boy broke her heart. She started crying and just didn't stop. We finally took her to the doctor and he prescribed some medicine for her. Something to calm her down, you know. We got home and thirty minutes later I found her in the bathroom with the empty bottle beside her."

Richard winced. He knew it was bad, but he hadn't realised how much so.

"That was our first trip to the ER. Stomach pumped. She had a psych consult, and they said she needed evaluation. She ripped the IV out of her arm and tried to leave the hospital. Blood was flying everywhere from that IV, she was still throwing up from the pills, and she was screaming about being in prison." Grace shuddered. "It was terrible."

"It sounds like it was."

"There were a few other episodes. They all lasted a few weeks, then she would get her meds adjusted, and she would be on an even keel again. Then you came along, and there were no more episodes. We figured she had grown out of it, and we were so grateful."

Richard wiped his eyes and stared at his coffee.

"Her episodes were attached to emotional upheaval. We thought she might have an episode when you got married, with the stress and everything, but she came through with flying colours. She acted perfectly normal, and that was a credit to you. You're so steady, Richard. So solid. We knew you were good for her."

Richard let out a harsh laugh. "I missed it, Grace. I missed the signs."

Grace patted his hand. "She was very good at hiding it, Richard. And when she did start to slip a little, she came to me. She said she thought she was going into a bad place, like she had before. I took her to a doctor, and he said she needed intense therapy. She didn't want to get it, so she went back to you, and I kept waiting for a call. An episode. A trip to the ER. Something."

"But it never happened. She just disappeared one day."

Grace smiled sadly. "That was her episode. You didn't miss it, Richard. She ran off and, for a long time, we didn't know where she was, either. I know you thought I did, but I didn't."

"Where did she go?"

"I'm not sure," Grace said. "She called me about three months later. Said she was happy again." Grace paused and fiddled with her napkin. "There was a man involved."

So it was true, then. Richard shook his head as he wondered which parts were true, and which parts weren't, and if he would ever know for sure.

"She said she left me for someone," he told Grace.

"She didn't leave you for someone, but she did meet someone when she was gone."

"Is there a difference?"

Grace studied him for a moment, then shook her head. "Not to the heart, there ain't."

Richard got up and refilled his coffee cup. Grace watched him the whole time, and when he sat down again she said, "The latest episode happened when you filed for divorce."

"It's my fault, then."

"It could only be your fault if you knew," she reminded him.

"So she came back and thought we could make it work, but then there was Rebecca."

Grace nodded sadly. "Yeah."

They sat silently, thinking about the woman on the seventh floor, the one Grace loved, the one Richard had moved on from, but still felt responsibility for.

"I think you should go through with the divorce," Grace said suddenly, startling him. "You've waited for her for three years. That's a long enough time, no matter what your momma says. Besides, there's Rebecca, and she doesn't deserve to be left hanging."

Rebecca was at his home right now, nursing wounds inflicted by his wife, and she had promised to wait for him. She had flown from Miami to find him, confronted his wife to claim him, and had reassured him every step of the way. No, she did not deserve to be left hanging.

"I feel guilty," he admitted to Grace. "I was her husband, and I didn't go looking for her. Then I filed for divorce, and sent her off the deep end. I feel like much of it is my fault."

"She's sick," Grace reminded him. "That's nobody's fault."

Richard nodded, though he wasn't entirely convinced. Grace patted his hand one more time and stood up from the table. "I'm going upstairs," she said. "Why don't you go see Rebecca, and come back tomorrow, when Amanda is a little more like herself."

Richard nodded and watched Grace walk away, knowing Amanda would never be herself again.

Rebecca was waiting for him when he got home. As his headlights washed over the house, she came out on the porch to greet him in her bare feet, even though it was below freezing. Her whole body hurt, her face worst of all. She had used ice packs and ibuprofen from his medicine cabinet, but the pain had hardly eased. The pain in her heart, however, was now for someone else, not for herself.

"How is she?" she asked as he came up the walk.

He shook his head and urged her into the house. "You're going to freeze."

"Is she going to be all right?"

Inside the house, the fire was roaring. Richard stood in front of it and warmed his hands while he thought about the things Grace had said, and where Amanda's life might be headed. "She's in the psych ward," he said, and Rebecca sank down on the couch, stunned.

"You mean, she's…they committed her?"

"Apparently this isn't the first time."

Rebecca felt horribly guilty, not only for the way she had provoked Amanda, but for the things she had said about her in the past. Hindsight was twenty-twenty, and right now hindsight was a vicious bitch hell-bent on reminding Rebecca of all the mistakes she made.

"I'm so sorry," she said.

"Her mother told me the whole story," he said, then explained everything to Rebecca.

She sat still as a stone, watching him and listening to every word, wishing like hell she had never pushed Amanda over the edge. But how could she have known? She didn't even know the edge was there.

"They are going to keep her?"

"She's in for at least two weeks."

Rebecca took a deep breath. Her ribs hurt. She went to the kitchen for an ice pack and came back to find Richard facing the fire, his back to the doorway. She watched him stand there, read defeat in the slump of his shoulders, heard the sighs that came from deep in his body, the ones that said he was more tired than he had been in a long, long time. It had been a long and draining time for all of them.

Richard heard her come into the room and turned to look at her. He was dead on his feet, but there were more things he had to say before he collapsed into bed.

"I want you to know," he said, "I'm going through with the divorce, Rebecca."

She sat gingerly on the edge of the couch. She had thought about that long and hard while he was gone, and she had decided that if he chose to stay married to Amanda she would have to live with that. It would break her heart, but she knew he was the kind of man who did the right thing, and she had no idea what the right thing might be in a situation like this. She would trust his judgement, even if that meant letting him walk away from her.

"Richard..."

"Yes, I'm sure. Amanda was gone for years, and my heart has moved on. No amount of explanations can change that. I'm sorry she's in this terrible state right now, and I'll do what I can to help, but I'm not going to stop the divorce because she came back."

Rebecca's heart swelled with happiness, even as a part of it broke for the woman he had once loved. Regardless of the trouble Amanda had caused, Rebecca wanted to see her get better, and she didn't want her to suffer the heartache of losing the man she loved.

But that was the same man Rebecca loved, and she didn't want to give him up.

She rose from the couch, put her arms around Richard, and kissed him on the forehead. "Let's get some sleep," she said. "The world will be clearer tomorrow."

Chapter Eighteen

They awoke the next morning to the sun streaming in through the windows. It was just like the days they had awakened to after a lazy night of lovemaking, the sunlight their only alarm clock. This time wasn't nearly as calm, as Rebecca stretched and cried out in surprise. The pain of her altercation with Amanda had caught her off guard, no matter how many ibuprofen she had taken.

"Whoa, now, easy," Richard said, touching her arms gently, looking into her face. The bruises looked terrible this morning, as he had known they would, but the cuts looked much better than they had when they had been fresh. Now that she was naked in the sunlight, he could see the bruises on her ribcage too, and the one really good one on her breastbone, almost directly between her breasts.

Amanda had to be insane with rage to do that kind of damage.

Rebecca smiled at him. Her lips were still swollen and one eye was looking pretty rough, but she was still more beautiful than any other woman he had ever seen. He leant forward and kissed her carefully, afraid of hurting her. She ran her hands through his hair and kissed him back, pulling him closer with every passing minute, until he was almost on top of her.

"Make love to me," she whispered, and he shook his head.

"No way. I'll hurt you more than anything else."

She smiled against his lips. "You can be gentle as a whisper, Mr Paris."

He protested as she lay down and pulled him over her. It wasn't just his fear of hurting her, and when she saw that scared look in his eyes she knew his hesitation was much bigger than it appeared.

"What did she say to you?" she asked softly, and Richard looked away, unable to meet her eyes.

"She said her lover was better than me. That she had learned there was more to sex than the missionary position." The words had been hard to hear and, now, they were even harder to say. Rivers of shame tore through him as he said them, wondering anew if they were all true, or if she had just set out to hurt him.

Rebecca sat up and forced Richard to look at her. "She lied."

"But…"

"She lied, Richard. You're a kind and attentive lover, and you're exciting, too. I've never met a man who would so readily share his fantasies with me, or ask me about mine, and do his best to make them all into a reality."

Though her words warmed him, the doubts still lingered. Rebecca knew what those doubts were like — she had felt more than a few of her own in the past. It would take a long time for them to fade, and there was no better time than now to start working on it.

"Make love to me," she said again.

Richard was almost afraid to touch her. He hadn't known until that moment how badly mere words could hurt, how paralysing a fear they could bring to the surface. He gently touched Rebecca's breast and she smiled at him, encouraging him to keep going.

"Rebecca," he murmured. "I can't, honey. I just can't."

She bit her lip and studied him. She knew full well it wasn't a rejection of her, but it felt very much like one, and she silently cursed Amanda for her ability to hurt both of them, even when she wasn't there.

"Then let's get dressed and go back to your office," she said. "We've got plenty of time to overcome this, and I'm not about to push you until you're ready."

"Isn't that always the man's line?" he teased, relieved she wasn't going to insist.

She carefully got out of bed and walked to the shower. She climbed in and Richard was right behind her, both of them under the water and using the soap, but neither one of them trying the sexual games that had happened the last time they were in a shower together. Now that Rebecca was moving around she felt much better, but she avoided the mirror. She didn't want to know how bad it looked.

She solved the problem of making herself presentable by wrapping a scarf around her neck. It was one of Richard's, old and thin, but perfect for what she needed. Her black eye would still be evident, but was there anyone in town who didn't know what had happened? Rebecca was sure the gossip wires had hummed well into the night and got an early start this morning.

Richard watched her move around the room, berating himself for not making love to her. Was he really going to let Amanda's anger keep him from enjoying the woman he wanted so much? But now she was dressed, and so was he, and she was looking at him from the top of the stairs.

"Hurry up, lazybones," she said.

Richard drove them to the office, where the same young man was there to greet them. The coffee in the back room was piping hot and Richard poured two cups. Rebecca wandered over to the layout room as she shrugged out of her jacket. He watched her bend low over the old press and study it. Her shirt fit snugly into the waist of her jeans. Her hourglass profile was accentuated by a thin leather belt. She had left her hair down today, the better to cover the marks on the side of her face, and when she arched her back to stretch, he watched as her breasts were thrown into sharp relief.

Her nipples were hard under her shirt.

Richard stared at them as she moved. She must have known he was watching her, for sometimes she seemed to glance sidelong at him, but she never acknowledged him. She just moved among the things he was so familiar with, taking her time, and every now and then she would stand in such a way he could have sworn she was posing for him.

When she moved from his office area to the rooms that never got used anymore, the ones so crowded with the flotsam of days gone by that Richard mostly just kept the doors closed and ignored the mess, he grinned and followed her.

He closed the door behind them.

The room was pitch-black without the overhead light from the next room over. He could hear the slight rustling sounds Rebecca made as she moved carefully in the room, perhaps turning around to look at him, perhaps trying to feel her way back to him. Finally the movement stopped and her voice came, low and careful. "Does the door lock?"

Richard reached behind him, felt for the knob, and found no lock there. He had never thought to look for one before. "No."

There was silence for a long moment. "Good."

Richard waited to let his eyes adjust to the darkness, but there was no adjusting to be had. It really was dark as a tomb in there, and it smelt like one, too—musty paper, dusty computers tucked away in corners, wood that was a century old.

Richard took a few steps forward, feeling his way with his shins and his hands, hoping he would brush up against something rather than slam into it. He took his time, working towards where he had heard her voice. If he stood quietly for a moment, he could hear her breathing.

When he reached something hard, he wrapped his hand around it. It was wooden, and smooth—maybe part of a frame of some old machine, something that hadn't been used in decades. He felt with his other hand and there she was, warm flesh under his palm.

He slid his hand down. And down.

She was naked.

Richard's cock was instantly hard. What he couldn't do in the glare of the sunlight was the one thing he couldn't live without, here in the utter darkness. Using her body as a guide, he stepped behind her and realised she was bent over the old printing press, her hands outstretched, her bare ass waiting.

"Fuck me," she whispered.

Richard pulled down his slacks. He listened for sounds from outside the door, any evidence of an interruption, but even as he listened he knew he didn't give a damn. There was a warm and willing woman right in front of him, her pussy already wet, and what else mattered?

He slid in with one long, smooth thrust.

Rebecca arched her back, pushing on to him, and smiled in the darkness. He fit her perfectly, like a key to a lock. She spread her legs wider and bent low over the machine in front of her, the metal parts cold against her hard nipples, the smooth rubber parts slippery against her body. Richard's hands were on her hips and he was pulling her back, fucking her hard, while she held on.

Richard rammed into her with all the force he had. He knew she was bruised and battered, but that paled in comparison to how wet and hot her cunt was around his dick. She wanted a fuck, and she wanted it hard. She slammed back into him, giving as good as she got. His balls made a soft slapping sound with every thrust, and he grunted softly every time he pushed in.

Rebecca spread her legs wider, desperate to get him deeper. He bent his knees and fucked her with an upward angle, a new sensation that made her shake with the impending orgasm. He was touching something within her, something that was hard to reach, and she was afraid to move, lest the pleasure disappear. "Right there," she whispered. "Right there, oh, God, don't stop."

Richard pumped in and out of her, nothing but his hips moving. He held her thighs hard with his hands when she started to squirm, not letting her move away from him, and not letting up. The metal rattled underneath her as she tightened her hands on it, pulling hard, the orgasm blossoming from the inside out.

Richard knew when she came. Though she didn't make a sound, he felt the pulses of her cunt around him, both sucking at him and trying to push him out at the same time. He held very still inside her for a moment, enjoying the sensation. When he moved again it was to pump hard, straight in and out, now intent on making himself come, too.

When he did come, he had to bite his lip to keep from hollering.

He held inside her for as long as he could. Then he rubbed against her, spreading her wetness all over them both. She giggled at the slippery feeling, and he shushed her with a loud stage whisper. "Somebody will come back here and see you naked," he warned.

"You would like that, wouldn't you?"

His cock twitched in response, making her laugh again.

Richard carefully pulled up his pants. He made his way back towards the door as Rebecca made herself somewhat presentable. When she gave the okay, he opened the door just a little, enough to let the light shine through, and looked at her.

Her hair was a mess, the way he loved to see it. Her cheeks were flushed, and in the dim light the bruised eye didn't look bruised at all. She gave him a wicked grin.

"I think I have ink on my tits," she said.

The rest of the day was spent flirting like mad while he tried to get work done. He pushed himself to finish more articles than he usually did, and Rebecca did her best to help him, though she was miserable at proofreading and admitted as much. She kept staring at him instead of at the papers in front of her. Every time he got up for something, she made sure to reach out and touch him. The constant scrutiny kept him hot, and the constant interruptions from townsfolk and employees kept the frustration high. Though he knew he was there to work, there was nothing he wanted more than Rebecca in bed, moaning on his cock.

When the office finally closed up for the day, Richard bade the last employee goodbye and locked the door behind them. He pulled the shades down and turned to the woman who had been waiting for this moment all day.

"You vixen," he growled, then he was on her.

They did it in his office chair. She sat on top of him, her legs draped on either side, and lowered her wet hole on to his dick. He slid in without the slightest hint of resistance, but when she pulled up on him she squeezed hard with her inner muscles. The result was like a firm handjob, only much, much nicer. He teased her nipples with his fingertips while she bounced up and down on him, her head thrown back. When she reached back to brace herself on the desk, all the paperwork slid to the floor, where it was completely ignored. She leant back against the computer monitor and when the keyboard got in the way, she pushed it aside, letting it fall to the floor with a clatter.

Richard stood up and grabbed her hips, pressing her firmly into his desk, running his dick in and out of her while she squealed with delight. She grabbed the edge of the desk, knocking over a cup full of pens and pencils. They scattered on the floor and rolled in every direction. Richard leaned over her, thrusting hard into her pussy and running his dick against her clit at the same time, stimulating her from the inside out. She bucked against him when she came, her mouth open wide with ecstasy, her eyes wild as they met his. He came right along with her, his balls throbbing as he emptied into her.

Someone knocked on the door.

The sound startled Richard so much he almost dropped Rebecca to the floor. She caught herself on the edge of the desk and lowered her feet to the ground, staring at the front door. The blinds there were closed but could someone see through anyway? Maybe from around the corner?

Richard pulled his pants up and shrugged into his shirt. "It's probably someone wanting to place an ad before deadline."

The sound came again, but this time it was an insistent pounding. Someone knew they were in there, and they weren't taking silence for an answer.

Rebecca quickly found her clothes and put them on. Richard waited in the inner doorway while she made herself look presentable, then he peeked out of the shade at whoever was beating down the door.

When he saw his mother, he sighed.

"Let me in, son! Damn it, it's cold out here."

Richard opened the door and Janette came inside, a whirl of wool and cold and anger.

She glared at him then shot a vicious look at Rebecca. "What have you done?" she almost yelled, and, though Rebecca's instinct was to fade into the office and avoid this confrontation, Richard stood his ground and calmly answered.

"I'm not sure you want to know what I was just doing, Ma."

His mother looked as though she wanted to slap him. "Don't be obscene."

"If this is about Amanda, Ma, you've got no cause to argue. She's in the psych ward at General."

"She's a very sick woman!"

"Yes, she is."

"And you're still leaving her? I figured you would be the good man I raised you to be, and come to your senses! You don't just leave your wife when she's in the hospital and in need of her husband's good care!"

Richard rubbed his eyes. "She's been gone for years, Ma. I'm sorry she's sick and I will do what I can to help her, but I'm not in love with her anymore."

"Oh, yes, you are. You're just blinded by that...that..."

"My name is Rebecca," she said from across the room, and won a glare from Janette.

"I'm not in love with Amanda," he said again, "and I'm not a martyr."

"You're a married man!"

Richard held up his hands. Both of them were bare of rings. "I haven't been married for a long time, Ma. The divorce papers just make it legal."

"It's not right," she said again, and Richard realised she didn't know any argument other than that one. She had lived her life based on a certain set of rules, a certain expectation of doing things, and she thought the whole world should work that way. When it didn't, she clucked and shook her head in consternation, but when it was her own son who broke the rules, she was hell-bent on bringing him back into line.

"Maybe it's not right," he agreed. "I wish the world worked that way, Ma. I wish we lived in a place where relationships lasted, and husbands and wives treated one another with respect. I wish this world knew nothing of divorce, or arguments, or illness, and everything worked out. But that's a utopia, Ma, and humans aren't capable of utopia in large doses."

She glared at him. "Don't you get all philosophical with me," she said, pointing a finger.

"If she hadn't left, Ma, none of this would have happened. If I had known she was sick before I married her, I would have been able to see the signs, and I might have been able to help her. But none of those things happened, and life is the way it is. I'm sorry if you don't like it, but I'm getting a divorce, and no amount of bickering or guilt-tripping is going to change that."

Janette had tears in her eyes. "You haven't even been to see her."

"That's where I'm going right now, if you will let us leave here and do it."

Janette shot a look of pure spite at Rebecca. The younger woman stood her ground but inside she shrank away from that look, hating the fact that Janette would never accept her, no matter how much time went by or how her relationship with Richard evolved.

Richard watched his mother leave. She practically ran to her car, got in behind the wheel, and made a show of wiping away tears before she started the car and drove away.

Even as he watched her he knew she would never come around, and that, as much as she loved him, their relationship would be strained from this point on, no matter what he did. It was something he would have to learn to live with, but he didn't imagine it would ever stop hurting.

"I'm sorry," Rebecca said, coming up behind him.

"You and me both," he said, and put his arm around her.

"Let's go get flowers for Amanda," Rebecca said. "I'll wait in the car while you go up to see her."

Richard looked down at her. "You sure?"

Rebecca was absolutely sure. In fact, she was much surer of everything than she had ever been. She understood that Amanda was sick, that she needed all the help she could get—and that included Richard's forgiveness. She also knew that no matter what was happening around them, no matter who didn't agree with their relationship, she was in this for the long haul. She knew Richard was in it for good, too.

"Daisies are good. Do you think we can find daisies at this hour?"

Richard led her out the door, wondering if the hospital gift shop was still open.

Chapter Nineteen

Before they knew it, Christmas arrived. Richard spent it in Miami, his first time celebrating Christmas in a place where he didn't have to wear a coat to go outside. Rebecca's tiny apartment was filled with lights. A Christmas tree was up in the living room, which meant one less place to sit, because she had moved a chair out to the balcony to make room.

On Christmas morning they sat on that balcony in the early sunlight, wearing pyjamas and drinking iced tea instead of hot cocoa. It was the strangest Christmas he had ever had, and quite possibly the happiest.

Amanda was still in the hospital, where she would probably stay for quite some time. Richard called Grace every few days to check on how she was doing, and he made sure to send weekly flowers, but he knew it was best for Amanda if he didn't contact her directly. She was just now stabilising, and he would do her more harm than good. Every time he hung up the phone with Grace he felt a twinge of guilt, and wondered what he could have done to see the signs. He thought he would always feel that guilt, no matter how much time passed.

Rebecca had gone back to Miami and immediately thrown herself into work. Her black eye was hard to cover with makeup and she knew her customers noticed it, but none of them asked what had happened to her. She had no idea what she would have told them if they had. How could she explain everything that had happened and break it all down into a small nutshell of a story?

She and Richard spent time on the phone while they were apart, finally talking about the future. She thought the notion of her moving to Iowa was a pretty clear-cut scenario. The paper couldn't move with Richard, but her job could move with her. Besides that, Crispin didn't have a single professional photographer, and she was pretty sure her prices would compare favourably with the bigger ones in Des Moines. She had started researching the possibility and also looking for rental properties, something she hadn't yet mentioned to Richard. She wanted to have all her plans in order when she came to the table with the idea of moving closer to him.

Richard had had much of the same thoughts, and he hadn't told her about them, either. He had approached an old colleague a few weeks ago and over drinks had discussed the future of the *Crispin Tribune*. Now he sat in front of Rebecca on the balcony, prepared to discuss it all with her.

"I like Miami," he said. "Is it really this sunny all the time?"

She nodded. "Most of the time. The storms can be good ones, though."

"At least you don't have blizzards."

She smiled at him over her tea. The ice cubes tinkled in the glass as she took another long drink.

"I've been thinking about the paper," he said. "I met with an old colleague of mine from the *Chicago Tribune* a few weeks ago, and ran some ideas past him."

"Oh?" Rebecca sat forward, surprised she hadn't heard about any of this before.

"I asked him what a good selling price might be," he said, and watched as her eyes widened. "He thought it would bring a pretty penny. After all the legal wrangling, it would give me more than enough money to sink into a new business."

Rebecca blinked at him, trying to process all this. "You're leaving the paper?"

"I'm thinking about it."

"But...but why would you do that? The *Tribune* is an institution in Crispin! You're the only one who can compete with the big boys out of Des Moines. You've got a special niche. You're needed there."

"Maybe it's time to move on," he said.

"Move on to what? To where?"

"Miami."

He watched her face as the words sank in. The shock was first, followed by the denial, then the utter happiness — but soon after that came something else.

"Richard," she said, shaking her head. "You can't do that."

"Why not?"

She smiled up at him. "Because I'm coming to Iowa."

Now it was her turn to watch the emotions flash over his face. After going through all of them, he gave a hearty laugh. "You're not coming to Iowa. You can't survive Iowa."

"I can too!"

"You hate winter, you can't drive on snow, and you wouldn't know what to do with all that space."

"You will miss winter, you hate driving in traffic, and you can't stand buildings so close together."

They smiled at each other, standing at a very exciting crossroads.

"But you know what this means?" he asked, and she nodded.

"It means we're making plans."

He leaned over and kissed her. She put down her glass of iced tea and grabbed at his shirt. He fell over her on to the floor of the balcony, where their legs tangled and their tongues met. He kissed her until the sun disappeared behind dark clouds and made the world grey.

She slipped her hands under his T-shirt and with one experienced move she yanked it over his head. She touched his bare chest, her fingertips trailing over one small bruise in the exact shape of her teeth. She fit her teeth to it again, this time using only her lips to mark him, a soft caress that made his nipples hard. She touched them with her fingertips and whispered into his ear.

"Ever made love in the rain?"

He laughed against her neck. "It's not raining."

"It's going to," she promised, and pulled his head down for another kiss.

Sure enough, the dark clouds didn't go away. Richard missed the play of the sunlight in the hollows of her neck. He kissed her there, taking his time and tasting the sweet flavour of her. His tongue found the place where her perfume had been last night and brought it back to life, the taste stinging his tongue, the scent filling his nose. She ran her fingertips lightly over his back and wrapped her legs around his, holding him to her while his touch sent shivers through her body.

"Ever made love on a balcony thirty stories up?"

Richard didn't even bother to answer that one. He kissed his way down to her shirt and started to unbutton it, one slow button at a time, dropping a kiss on her skin with each bit of skin he revealed. When the shirt was open and she was laying there half-naked before him, he started to work on her nipples, laving one with his tongue while playing the other with his fingertips. She arched up into his touch and growled low in her throat, the smile still on her face.

The first drop of rain touched her bare skin, and, though it was warm outside, she shivered.

Richard kissed his way down her belly until he reached her pyjama bottoms. Rebecca wiggled out of them but before they were down to her feet he was spreading her legs and pressing his face between them. He breathed deeply of her scent, mostly all her but a little of him, and with a wicked grin he remembered what he had done to her last night. He licked her slowly, nibbling at her pussy lips, pulling on them, making her wet and making her moan. She tangled her hands in his hair and held him closer, moving her hips up, urging him to touch her where she needed it most.

He slid his tongue down instead, and lightly touched the rosebud of her ass.

She jerked hard. She spread her legs wider as the rain started to sprinkle over her, cool drops touching her skin. They tickled as they slid down her sides. She opened her mouth and tasted the drops as they eased over her lips and peppered her tongue.

He held her tight as he ministered to her, revelling in the little moans and the wiggling of her body against his tongue. Soon the rain was coming down harder and had soaked his pyjama bottoms, so he worked them down his body with one hand and kicked them off to a corner of the little balcony. His dick was hard and pressed against the smooth concrete, the cold making him a little softer, even as the woman writhing underneath him kept the passion at a fever pitch.

"I need it," she panted, and he didn't make her wait any longer. He slid his tongue up and pressed it hard against her clit, running it around and around the sensitive little button, until she was gasping for air. He slipped one finger into her ass, giving her no warning about what he was going to do, and the sudden shock sent her into an orgasm that knocked her breathless.

Her body tightened around his hand, pulsing with the pleasure. When she finally lay still, he moved above her. The rain was pelting them now, no longer gentle. Richard hovered over her as the drops stung his shoulders and ran all over his body, a shower from the heavens.

"Fuck me," she breathed, the words he loved so much to hear, and he slid into her.

She tried to wrap her legs around his hips, but the water made him too slippery. She tried to hold on to him with her arms, but faced the same problem. Finally she lay back on the balcony, reached above her head to grab at the bars of the railing, and planted her feet against the concrete. She bumped her hips, rising up to meet him, and watched as his face went slack with pleasure.

"God, that's good," he murmured.

The rain kept falling and she kept moving, grinding against him as he held still. She watched the rain drip from his forehead and nose, traced the drops as they slid down his arms, and tasted the water that dripped from his chin. She loved the way his skin slipped against her, as if their whole bodies were fucking.

Richard opened his eyes and smiled at her. Her hair was dark with the rain, her face covered with tiny drops, her lips open to take them in. Her hips bumped against his over and over, her eyes pinned to his face, as he approached the pinnacle. When she ground her pussy against him one last time he did go over the edge, calling out into the rainstorm as he filled her.

She kissed him as he came back down to earth. When he moved away from her she was startled by how hard the rain was. He had shielded her from it with his body but now the protection was gone the drops were stinging against her skin.

She stood up and let it wash down her body. Richard stood watching her, unheeding of the rain that cascaded down his body, and she admired the way he looked now, so trim and fit. He had lost weight during their marathon sex sessions, and he swore his body was harder than it had been in years. She walked to him and wrapped her arms around his middle.

"Now you've made love in the rain," she teased.

The torrent got worse, and the first blast of lightning lit up the sky. The vivid light blinded them both. Rebecca ran for the door, pulling him with her as she slid it open and stepped inside. The sudden absence of the rain set off chills in her body, and she hurried to the bathroom for her robe. She threw a towel at Richard and admired his body as he dried off. He luffed his hair, then sat down on the couch, naked.

"So you're coming to Miami," she said, picking right up where they had left off.

"Yeah."

"But I'm coming to Iowa."

She said it with such a matter-of-fact tone that he wondered how much planning she had already done, and when she was going to share it with him.

"Tell me about these plans," he said. "You've obviously done some thinking."

"I have." She sat down on the coffee table in front of him. "I've looked into the photography business up there, and it seems a bit lacking. Crispin could use my services. And it would allow you to stay with the paper, and avoid all these weekend trips to visit some chickie down south."

Richard grinned at her. "You've got it all figured out, then?"

"I even found an apartment. It's a very reasonable price. I knew the cost of living there was much less, but I had no idea how expensive Miami really was until I started doing some research."

"Who says you need an apartment?" he asked.

She stared at him. Was he offering what she thought he was?

"I can't stay in your house," she said. "You're not quite divorced yet, remember? It could cause problems for you."

"What if I said I was going to sell the house?"

Rebecca shook her head. They had both made huge plans in the hopes of surprising one another, and now all those plans seemed helter-skelter.

"You're selling?"

"I think we should start in a place of our own. Not a place that has so many memories."

"But they're good memories."

"Yeah, they are...but there are bad ones, too. You can point out the spot on the floor where Amanda pinned you down and hit you. I can show you where she left the note. I can point out the place where our wedding picture used to be. Is that really the kind of memories you want to creep into our lives? Because they will, you know. It might not seem that way now, but the first time we have a good argument something will come back. I can almost guarantee it."

Rebecca nodded. "Okay. So where were you planning on going?"

"Miami."

She snorted with laughter and slapped him on the knee.

"If you are really dead-set on coming to Crispin, I'm not going to stop you," he said. "But know the town won't be all that accepting at first. Most of the people there are going to love you, but the ones who don't will make a lot of noise."

"I already expect that, and I'm ready for it."

"Then can you come to Iowa? I can set up a meeting with the realtor, and we can look around. See what we like."

She shook her head in amazement. "Just like that...you can move out of the house you've lived in for so long? Just like that?"

"I was going to come to Miami," he pointed out.

She reached out and took his hand. "I'll get plane tickets as soon as the offices open."

He kissed her fingers. "Merry Christmas, my love," he whispered.

The first five houses they looked at were not suitable for them. Either they were too modern, or too traditional, or filled with too little space. Though they hadn't yet discussed children, Richard was more than open to having them, and Rebecca thought more and more about a little one running around, one with his eyes. When the realtor had asked how many bedrooms they required, Richard immediately replied, "Three," which brought a dazzling smile from Rebecca.

The sixth house was the one that made them both gasp as they walked through the front door. A massive fireplace sat in the corner of the living room. The ceilings were high, adorned with rough-hewn wood beams. The kitchen was open, separated from the rest of the house by a long marble bar. The counters were exquisitely carved, and the wallpaper was dramatic, a perfect complement to the dark cherry wood on the floors. It was a bit out of their price range and far too luxurious.

The realtor watched their reactions, raised an eyebrow and said, "I'll give you a moment." She walked out of the room and they looked at each other, their eyes wide.

"I want this house."

"I want it too, but can we afford it?"

"If I sell the farmland too, we can."

"But will that bring enough to make our payments low?"

He smiled at her. "It will pay for the house outright."

That stunned her. "How much is land out here worth, anyway?"

Richard beckoned the realtor inside and told her they wanted the house. By the time the end of the day was out, the For Sale sign had gone up on his property, and their offer for the house had been made. She signed her name on the contract, right beside his, and that alone made her both happy and incredibly scared. This was the real deal, and now there was no denying it. That night Rebecca lay in bed beside Richard and fretted. "What if we don't sell it in time?"

He rolled over her. When he slid into her, she wasn't thinking about money or houses or contracts. She was thinking about how perfectly he fit, how he could stroke the fire to life inside her with just a simple touch. Her whole body came alive when he moved within her.

He murmured against her lips, "We need to think about how we're going to fill up all those bedrooms."

She arched up to him, more than ready to get started.

Epilogue

Despite the bitter cold and the impossible amount of snow, springtime did eventually come to Iowa. On a bright April day, Richard pulled into the driveway and studied the front of their new house. There were flowers everywhere, tumbling out of planters, bursting from the flower beds, even trailing down from hanging pots. The yard was alive with colour, and now that the trees had leafed out in the warmth of the approaching summer the shade was heavenly. Red maples lined the road and giant oak trees stood sentry in the backyard. It wouldn't be long before he would have to mow the lawn again.

He climbed out of the truck. Rebecca's car was parked at the back of the drive, the new paint job gleaming in the afternoon light. The front door was open, and through the screen he observed Rebecca as she moved around the kitchen, singing to a song on the radio. He let himself in quietly, not wanting to disturb her, as she danced across the floor, her hips moving, her feet shuffling. When she turned and caught sight of him she blushed, then put down her dishtowel and came into his arms. Her kiss tasted like coffee, and the kitchen smelt like cinnamon.

"How was work?" she asked, and he sat down at the kitchen table. She watched as he poured a cup of coffee. She thought she would never get used to the thrill of waking up with him every morning, living in this house with him every day, and expecting him to come home every night. It was a dream come true.

"Work was interesting. The new computer system kept going down, and I had no idea how to fix it, but you know Mike? The new boy we hired from the high school programme?"

"Yeah?"

"He fixed it. I've never seen anything like it. He took one look at the thing and touched a wire here and there, and then we were off to the races." Richard took a sip out of his coffee. "That kid reminds me of how old I'm getting."

"You're not old."

"I don't know where the modem is, much less how to fix it."

"I don't, either. Does that make me old?"

"You will never grow old. How was your day?"

"I spent the day at the high school, taking graduation pictures."

"It starts that early?"

"Oh, yeah. They already have their caps and gowns."

"This is the last time you will have to do that, you know. As soon as that book comes out, you won't have to take graduation pictures ever again."

Rebecca smiled at him. His belief in her was so strong, he was certain her book of Iowa photographs would sell like hotcakes and make them millionaires. She was pretty sure it didn't work like that, but the fact that he believed it could was inspiring.

She pulled peach cobbler out of the oven. Richard's stomach growled at the sight of the tender peaches and golden crust. She looked over her shoulder. "Hungry?"

"As a bear."

She spooned the warm cobbler into bowls and pulled the ice cream from the freezer.

"I got something in the mail today," he said, and pulled a manila envelope from his coat. He hung the coat on the chair, taking his time, and turned back to see her looking at the papers. She flipped through them for a moment before her eyes met his. "Is this what it looks like?"

"That's what it looks like."

Rebecca's eyes swam with tears. She put the papers down on the table and leaned over them, her hands touching the signatures. "I knew this was coming," she said. "And it makes me happy, but it makes me sad, too. Is that weird?"

"I cried when I got them," he admitted, and she looked up into his eyes.

"You cried?"

"It's always hard to accept when something ends," he said.

She reached out and put her hand on his. "How is she?"

"The same."

In the weeks since they had moved to the new house on the outskirts of Crispin, Amanda had been moved to a hospital in Des Moines. Her condition hadn't stabilised with treatment, and now they were trying new medications, plus intense therapies that might give her a halfway decent life. The illness that had plagued her since childhood was worse than ever, and that fact made

Richard feel guilty every time he thought of it. He knew it wasn't his fault, but there would always be that lingering doubt in the back of his mind, the question of what he might have missed, what he should have done.

It also fostered a deep determination to do the right things with Rebecca.

"I think the wondering was easier than the knowing," he said. "When she was gone, I didn't know how bad it could get. I almost wish she hadn't come back."

"You don't mean that."

"No, I don't."

Richard held her hand as they looked at the papers. Those documents meant the end of an important part of his life, and he wasn't ashamed to mourn for that. But they also meant the chance for a new beginning, and he was grateful he now had the opportunity to try again.

He reached into his pocket and pulled out the little black box. He set it on the kitchen table, right on top of the papers. Rebecca looked up at him with startled eyes. They had talked about what the future might hold, and they had talked often about having children, but she hadn't expected this to come so soon.

She pulled her hand away from Richard and slowly picked up the box. It was heavy in her hand, soft and warm from being against his body. "Richard…"

"Open it," he said.

Rebecca took a deep breath and opened the box. The ring caught the light from the high windows and sent rainbows of colour over her hand. Tears stung her eyes and she wiped them away, gazing at the ring. The diamond was huge, the kind of ring she was sure he couldn't afford, but that didn't stop her from pulling it from the box and staring with awe.

"Rebecca," he said.

She couldn't look at him. She couldn't do anything but stare at the ring, soaking up the reality of it, the dream she hadn't dared put voice to in all those long months of togetherness. Richard watched her, smiling at her reaction, happy he had given her something she wanted so badly. Maybe she hadn't said it before, but he had seen it in her, the longing that said she needed the next step.

He needed that next step, too. He needed it more than he could ever put into words.

"Rebecca, baby. Look at me."

She finally looked up at him and wiped the tears from her cheeks. She knew what he was going to ask, but was there really any question?

"Yes," she whispered.

"I haven't asked you yet," he teased, and she teased right back.

"This ring does all the asking you need."

He came around the corner of the table, and she shook her head. "You're not getting down on one knee, are you?"

He grinned and knelt to the floor. Inexplicably, Rebecca started blushing. The red in her cheeks made her look so young and happy, and the beauty of her took Richard's breath away.

"Rebecca," he said, and to his surprise she knelt down on the floor with him.

"Yes."

"Will you be my wife?"

"Yes!"

She threw her arms around him. Richard buried his face in her shoulder and laughed. He pulled the box from her hand and took out the ring, then slid the diamond on her finger. It looked good on her, just as he had known it would.

"We've got a wedding to plan," he whispered in her ear, and she laughed with him, the tears still falling. He helped her up from the floor and together they stood in the kitchen while the cobbler cooled and the ice cream melted. The flowers outside bloomed in a chaos of colour as they both thought about the wintertime that had just passed, the stranger she had been, the blizzard that had trapped her, and the beautiful things that could happen to two people during a week in the snow.

About the Author

Gwen Masters has seen hundreds of her short stories published in print and online, and her erotic novels have been translated into half a dozen different languages. When she's not writing smut, she is diving into research on interesting yet obscure topics, hopping a plane every few weeks, and masquerading as a serious news journalist. She splits her time between a home on the Georgia coast and a little place on the outskirts of Philadelphia.

Gwen Masters loves to hear from readers. You can find her contact information, website details and author profile page at http://www.total-e-bound.com

Total-E-Bound Publishing

www.total-e-bound.com

Take a look at our exciting range of literagasmic™
erotic romance titles and discover pure quality
at Total-E-Bound.